THE LUCKY ONE

A Carolina Connections Novel - Book 3

SYLVIE STEWART

Rolling Hearts Press

ALSO BY SYLVIE STEWART

The Carolina Connection Series:

The Fix *(Carolina Connections, Book 1)*

The Spark (*Carolina Connections* Book 2)

The Game *(Carolina Connections Book 4)*

The Way You Are *(Carolina Connections Book 5)*

☘ ☘ ☘

The Nerd Next Door *(Carolina Kisses, Book 1)*

Then Again

Happy New You

Game Changer *(July 2019)*

About That

Full-On Clinger

☘ ☘ ☘

Between a Rock and a Royal *(Kings of Carolina, Book 1*

Blue Bloods and Backroads (*Kings of Carolina*, Book 2)

COPYRIGHT

First Print Edition: 2017

Edited by Heather Mann

ISBN: 978-0-9989260-1-8

Murphy's Law:

Nothing is as easy as it looks.
Everything takes longer than you expect.
And if anything can go wrong,
It will at the worst possible moment.

Chapter One

HELLO, MY NAME IS SATAN

BAILEY

"I swear his eyes are following me."

"It *is* a little creepy, I'm not gonna lie," said Mark, glancing over my shoulder.

A shiver ran down my spine and the hairs on the back of my neck stood at attention.

Mark took in my expression—which I'm sure was one of intense revulsion—and laughed right in my face, his straight white teeth not even attempting to bite his tongue. This was entirely unsurprising.

Mark's day is not complete unless he has tortured me in some way. He's the twin brother I never had and certainly never wanted. I already have an older brother, but Mark somehow worked his way into my life and I can't seem to get rid of him and his ridiculously bulky bod no matter how hard I try.

Still smiling at my pain, Mark shook his head and asked, "If he freaks you out so much, why the hell did you say yes?"

I glared at him, hands on my hips. "What in the hell was I supposed to do?! There were tears! Wet, sloppy tears!"

This did nothing to tame his smile. "You are such a fucking pushover," he whispered in my ear before skirting around me and approaching the creepy son of a bitch.

"Ha!" I declared as I turned around, completely forgetting to keep my gaze averted. "Shows how much you know. I talked the kid down from a puppy!" I was actually quite proud of myself, despite my lack of forethought.

Turns out I can't stand lizards. Who knew? But the joyous expression on my nephew's face and the complete cessation of all waterworks was my prize to revel in.

Totally worth it.

I'm sure I broke every babysitting rule in the book, but desperate times call for desperate measures. It looked like my brother and his new wife just got themselves a pet gecko.

Whoops.

"Okay, little man. Everything is all set up," Mark said to a nearly-vibrating Rocco. "The light will keep him nice and warm, he's got a good place to hide in that log, and your Aunt Bailey will show you how to feed him the crickets." Mark's smile turned evil as his eyes found me again.

What in God's name had I been thinking? To be fair, I had assumed these crickets would be dead when the twelve-year-old sales associate had pushed his glasses up on his nose and mentioned we'd need to stock up. By the time I realized we would instead be bringing home a plastic container teeming with live insects, it was too late. Rocco, my adorable nephew, had fallen in love.

"Fist bump," Mark requested of Rocco, whose attention was

completely captured by his new pet. Rocco extended his little fist without letting his eyes stray from the tank. "Thanks, Mark."

"Sure thing," Mark replied, ruffling the kid's dark hair. Then to me, "I gotta get back to Fiona."

"Is she feeling any better?" I asked, leaning against Rocco's dresser.

"Eh, hard to say."

Mark looked slightly distressed at the thought, and I marveled for the umpteenth time at the transformation my once-slutty friend had undergone since meeting his girlfriend, Fiona. Gone was the arrogant manwhore and in his place was an arrogant, pussy-whipped little douchebag. Ah, it warms the heart.

"I picked up an antibiotic for her, so hopefully that will start working soon," he said as he gathered his things.

I felt a sympathy pain in my throat just thinking about Fiona and her bout of strep throat. I cursed the damn virus for forcing me to step in and babysit Rocco while my brother, Nate, and his new wife, Laney, were off on their honeymoon. The same virus that, today, revealed just how ill-equipped I was to care for a child without becoming the biggest sucker known to man. "Well, tell her I hope she feels better and not to worry about Rocco—I got this."

Mark stopped in his tracks on his way to the door. He cocked his head, his eyebrows arching and his mouth sporting that damn smirk I wanted to knock off his stupid face. "Oh, I can see that."

I flipped him off, confident that Rocco's attention was elsewhere.

Mark's smug cackle echoed in the hallway outside Rocco's bedroom. "I'll let myself out!"

"You do that, Buffy!" Asshole.

Damn. It was just me and the kid again.

It's not that I don't like kids—I love my new nephew. I'm just not all that comfortable around tiny humans. I think I'm always waiting for them to judge me and find me inadequate somehow.

I'm the youngest of two kids, and I was never the babysitting type. My teen years had been spent sketching, reading, and plotting to get Nate in trouble whenever possible. And I'm a total daddy's girl, so I never pursued anything Riordan Murphy would consider "girly," much to my mom's disappointment. Babysitting, makeup lessons, and trips to the mall were eschewed in favor of hanging out at building sites with my dad and rocking out to heavy metal while painting and drawing. And, although my taste in music evolved as I reached adulthood, the rest pretty much stayed the same.

Everything I knew about taking care of a child consisted of lessons learned through trial and error over the last twenty-four hours.

I had been minding my own damn business last night, scarfing down cold pizza and channel surfing, when my phone had rung. I'd been ready to let it go to voicemail when I saw it was my brother. I hit the accept button; I should have let it go to voicemail.

"What in the hell are you doing calling me on your honeymoon? Did Laney come to her senses and leave your sorry ass?"

"Oh, thank God!" Nate sounded winded.

"What is the matter with you?" I set my pizza slice back on the paper plate and sat up on the couch.

"Mark just called. Fiona's got strep throat, I guess, and she's afraid she's going to pass it to Rocco. We need somebody else to go stay with him."

"So, call Mom," I told him, shaking my head at his stupidity.

"I already did, dumbass. She and Dad are in the Keys this week."

Oh yeah, I'd forgotten that.

"So, call Gavin." I leaned back once again, confident that I'd solved the world's problems. Gavin is Laney's brother, and he loves his nephew to death. He'd drop anything if Rocco needed him.

I heard an audible sigh. "Bay, do you really think I'd be calling if I hadn't already exhausted all other options?"

Good point.

"I take it Gavin's unavailable."

"Everybody is unavailable! Gavin's working, Laney's folks are in Virginia, Mom and Dad are in Florida, Mark is taking care of Fiona and covering for me at work. And if Laney finds out, she'll insist on flying back home and skipping our honeymoon! That is not happening."

"Well, not to be insensitive or anything, but what about Rocco's actual father?"

"Are you kidding me right now?!"

Admittedly, it wasn't my best idea. Rocco's biological father lives in California. That's one long-ass plane ride from North Carolina. As far as I know, he only sees Rocco a couple times a year. Not the best option.

"Fine." I sighed loudly and waited for him to rant some more as I took another bite of my pizza.

"Think of it this way—I will owe you huge."

Oooh, I hadn't thought of it like that. "I'm listening," I mumbled over a mouthful of pepperoni.

"You can't get much better than that and you know it." His voice dripped with desperation.

"True. Okay, what do I need to do?"

He sighed with relief. "You know Rocco—he's easy. Mark and Fiona have all the notes Laney wrote. Just follow those and you'll be fine. I'll Facetime Rocco and make sure he's feeling okay about the change. If he gets upset or worried, just call and I'll talk to him. Fiona should be better in a few days and can take over again." He proceeded to give me basic instructions and told me Mark would be at their house with Rocco until I could get there.

"Enjoy the honeymoon, Romeo, because your ass is mine when you set foot on U.S. soil again."

"That sounds creepy, even for you, Bailey."

"Go call your kid." I hung up on him and began making my mental checklist of things Nate owed me. This was like shooting fish in a barrel.

When I pulled into Nate and Laney's driveway a half-hour later, I spotted Fiona sitting in the passenger seat of Mark's black pick-up truck. I parked and approached her window.

"Knock knock!" I banged on the glass with my knuckles, startling the snot out of her. Fiona's head snapped back into the headrest and her blond hair flew around in every direction.

"Goddamn you!" she yelled and then grabbed her throat with both hands.

I covered my mouth to hide my grin while she rolled the window down.

"Just for that, I'm going to cough on you!" she said in a rasp. I backed up a step.

"You sound like shit," I told her.

"Yeah, no kidding. I feel like shit too." She smoothed her uncharacteristically messy hair and then reached for a tissue from a box on the bench seat.

"So," I began, suddenly feeling self-conscious. "How is Rocco feeling about having his clueless new aunt stay with him?"

She blew her nose delicately, as only Fiona could do, and then gave me a scolding look. "Bailey, he'll be fine. You'll be fine too. Don't worry so much. He's six—it's not rocket science."

Ha! Fiona is a natural with kids, and she's known Rocco since he was a baby. I just met the kid last year when Nate started dating Laney. Granted, Rocco has become a semi-permanent fixture at my parents' house since then, but they're both naturals too. How did I end up missing this gene?

"Yeah," was the only reply I could come up with as I nervously eyed the front door of the house. "Welp, wish me luck. Hope you feel better." I turned toward the house.

"Just remember—you're in charge, and 'no' means 'no'! Ow," she rasped, clearly having forgotten to take it easy again.

"I don't think you really understand that phrase, Fiona, but thanks!" I called back to her as I climbed the porch steps.

And over the next twenty-four hours, I learned that "no" means many things, but not one of them is actually "no." For example, "No, raw brownie batter can make you sick" actually means, "Let's try it and see!" And, "No, you can't go outside in your underwear" gets loosely translated into, "Just stay in the back yard."

Turns out I am awesome at saying "no," but terrible at meaning it. If they gave out awards for being a big fat fucking sucker, I would sweep the floor with all y'all's asses!

So, Rocco and I came to an understanding. He would do whatever he damn well pleased and I would repeat the phrase "just don't tell anyone" every six minutes. Which worked out pretty well until I'd come up with the brilliant plan to stop by the pet store to "just have a look."

What?! Nobody warned me that small humans are incapable of walking out of a pet store without some manner of little vermin to slobber all over. Thus, our current situation, which had required Mark to make a return trip to Laney and Nate's to set up a freaking terrarium for a creepy-ass reptile. Oh, and to taunt me.

I pushed off the dresser and sidled along the wall to keep my distance. Rocco was still transfixed by the gecko.

"So, uh, what are you gonna name him?" I asked.

He spared me a glance. "I dunno. What do you think we should call him?"

"Um, Satan?" I offered.

Rocco laughed, even though I hadn't been joking. "Very funny, Aunt Bailey."

"Okay, then *you* come up with a better name," I challenged, finally beginning to relax somewhat in Satan's presence.

Rocco quirked his lips to one side in thought and then said, "Gecko."

"Seriously?" I couldn't help myself.

"What's the matter with that?" He was genuinely perplexed.

"That would be like your mom naming you 'Human,'" I explained.

He scrunched his dark eyebrows. "Oh. Well, then you come up with something." He shrugged.

"Quasimodo," I said with a smile. That right there was gold.

"Quasi-what?" he asked, the "s" coming out as a "th" sound due to his lisp.

So, I guess that was a no. "Well, it could be a girl…"

"No," Rocco said, matter-of-factly, with a single shake of his head.

I snickered. "Fine. Just think about it and we'll decide later."

That seemed to be acceptable because Satan once again captured his attention.

My phone vibrated in my back pocket, signaling a text. I checked to see who it was from and immediately wished I hadn't. I blew out a breath and returned the phone to my jeans. I was operating under the theory that if I ignored the caller, he would go away.

Before I could spare the troublesome caller more thought, I was attacked at the kneecaps by Rocco, who wrapped his arms around my legs in a giant hug.

"What's that for?" I asked, wondering if I was being set up for another giant babysitting fail.

He peered up at me with huge brown eyes and an earnest look. "I forgot to say thank you for my gecko."

Well, shit, now I was going to have to make another batch of brownies.

Later. Right now, my nephew needed a hug.

☘☘☘

Two hours later, Rocco was tucked safely into bed with the still-unnamed reptile by his side as I collapsed on the couch. This babysitting thing was no joke. I was exhausted.

Thankfully, I only had to make it through one more day before the school week started. I was modifying my work schedule so I could get Rocco off the bus in the afternoons, but it still meant I'd have several kid-free hours to myself.

With Nate gone for the week, Mark and some of the other guys were picking up the slack at Built by Murphy, my family's construction and contracting company. Nate, Mark, and I all work there, along with Gavin, although he only works part-time.

My father started the company when he was my age, and over the last thirty-odd years it's grown into a sizeable local operation with a stellar reputation. Nate and I knew from a very young age that our dad's hope was to pass the company along to us, and we've done little to discourage that—even though I know we've both had reservations.

Nate reconciled his last year when our dad had a heart attack and Nate was forced to return home to North Carolina and take over the construction side of the business. After some false starts, he found his groove and hasn't looked back.

I, on the other hand, have not come to terms with my feelings about the company. Perhaps I should rephrase that. I know exactly how I feel about it—I just haven't told the most significant person about my feelings. I'm generally very good at telling people exactly what I think—sometimes too good. Except when it comes to my dad.

One day, I'll work up the courage to tell my dad I'm leaving the company and pursuing my real dreams. One day.

Until then, I had Sunday with Satan and my nephew to survive.

Chapter Two

DELICIOUS

JAKE

Her hand slid down my chest, brushing over my sternum on its way to where I needed it the most. She didn't disappoint. My cock pulsed in her hand as her grip tightened and I groaned in her ear.

"You are so fucking sexy," I told her.

I could feel her smile against the skin of my shoulder and I let my hands explore the perfect round globes of her ass. My fingers flexed along with my cock.

"I need you," she whispered, nipping my skin.

"I need you too," I returned.

"I need you to run to the store, Jake. We're out of coffee."

WTF?

I looked back at the blond goddess in my arms, but the bed was empty next to me.

I blinked.

"Sorry, I'd go but I need to get ready so I can cover the lunch event for Fiona today. Poor girl."

I looked to the doorway of my bedroom and saw my mother adjusting her robe while she checked her phone.

Shit.

I took a quick look toward my junk to make sure my painful hard-on wasn't on display. Thankfully, the bedding disguised my awkward situation.

Damn. I'd had that dream again.

Ever since the night of Nate and Laney's wedding, I'd had the same dream. It always involved the blonde and it never ended how I wanted it to.

"What?" I shook my head to clear the cobwebs and looked back to my mom.

"Sorry, sweetie. I have to cater a lunch event on my own today since Fiona's sick and can't make it. We're out of coffee and I'm not going to make it without caffeine. Can you run and grab some? Please?"

Only processing about two words of what she said, I ran my hands over my face and nodded in agreement.

"Thank you so much!" My mom turned and sped down the hall toward her room.

I had to get my own place. And soon.

♣ ♣ ♣

That damn dream was still gnawing at me twenty minutes later while I walked through the coffee aisle of Food Lion.

A quick check of my phone confirmed what I already knew—no responses to my multiple text messages.

What in the hell was wrong with me? I didn't pursue women who made it clear they wanted nothing to do with me. It was way past time to move on.

Yet…I couldn't bring myself to do it.

It had been three weeks since I'd seen Bailey Murphy. Three weeks of unreturned calls and texts that had turned me into one of "those" guys. I shoved my phone back into my pocket and scrubbed my hands over my face and into my hair.

I still wasn't used to how long my hair had gotten. I'd sported a buzz cut ever since I joined the Marines out of high school, and I'd only recently decided to let it grow out a bit. That was just one of many changes I'd made lately.

One short month ago, I'd moved back to Greensboro from Clearwater, Florida, where I'd been living and working for the last several years.

The move itself had been an exhausting one. I'd driven straight through the night in a rental truck with all my personal shit in it, despite the fact that I'd worked a full day tying up loose ends with my condo and business. I proceeded to spend the following week coordinating the delivery and storage of my business's heavy equipment, only to find myself rising with the sun to catch meetings with my new business partner here in Greensboro. Then I had to fly back to Florida to get my truck and make the ten-hour drive here.

My back ached, my head hurt, and I had a mountain of paperwork to go through. But, apparently, none of that got me a get-out-of-jail-free card when Saturday rolled around and I was reminded by my brother, Mark, that I had a wedding to go to.

"Can't you just tell them I'm sick or something?" I pleaded with my little brother.

"What are you, nine? Act like an adult and get dressed. You're giving Mom a ride to the reception place on your way. She's catering."

That fact made me feel a little more energized. Our mom and Fiona, Mark's new crazy-ass girlfriend, were starting up a catering business together—which I thought was an awesome idea.

In addition to being an absolute blast to hang around, Fiona is an amazing cook. If it hadn't been so fun to watch her and Mark annoying the shit out of each other while simultaneously panting over one another, I would have totally tried to get in there. If anybody deserved a happy ending, though, it was those two. Or those three, if you include our mom getting a new job. And the fact that Fiona and our mom get on so well was a bonus.

Life hadn't been great in our house when Mark and I were growing up. Our parents had a toxic relationship, due to my dad being a giant asshole, and the situation left our mom struggling with depression while assuming the role of primary breadwinner and caretaker. We'd survived, but, I'm ashamed to admit, I bolted as soon as possible after my high school graduation—leaving my fourteen-year-old brother to hold shit together.

Everything eventually worked out okay, but I would always regret not stepping up for my family when I should have. So, seeing my brother in love with a cute little hellion and my mom finally beginning a career she enjoyed helped mend my soul a bit.

It did not, however, make me any more excited to attend a damn wedding.

But I'd gotten to know Laney and Nate, and they'd both helped out tremendously when we'd all found ourselves in a bad situation a few months back. The least I could do was celebrate their big day with them and buy them a toaster or something.

That's how I found myself in a suit and tie, sitting in a church pew with complete strangers while my little brother stood up with Nate and his soon-to-be brother-in-law, Gavin. I'd just resolved to make it an early night when the music started and the entire congregation's gaze shifted to the back of the church.

My breath actually caught in my lungs and I had the brief inclination to put a fist to my own chest. There stood one of the hottest chicks I'd ever laid eyes on. She was tall and blond with a perfect rack and a stunning face. She was wearing a blue strapless dress that showed off acres of creamy skin along her neck and shoulders. A pair of hot-as-shit high heels perfectly accentuated some of the longest legs I'd ever seen.

My plans changed in that instant. I might still make it an early night, but hopefully I wouldn't be doing it alone.

☘ ☘ ☘

"I got your coffee!" I called out to my mom when I returned home.

She hustled in from the back hallway and reached up to plant a kiss on my cheek. "You're a life-saver, Jake."

"Why, yes, yes I am," I told her as I handed over both the grocery bag and a large latte I'd gotten at a drive-thru on the way home.

She gave a little gasp and then shrugged. "That's it. You're now my favorite son." Taking both items in hand, she retreated to the kitchen.

"What do you mean?" I called after her. "I thought I already was your favorite!"

She turned to smile at me when I followed her into the small kitchen and I watched as she took her first sip and relaxed her slim frame back into the countertop.

"So, anything else I can do to help? Looks like you've got a busy day," I offered.

"Thanks, but no. I think I have it covered. It's just a small luncheon and it's recipes we've done before. Mostly cold things that have already been prepared."

I nodded in response and took a seat at the wobbly kitchen table. She needed to get rid of this damn thing. It was the same one I'd grown up with, and it was past time for a fresh start.

"I just feel so bad about Fiona, the poor girl."

"What's wrong with her?"

She waved her hand. "Oh, nothing really—she's just got strep throat. She'll be fine, but I know she's feeling awful about not just the lunch but about Rocco too. She was supposed to be watching him while Nate and Laney are gone."

I'd forgotten that the happy couple had postponed their honeymoon to make sure their son, Rocco, got settled into his first year of school okay. I thought it was kind of nice that they'd done that, and I guess it made sense since the kid was kind of sensitive.

"That sucks. So, who's watching Rocco then?" The kid was a hoot—he had more questions than the world had answers, and he knew everything there was to know about turtles—both the real and mutant-ninja variety.

"Bailey, I think. Nate's sister. You may have met her at the wedding."

I practically choked on my own tongue.

"Anyway, hopefully Fiona will be better soon—until then, though, I think I'm going to be busy," she said with a shrug and then left to finish getting ready, I assumed.

But my mind was not focusing on my mom's new job and her busy day anymore. No, I had new plans for my Sunday. Plans that involved a sneaky blonde who thought she could give me the slip.

Was my behavior a little stalker-y? Perhaps. But I wasn't about to let Bailey and the best sex of my life go without doing my damn best to secure a date and who knows what else—at the very least, a replay would be nice.

When it comes to women, I'm a middle-road kind of guy. Yes, the occasional one-night-stand is not unheard of, but I tend to leave that decision up to the girl. Left to my own devices, I'm what you might call a serial dater. I love taking girls out. Sometimes it's just one PG date with no follow-up, and other times we hang out for a few months and run the full gamut of the motion-picture rating scale. If a girl wants to spend a night or seven, that doesn't faze me one bit—I enjoy waking up to a soft, sweet body warming the bed next to me.

And who doesn't love morning sex? These guys who cut and run the night before don't know what they're missing. I prefer to let a relationship run its course and then move on. It's not that I'm not open to a long-term relationship—I just haven't found one that fits. And I'm not actively looking either.

I'm in my early thirties. I figure I'll get there one day, but it's not worth dwelling on—especially when I've got so much else going on in my life.

But Bailey Murphy? I wasn't willing to give up on her just yet. I rose from the cheap kitchen chair and made my way to the hall bathroom to shower and shave.

I had a girl to call on.

Damn if there wasn't an actual spring in my step.

♣♣♣

Given the unreturned texts and calls, I determined that showing up without warning at Laney and Nate's house would not be received well by my reluctant conquest. A small bribe might be in order—and who doesn't like burritos?

While I waited for my takeout order at Barberitos, I tried to develop a plan of attack and anticipate Bailey's reaction. This could go any number of ways, from a coy tilt of the head and an invitation to come in, to an abrupt slam of the door in my face.

Perhaps burritos weren't going to cut it.

"Jake!" The kid at the counter called my name. I went to retrieve my order when a strong hand grasped my shoulder. I turned and found myself faced with the shit-eating grin of my new business partner, Jax Crosby.

"I thought that was you," he said, extending his hand for a shake.

Jax is one of those guys who is consistently two steps ahead of the game and enjoys the hell out of being so. Shit-eating grin is his go-to facial expression.

"Hey, man, how's it going?" I replied, taking his hand. I quickly grabbed my bag of food as we moved out of the way to make room for the other customers.

"Good, good," he said in his lazy accent. "I was gonna call you this afternoon." He scratched his shock of wild blond hair and threw his chin out toward me. "Got a lead on a landscaping project. Thought we could talk it over if you've got time."

Shit. I had a bag of hot burritos and a sexy girl to attend to, but this was my job—my brand-new livelihood. It was nothing to dick around with.

He seemed to sense my hesitation before I could mask it. His gaze transferred to the oversized brown bag of goodness in my hand, and his lips twitched up on one side. "Aaah, I see how it is," he drawled. The guy missed nothing.

"Nah, man. It's fine. I've got time," I tried to protest.

He was shaking his head before I could finish the first word. "No way. Far be it from me to stand in the way of a man and his mission." Out came the grin again.

I couldn't help but return it. "Well, I have to admit—I do have something quite…delicious waiting for me." I raised the bag of food in mock acknowledgment.

"Carry on, brother." Jax patted my shoulder and turned toward the counter. "Call me when you're done and we'll chat then," he finished as he sauntered over to place his order.

"Will do." I walked out the door and to my truck.

My thoughts lingered on our brief chat. A potential customer was nothing to ignore, especially since I was unknown in this town for my professional work. I'd busted my ass learning the ins and outs of the landscape design industry and I was determined to make a go of it here in my hometown.

As I steered the truck north, I vowed to myself that I would call Jax as soon as I got back to my mom's house later—which reminded me, yet again, that it was high time to get my own place.

But it wasn't like staying with my mom was a hardship. I loved having concentrated time with her after my long absence and infrequent visits home the last several years. It was inexcusable when it came right down to it, but I had been so used to avoiding my family back when my dad was around that I hadn't ever truly transitioned to normal visits once he'd left.

All of that was in the past now, and I could enjoy time with my mom and brother. But that didn't mean I had to permanently crash in my old twin bed, surrounded by plastic debate-team trophies my mom kept as a shrine honoring Mark's old days as a teenage loser.

Damn, I had to be careful what I said about my baby brother these days—that dude could kick my ass if he had a mind to.

I pulled into Laney and Nate's driveway and put my truck in

park. One deep breath and then the burritos and I were on our way to the front porch. But before I could even raise a finger to the doorbell, an ear-piercing scream tore through the house and had me dropping the bag to the concrete while my fists automatically pounded on the door for entry.

Chapter Three

CLICHÉS AND CHUPACABRAS

BAILEY

"Well, where did you see him last?" I asked in a panic, trying and failing to hide my crazy.

Rocco, looking equal parts guilty and devastated, brought his eyes up to mine while his lower lip quivered. "I just wanted to hold him."

No no no! I was a dead woman. Not only had I bought my nephew a contraband pet, I'd now inadvertently broken the boy's heart! Although, I was a tiny bit proud of myself for being more concerned about these issues than the one of a *goddamn lizard* being loose in the same dwelling where I was expected to sleep tonight!

"It'll be okay," I promised with completely false sincerity. "We'll find him."

"Promise?" Rocco asked, his face the picture of despair.

This kid had a lucrative career as either a beggar or an actor ahead of him. Either way, he'd clean up.

"Promise," my mouth said while every other part of me screamed at it to shut the hell up and get out of the house.

Nate was going to owe me huge after this mess.

"He's probably just scared and hiding somewhere," I told the kid.

He latched onto that idea right away and got down on hands and knees to look under his bed. "You think?"

"Yeah. Definitely." I joined him down on the carpet, careful to let his face be the one closest to the potential hiding place of the devil.

What?! He's the one who wanted the damn thing.

"Not here," Rocco said as he lifted his head up and peered at me with concern.

Now that I knew it was safe, I made a half-hearted attempt to glance under the bed as well.

"There he is!!" was the last thing I heard before my head swiveled of its own accord and I found myself eye-to-beady-eye with the leathery form of Satan Quasimodo Holy Shit Motherfucking Gecko.

I vaguely recall wondering who was screaming before black spots swam in front of me and a horrible pounding noise echoed through my brain. There wasn't anything after that.

I assumed the lizard ate my brain.

At least my death was a swift one.

☘ ☘ ☘

"Did she hit her head on anything?" I heard a deep rumble by my left ear. I'm relatively certain lizards don't talk.

"No, she was already down on the floor. She just screamed like a monkey and then fell asleep. It was weird." This voice belonged to my nephew for sure.

It seemed I was still alive. I opened my eyes, and upon seeing the owner of the rumbly voice, I closed them again immediately. If it was possible, I became even more light-headed.

Crap. I couldn't handle this today.

"Bailey," the rumbly voice beckoned.

I played possum.

"I know you're awake. Come on—I'm worried." I did sense a tone of concern in that rumble, so I felt somewhat compelled to act like an adult.

I opened my eyes again and saw gorgeous hazel ones staring back at mine. "It's okay. I'm fine. Nothing to see here." I tried for nonchalance.

Then I remembered the gecko and sat up like a shot, cracking my head on Jake Beckett's very chiseled, very sexy, and very hard chin in the process.

"Ow," we said in unison.

"Damn, woman." Jake rubbed his dark stubbled chin. "What's your hurry?"

I held my aching head and looked around frantically for Satan, trying to ignore both the hot guy and my dizziness. *Priorities, people!*

"Rocco, where is he?" I demanded.

"He ran away when you screamed. I think he's behind the dresser."

"Would somebody care to explain what's going on?" Jake asked from his kneeling position on the floor of the bedroom. "I heard you shrieking—you were passed out cold when I came in. Are you hurt?" His brow was creased in concern.

Sigh.

Without my permission, my eyes wandered from his face straight down to his thighs, which were straining the confines of the denim covering them. I had to close my eyes again and give myself an inner head-smack.

No thinking about the sexy man. No! Just grow up and breathe like a normal person.

I cleared my throat and opened one eye.

"Um, hello, Jake."

He just raised an eyebrow in response.

"I'm fine. Really. We were just looking for Rocco's lizard and it surprised me—that's all."

"And you passed out?"

I gave a nervous titter. "Well, I don't know if I would say I 'passed out.' I was just relaxing with my eyes closed." Time to redirect. "What are you doing here, anyway? Wait—how did you get in?"

He gave me a brief scolding look that creased his brow once more. "You left the front door unlocked. I took the liberty of letting myself in when it sounded like you'd been attacked by a chupacabra."

The man grinned cockily at me.

Shit. He was sexy when he grinned. And those cheekbones…dammit.

"What's a chupacabra?" asked Rocco, who was now peering behind the dresser.

Jake chuckled. "It's this cool creature with big fangs and spikes down its back. It likes to eat goats."

"Awesome," Rocco replied, trying to shove his head between the wall and his dresser.

I raised my eyes to the ceiling. I will never understand boys. Or men.

"What are you doing?" asked Jake.

"Trying to get my gecko to come out."

"Since when do you have a gecko?"

I had to wrest control of this situation immediately. I called on my inner bitch who could usually be found lurking just beneath the surface, right where I needed her. I cleared my throat again. "So, as you can see, we're all fine here. I'm sure you have things you need to do today." Subtlety is not my specialty, but he had to go.

I tried to stand up, but my head had other ideas and decided to pitch forward. Jake grasped my arms to prevent me from face-planting on the rug.

"Easy there." He stood and supported me while he steered us to Rocco's bed. "The only thing I have to do today is take you to the ER."

Shit.

Why couldn't the damn lizard have just finished me off?

☘ ☘ ☘

"So, let me get this straight. You babysat the kid for a grand total of twelve hours before purchasing a pet and $200 worth of supplies as a bribe? Wow. Just, wow. I believe that's a record." Jake leaned back in the waiting room chair and crossed his arms over his chest. The short sleeves of his gray t-shirt rode up with the action, revealing taught, tanned skin over the muscles residing there.

I whimpered a bit to myself and then forced the image aside. He was just a man, for God's sake. Or a god, for man's sake? Either way, he was heartbreak waiting to happen.

"You sound like your stupid brother. I already explained that there were tears. I panicked, okay?"

He muffled a laugh with a fake chin scratch.

"Bailey Murphy?" a nurse called from an open door. I stood and noticed Jake rising out of his seat as well. I stopped and gave him my best "hell no" look.

"So, you'll be flying solo, then?" He stopped in mid-stand.

I gave an emphatic nod and raced on over to the door before he and Rocco could follow me.

Couldn't he take a hint? What was wrong with him?

Unfortunately, the answer to that was nothing.

I followed the nurse through the maze of hallways and was led to a small room where she proceeded to take my vitals and ask me a series of questions—when did I eat last, have I ever fainted before, what was I doing when I fainted (I may have lied on that answer), could I possibly be pregnant, do I suffer from low blood sugar. Yada, yada, yada.

My answers all checked out and there was no indication anything was wrong with me. So, I proceeded to wait forty-five minutes for the doctor to come in and pronounce that I was fine. Just like I'd said I was.

I was sent back out to the waiting room with instructions to drink plenty of fluids and eat several small meals throughout the course of the day. And all of this fabulous advice was mine to keep for the low, low price of $75 plus whatever bill was sure to come later.

You could say I was displeased, so can you blame me for giving Jake the silent treatment all the way back to Laney and Nate's?

"I forgot," Jake announced from his position behind the wheel of his fancy-ass truck. He apparently didn't understand the rules of the silent treatment. "I brought Barberitos over earlier for you guys. I think I ended up leaving it in the hallway on my way in."

Hmm. Perhaps he could eventually be forgiven.

"Oh?" was all I gave him for the moment.

"What's a barberito?" asked Rocco from the rear seat where he was playing on his tablet.

"Only the best burrito in town." Jake smiled and glanced toward the back.

"Gross."

There was just no accounting for taste.

Jake shrugged it off. "I'll eat yours, dude."

Ha! Like I was letting that happen.

I was struck again by the thought that everyone in the world seemed to be good with kids but me. And how unfair was it that Jake Beckett was not only hot as sin and a wizard in the sack, but he was also nice to small people and fainting women?

What was I supposed to do with that?

We finally pulled into the driveway and I hopped out quickly to avoid any awkward assistance that might be offered. Seeming to need no invitation, Jake followed us inside and closed the door behind him.

I took a deep breath and firmed my back as well as my resolve.

"As you can see, we're all fine. I appreciate your concern—and the burritos—but everything is under control. We'll go ahead and get on with our day and you can get on with yours." I held my hand out toward the door like some damn restaurant hostess.

"Uh-huh," he replied and had the nerve to lean against the entryway wall and put his hands in his pockets.

What was this? Was he posing for a bachelor-of-the-month calendar?

Gah!

I performed the hostess gesture yet again.

This time it received a grin.

"What?!" I demanded.

He looked me up and down. "Uh-huh."

I became acutely aware of my attire and general appearance in that moment. I could feel the heat rising to my cheeks.

My hair was in a messy ponytail and I was dressed in athletic shorts and a men's t-shirt. I didn't need to look down to know there was a ketchup stain on the hem and a dinosaur riding a bicycle on the front. I have no explanation.

I urged myself to ignore Jake's look and not even attempt to interpret it.

This moment perfectly captured the reason all Jake's texts and calls had gone unanswered over the past three weeks.

He wasn't texting *me*.

He was texting the girl from the wedding.

The girl I'd pretended to be for one night.

The girl I would never be.

The one I couldn't afford to be.

☘☘☘

It wasn't really my fault. It was the fault of every movie ever made, every book ever written, and every damn talk show ever produced. When you're single, on the cusp of thirty, and your only sibling is getting married, things happen. Things like clocks ticking, insecurities blooming, little green demons taking up residence in your mind—all things you never knew were inside you until that day.

So it happened that, on the day of Nate and Laney's wedding, I'd awoken not feeling quite like myself.

Part of the reason, I knew, was that I would be required to wear both make-up and a freaking dress to the wedding. Bailey Murphy does not do girly shit. But when a tiny, blond force-of-nature threatens your very existence if you don't don the assigned attire (and smile while doing it), you obey. I'd seen Fiona in a temper and it was no joke. She took her maid-of-honor responsibilities very seriously and I was not about to provoke her.

I'd shown up to fittings, as instructed, and I'd done all the oohing and ahhing at the bride (who did look stunning in her gown, by the way). And I had enthusiastically participated in the shower and bachelorette party, although I didn't indulge as vigorously as a certain bride-to-be who had to be carried into the house by my big brother when the night was over.

For the entire week leading up to the big day, I'd walked back and forth across my living room in a pair of ridiculously high heels, determined that I would not humiliate myself by falling on my face in front of everyone I knew.

I'd thought I was prepared.

I was wrong.

I felt a twinge of something when I woke up, but I brushed it aside, as there were many things to be done—the worst of which involved Fiona plucking errant eyebrow hairs from my face that I insisted I needed to keep for warmth when winter came. She didn't share my feelings.

But, as the day progressed, there was no denying what was happening to me.

I was falling victim to the oldest cliché in the book. My brother was getting married, my friends were in happy relationships, and I was single and about to turn thirty. I could almost physically feel the cloak of the proverbial Old Maid descending upon my shoulders.

And that right there was how a tall, handsome, smooth-talking guy by the name of Jake Beckett worked the second oldest cliché in the book and got laid by a bridesmaid.

Chapter Four

PICKLES

JAKE

Damn, this girl was practically squirming with discomfort. At least now I had confirmation that she wasn't completely immune to me. I could feel the connection between us pulling tight—I hadn't imagined it. There was a different reason she hadn't been answering my attempts at communication since the wedding. And I was going to uncover it.

I was finding it hard to turn down this challenge.

While Rocco was off doing God knows what, I took my time looking Bailey over, and I'm not sure her cheeks could have flamed any brighter. It was cute, but I'd already seen her naked so I didn't understand the bashfulness.

I pried myself off the wall where I'd been leaning while checking her out. She had this messy, athletic thing going on—quite a departure from the polished-goddess look she'd rocked at our last encounter. But, hey, it was Sunday and she was babysitting a six-year-old. It's not like I expected her to be wearing heels.

I knew she wanted me to go, but that was too damn bad. I had burritos to eat, a potential date to secure, and a gecko to rescue before I left her alone.

"So, Bailey, which one do you want?" I approached her deliberately, almost prowling. I admit I may have been laying it on a bit thick.

The squirming increased.

"Which what?" she practically whispered as I got nearer.

Damn, I bet she'd light up if I touched her. I'd been dreaming about it for weeks, so it was going to be damn hard to keep myself in check.

"Meat or no meat?" I asked quietly. This was fun.

I actually heard her attempt to swallow and I watched her throat work.

"Wh…what?"

Once I was right in front of her, I bent down slowly but let my eyes remain on her face.

Then I picked up the Barberitos bag and straightened again, casual as can be. I shrugged, like a bit of an asshole. "Burritos. I didn't know which kind you liked so I got a variety."

Her eyes finally focused on the bag and she gave her head a tiny shake. Then she shot daggers at me with her piercing blue eyes.

I deserved it.

She smoothed a hand over her hair and turned around abruptly to stalk to the kitchen. "There'd better be a pork one in there."

I couldn't help but chuckle. "Hey, Rocco!" I yelled. "Come eat some chips!"

It took a third of a second for the kid to emerge and race by me, snagging the brown bag on his way. I followed them to the kitchen, pleased with the progress I'd made so far.

☘☘☘

After the burritos were consumed, I still had two more things on my list to attend to. First, I was finding the gecko for Rocco so there would be no more fainting spells. How a person could be so freaked out by such a tiny thing was beyond me. But women are impossible to understand, as everyone knows.

With Rocco's help, I retrieved the little guy from behind the dresser where he had, indeed, been hiding. I had to admit, it was pretty cool-looking.

"What's his name?"

"We haven't decided yet. Aunt Bailey wants to name him Satan."

I barked out a laugh. "That doesn't really suit him, does it?" I lifted the creature up and looked into his tiny face.

"What does he like to eat?"

Rocco scratched his head. "Um, mostly crickets, I guess."

"That wouldn't be a very good name," I replied. "Well, then, what about one of your ninja turtle names?"

He gave me a look that said I couldn't be more of an idiot if I tried. "He's a lizard, not a turtle, Jake," he explained patiently.

Moving on.

"Well, what do *you* like to eat? Besides chips."

He seemed to think about this for longer than necessary. "Pizza, cookies, Pop-Tarts, Cheetos, pickles, candy, strawberries, cheeseburgers, olives, graham crackers, milkshakes, Goldfish, marshmallows, cereal, bananas, and yogurt. But it has to be the squeezy kind."

Okay then.

Bailey stood in the doorway. "Is it safe to come in yet?"

"All clear. We're just trying to come up with a name for this little guy."

She took a half step into the room but clearly wasn't willing to come any closer. "Rocco rejected all my ideas."

"Cuz you wanted to call him Satan and Quadiosmar," Rocco protested.

"Well, you wanted to call him Gecko! And it was Quasimodo," Bailey retorted.

"Seriously?" I looked back and forth between the two. Pathetic.

"You need to give him a happy name, one that's fun to say. Like Popeye or Gizmo—or one of your favorite foods we were talking about," I prompted.

"Well, then his name is gonna be Pickles because I love pickles and he's kinda green."

"Perfect," Bailey and I said in unison, and I saw her glance my way.

I held the gecko out to Rocco. "You put Pickles back in his tank. I gotta go, but I'll see you soon, kid." He took the little guy from my hand. "Hold onto him so he doesn't escape again," I warned. "Maybe you should call him Houdini."

Rocco gave me a puzzled look.

"Or not."

I turned and motioned for Bailey to follow me out into the hall.

She muttered something unintelligible but did indeed follow.

At the front door, I turned around and I swear I caught her cringing.

What the hell?

Before I could utter a word, she cut in, "Look, Jake, I'm sorry I didn't return your calls—or your texts. I had a…great time at the wedding." She ran her hand over her hair again in uneasiness. "But

I've got a lot going on and I just don't have time for a…*thing*…right now."

Huh. Well, that summed it up, now didn't it. The old "it's not you, it's me" brush-off. But my instincts said she was still as hot for me as I was for her. I'd have to either bow out gracefully or work this from another angle. I was hoping for the latter.

I was clearly a glutton for punishment.

I put my hands up in a classic "I'm unarmed" position. "Okay, enough said. Sorry if it felt like I was some crazy stalker." I laughed.

She didn't.

Oh.

"How about if we just hang out as friends, then. You know, grab a coffee, meet up with the gang for drinks…"

"Yeah," she said as she began walking slowly toward me. Ah, maybe this wasn't dead yet.

Then she reached one arm around me, and I swear I was a millisecond from swooping down and kissing her when I realized she was reaching for the fucking doorknob.

I'd been shut down and now I was being thrown out on my ass.

It was a tough day to be Jake Beckett.

☘☘☘

Fortunately, I had enough going on in my life to provide more than adequate distraction from the complete blow-off I'd just received.

I owed Jax a call to talk about the upcoming landscaping opportunity, and I knew that should have been my top priority all along. Perhaps Bailey was a distraction I just didn't need.

Everything in me hoped that moving back to Greensboro to start over was the right move. I'd worked damn hard to perfect my craft and establish important connections back in Clearwater, so it wasn't a decision I'd come to lightly. But I generally trust my instincts, and they told me to go home and reconnect with my family.

When I'd been home in the spring to deal with family shit, I'd managed to forge the beginnings of a relationship with Jax, who just happened to be Fiona's boss. She answered phones for him at his landscaping and lawn care business—when she wasn't doing her catering thing or making my brother nuts, that is. I'd done my homework, and Jax was the best of the best in this area.

So, I'd put together a business plan and presented him with an idea for a partnership of sorts. He wasn't lacking in customers, but he also wasn't taking full advantage of the opportunities out there. The man knew grass and a lot of vegetation, but he didn't know design. That's where I would come in.

I figured if we pooled our talents, we could build an even bigger business. But why would a guy with an already successful business want to take a chance on an unknown like me? Well, that's where all my references came in nice and handy. There are a lot of very pleased retirees on the Gulf side of Florida whose acquaintances I've met. Turns out older women love a little bit of North Carolina charm. And it doesn't hurt that I know my shit inside and out.

"Damn, Beckett!" Jax had said when he'd read the first page of my references. "Exactly what did you have to do for Ms. Caroline Shaw to declare you—" He lowered his eyes back down to the page to read, "'the sharpest young man I've ever had the pleasure of working with'?" He gave me a sly, conspiratorial grin.

I returned it. "I swear to you, man, I managed to resist all her charms and focus on the job." It hadn't been hard. Ms. Shaw is seventy-four.

Jax laughed and slapped his desk.

"Alright. Hit me with it." He leaned back in his chair and folded his hands behind his head.

This was my opening.

I knew my references had caught Jax's attention, but he's a smart guy and that alone wasn't going to do it. Luckily, my plan was as low-risk as possible for him.

"The way I see it, you've got the connections and the customer base in this area. You know the customers and they trust you. But they're going elsewhere when they decide they want a water feature or a landscape screen. And where do you think they're going for a tiered garden or an entertainment niche?"

One corner of his mouth quirked up. He knew exactly where I was going with this.

"Bixby's. That's where they're going. Or Northwest Garden Design. They're not half bad, but we both know Bixby's is shit. I can run circles around that crew," I said. I'd done my homework. "And I have the certification and experience."

Jax threw a chin out to me. "I'm no horticulturist and I don't run a nursery, as you well know. You think you're the first one to bring this to my attention?"

"Nope," I responded. "But I think I'm the right one."

He barked out a laugh at that one. "Okay, Beckett, show me the specifics."

And that was how I'd secured my ticket home to North Carolina and, hopefully, a rebuilt relationship with my mom and brother in the process.

I'd returned to Florida to get my shit in order and plan my big move, and I didn't want to look back. Now, it was months later and I was finally ready to roll with this new endeavor. Step one was to secure my first client.

Jax picked up on the first ring.

"Yo, Beckett! How'd your little project go this afternoon?" He chuckled.

"Unfortunately, it didn't," I replied, the wound to my pride feeling fresh again.

"Ouch. He struck out, ladies and gentlemen!"

"Not so fast. It's only the first inning. I need time to warm up before I go back in."

"Well, in the meantime, let's get down to business then."

I was definitely ready for that.

Chapter Five

WHITE LIES AND SNOWFLAKES

BAILEY

Like any remotely sane human being, I detest the very concept of Monday mornings. And this particular one had an extra layer of poo piled on top because not only did I have to get myself up and ready to go, but I also had to contend with a six-year-old who didn't want to leave his new pet at home while he went off to kindergarten. How do parents do this shit?

The previous night, he'd even tricked me into letting him sleep with me, an experience I was loath to ever repeat. At one point, I'd awoken with his butt on my pillow—thank God he'd had underwear on at least, even if that was the only item of clothing he wore. I was beginning to think Laney and Nate were just throwing money away by purchasing clothes of any kind for this kid.

"If I was him, I'd be lonely here all by myself." *Sniffle*.

"Rocco, he's a lizard. Lizards don't get lonely." We'd belabored this point for the last ten minutes. I believe my foot was actually tapping with impatience at this juncture. I was a walking, talking cliché.

"How do you know?"

"I just do." Lord, help me.

"How?"

"Because," was my brilliant comeback. I'd had a child for two days and I was already using the "because" excuse. This was humiliating.

"That's not a real answer, I don't think." Rocco drew his little brows together in thought.

"Buddy, we have exactly two minutes to get out of this house before you miss the bus and I'm late for work. What's it gonna take? Just lay it on me."

He didn't even hesitate. "I think a Tootsie Roll might work."

"Done. Let's roll." No pun intended.

♣ ♣ ♣

"So, I hear my brother dropped in on you yesterday."

Mark waltzed into my office mid-morning, ready for some verbal sparring, I'm sure. I ignored his remark completely.

"Please, for the love of God, tell me Fiona is better," I begged.

He just grinned in response.

"What does that face mean?" I made a circular motion in the general direction of his annoying mug.

"It means I'm not answering until you tell me why Jake came over to see you yesterday. I thought you said nothing really happened at the wedding." He wagged his finger at me. "Was somebody fibbing?" He flopped into the chair across the desk from me. "Spill it, Murphy!"

"Nothing happened. Nothing is going on. I have no idea why

he stopped by. And if you don't tell me how Fiona is, I swear I'm going to punch you in the throat—and then again in the dick for good measure."

"Jesus. Somebody's touchy this morning." He wisely scooted his chair back. "Oh, and by the way, you have a Cheerio in your hair."

I put my head in my hands, not even caring that there was actual *food* in my hair. "Mark," I whined, "remember when I said, 'I got this'?"

He cleared his throat in a failed attempt to muffle his laugh.

"I don't have this. I mean, I *really* don't have this."

I chanced a peek at him and was surprised to see a thoughtful expression. "Admitting you have a problem is the first step," he said, solemnly.

I threw a pen at him. "This is not funny!" I lowered my voice to a whisper for some stupid reason. "He's winning. And I mean, like, it's a shutout."

"Wait," he said. "Are we talking about Rocco or the lizard?"

I threw another pen at him. "Rocco! Both! That kid is walking all over me and I'm so exhausted and out of my element. When can you guys take over again? I am waving the white flag." I mimicked my surrender. "He had Tootsie Rolls for breakfast. The Cheerio is from *my* breakfast."

Mark twisted his mouth to one side and scooted the chair back a bit more.

This couldn't be good.

"Um, well, I hate to break it to you, but Fiona still has a fever, so it's gonna be at least a couple more days."

Since there really was no other option, I face-planted on my desk and prayed for a black hole to swallow me up. However, knowing there was actual work to be done, I made myself rally after a few minutes of well-deserved wallowing.

And since Mark had nothing useful to contribute to my crisis, I shooed him the hell out of my office before he could quiz me further about Jake's visit the day before. More threats to his man parts may have been involved.

Is lying to your kind-of best friend/brother/co-worker really all that wrong? I was going with no.

I just couldn't bring myself to admit to Mark that I'd shamelessly jumped his hot brother and broken all my rules regarding sex and men. I was still blaming the damn wedding anyway.

☘☘☘

I'd made it through the wedding ceremony without tripping or humiliating myself, which I considered a huge accomplishment deserving of at least two glasses of champagne. I am in no way a big drinker, contrary to what my name would suggest.

I'm convinced my parents were drunk when they named me, which makes me question the professionalism of the hospital staff, among other things. My first name is a brand of alcohol and my last name is synonymous with a very rich tradition steeped in "the drink." So, you'd think I could hold my liquor quite well. You'd be wrong.

It had been at the reception, while I watched my beloved ass of a brother dance with his beautiful bride, that I'd first spotted Mr. Tall, Dark, and Smartass. The smartass part was only confirmed later, but I had my suspicions from the beginning. Nobody can sport a cocky grin like that and pull off a convincing level of sincerity.

He was watching me.

This was something I was not used to—at all. At one point, I actually looked behind me to see if perhaps I was acting as a human shield to the intended recipient of "that look." But, no, there was no one. Therefore, I looked like a complete jackass—which is not uncommon in the life of Bailey Murphy.

The tall, hot dude was amused by my not-so-subtle move.

This was uncharted territory. Guys like this did not look at girls like me. First, he was incredibly tall—probably six-three or six-four. And despite his body being covered by a well-cut dark suit, there was no doubt he was built. It was Muscle Town under that suit jacket.

And that face! It was like Nate and Laney had hired actors to come in and pose for their perfect wedding spread in *People Magazine*. This guy had dark, perfectly messy hair, a five o'clock shadow, and killer cheekbones. He'd done very well in the gene pool drawing.

He also looked vaguely familiar, but I would remember if I'd seen him before. He must have been one of Laney's relatives. Whoever he was, he was doing a great job of making me acutely aware of every single solitary cell in my body—they were all abuzz.

Unsure of what to do with my hands, since they had suddenly become alien appendages whose function I'd completely forgotten, I desperately grasped at my champagne flute and chugged the contents.

This sent me sputtering. Brilliant.

By the time the choking-induced tears had dissipated, my mystery man was gone.

I should have been relieved to no longer be under his scrutiny, but I'm afraid my feelings more closely resembled regret.

☘☘☘

"Tell Doug the guys from Nussbaum's are coming in the morning so that drywall better be ready," I told one of the crew members over the phone.

I was trying to wrap things up and slip out early. I had to meet Rocco's bus in an hour so I didn't have much time to spare—but I'd take what I could get.

I shut down my laptop and hoofed it out into the fall sunshine. There is no place like North Carolina to enjoy fall and spring—the sun can't help but shine on our little state. Today was no exception, and my mood lifted in response. My red coupe was waiting half a block down the road and I jogged toward it.

Five minutes later, I was turning off Spring Garden and parking in the lot beside the Shearwater Gallery. If I timed things right, I had about thirty minutes. Thirty minutes I could spend exploring my favorite exhibit of the year—the paper arts exhibit.

Imagine the most beautiful snowflake you've ever seen. Now, imagine that someone cut an exact replica of that snowflake out of mountains of crisp, white paper. Multiply that by a thousand and picture yourself standing in the middle of this colossal, intricately crafted snowflake as it curves and twists around your body. Yeah, that's it.

This wasn't my first time visiting these masterpieces. I'd been coming at least once a week since the exhibit opened, each time discovering a new detail I'd missed on my previous visits.

This, right here, was what I wanted. Well, not paper art in particular, but to have *my* creations, *my* paintings, exhibited where they could make a person feel just how I felt standing beneath this vast gossamer snowflake.

The only thing I'd ever wanted was to be an artist. What my dad has always referred to as my "hobby" is, in truth, my passion.

When I'd gone to college, it was just assumed that I would major in something that would benefit the company in some way. So, I'd told myself that majoring in interior design and space planning would be enough to satisfy my need for creative outlet. Turns out, not so much.

My job at Built by Murphy consists mostly of a series of endless space-planning projects, meetings, and consultations. Deciding to move a half-wall ten inches to the right was about as creative as I got to be on a daily basis.

I checked my watch again, realizing that I'd lost track of time. I'd have to speed a bit to make it in time to meet the bus. I stroked the air in front of one particularly intricate curve of my snowflake before turning and racing to catch that bus.

♣ ♣ ♣

I was just pulling a pizza out of the oven when my phone rang that evening.

Part of me wanted it to be Jake and the rest of me cursed that part.

The rest of me got its wish.

"Hey, how's the honeymoon?" I asked with a grin. I plopped the pie on a cutting board and shook off the oven mitt.

"Oh God—it's gorgeous down here! I don't know if I can ever come back to real life," Laney sighed.

I could perfectly picture her lounging on a beach chair with an umbrella drink and a sun hat, Nate panting all over her.

"I'm glad you're having a good time. Is my brother behaving himself?"

"Um, no," she said with a giggle.

Yuck!

"Gross!! Blech—just don't!"

She laughed outright. My fault for asking.

"Okay, I'm sorry," she replied. "I'm actually calling because Nate and Fiona are miserable liars and they finally had to spill the beans that Rocco is with you. I should have caught on sooner when Fiona claimed for the third time that my kid was in the bathroom and couldn't come to the phone." She laughed at herself.

At least one of us seemed unhorrified at the notion of me caring for a child.

"Well, you found the little sucker. I was just about to call him in for dinner. You want to talk to him?" I failed to mention that he probably wouldn't eat his dinner considering the two Pop-Tarts he'd had after school. What was wrong with me?!

"Definitely, but I wanted to say thanks first. I feel really bad that you had to take over like this. I know it's not fair to you. And we can totally come home early if we need to."

I pulled a face even though I knew she couldn't see me. "Shut up—no way are you coming home from a tropical paradise to supervise bath time and make frozen pizza." I realized after I uttered that statement that I probably should make the kid bathe at some point in the week. I'd figure that out later, though. "And, besides, Nate said he owes me and I'm not about to lose that IOU! I've got plans for that bad boy."

"Did you just call your brother a 'bad boy'?"

"Eww, no—get your mind out of whatever nasty gutter it's swimming in right now. I'm going to have to take a shower to get rid of this crawling skin, you big ho-bag!"

She was giggling again. She was probably drunk.

"Rocco!" I yelled. "Come talk to your mom!"

"Mommy!" he screeched as he raced to the kitchen and snatched my phone out of my hand.

"Mommy, you'll never believe it! I have a new friend and his name is Pickles!"

Shit.

Well, I may have just lost my IOU.

Chapter Six

CURIOUS

JAKE

"It really depends on your personal tastes and which type of shrubs you prefer. Personally, I can't resist any of the flowering ones, but the coloring on some of the others we discussed can be phenomenal as well," I said as I turned the tablet toward Mrs. Emelia Vaughn, owner of a gorgeous colonial in Old Irving Park—and my potential new client.

"Hmm," was her only response. She rose one perfectly manicured finger and lazily swiped through the photos on the screen.

She'd been tough to read throughout our entire exchange, and I'll admit I was beginning to get worried. Had my charm failed me? Was it only potent in Florida?

My instincts were always spot-on with clients. I knew when to back-slap or fist-bump the men and when to lay back and project a casual, confident air. Likewise, I knew when to be respectfully professional with women or be affable and flirty. But Mrs. Vaughn had me in a state of self-doubt.

Jax had explained that his crew had been caring for the Vaughn's lawn and landscaping for over ten years. And, because of that, he'd felt comfortable offering a consultation should they be interested in redesigning their landscaping.

It so happened that their daughter had recently gotten engaged and they were planning an outdoor ceremony in their spacious back yard. And so, as one might expect from a well-established family such as theirs, the yard would need to be re-designed to be suitable to host such an affair.

That's where I came in.

I felt the first bead of sweat drip down the center of my back. I held back the urge to fill the silence. *Just wait her out, Beckett.*

After what felt like an eternity, she finally raised her steel-gray eyes to meet mine. "You mentioned a cascading waterfall, Mr. Beckett?"

And that's when I knew I had her.

♣ ♣ ♣

Later that evening, the door to my bedroom swung open and Mark barreled in, uninvited—his bulk making the room half the size it had been.

"Uh, can I help you?"

"No, shithead. The question is, can I help you?" he said with a grin as he stretched his neck from side to side. He'd clearly just come from the gym.

I was lying on my old twin bed, poring through job applications for my new venture. I'd be using some of Jax's guys, but we had to hire additional crew with experience in the types of installations we'd be doing.

"You can help me by getting out of my room and letting me get back to work, dickwad," I told him as I returned my attention to the paperwork. What can I say? When it comes to brothers, insults and physical assault are often the only forms of affection we understand.

"Hey," he fake-punched my arm. "It's my room too. Speaking of which, isn't it about time you moved out?" He looked around with an air of disgust. What an ass.

"I'm working on it," I told him. "What do you need?"

He cocked his head and the grin returned. "Like I said, it's not what *I* need. It's what *you* need."

"Cut the cryptic bullshit and spit it out, for the love of God." I scowled at him and finally closed my laptop, setting it and the papers on the bed beside me.

"I need you to go over to Laney and Nate's place tomorrow."

"Uh, how exactly is this helping me?"

He went for the punch again but this time I blocked him and got in a hit to his ribs. He just laughed it off.

God, he was so damn jolly these days it was making me ill.

"Come on, big brother. You're not fooling me. You've got a thing for Bailey. My guess is you got rejected when you went to see her the other day, so I'm giving you an opening to get back in there."

"How did you know I went over there?" I hadn't told a soul.

He shrugged. "Eh, word gets around. The kid has a big mouth."

Damn.

"And what would make you think I have a thing for Bailey, anyway?" I tried for nonchalance, not quite achieving it.

He just cocked his dumb head again and gave me his best "don't even try it" look. "Uh, because you had your tongue down her throat and your hand up her dress at the wedding reception. How's that?" His grin could have blown Jax's out of the water in the shit-eating department.

Double damn. I didn't think he'd seen that much.

Mark put his hands up in defense.

"Look, Bailey claims nothing happened beyond that, and I'm gonna choose to respect your privacy on that one. But I'm actually trying to help you. I think you two would be good together."

Who was this sappy dude and what had he done with my brother?

I feigned disinterest. Little did he know, he was right on the money with his guess that I'd been shut down.

"To be honest, it wasn't until I saw you two going at it that I knew for sure Bailey was straight." He barked out a laugh.

Huh?

"What does that mean?"

"Well, you know. She's kind of a mess."

"No, I don't. What the hell are you talking about?"

"Oh shit," he suddenly covered his mouth. "The wedding was the first time you met her, wasn't it?"

"Yeah, so?" Why did I feel like he deserved to be punched right then?

He laughed. "I hate to break it to you, man, but Bailey is basically a dude with tits."

WTF?

"But at least they're real—I think—so that's something."

Yup, I'd definitely have to punch him.

☘☘☘

Three days after my first attempt, I found myself standing once again on this particular porch in a renewed effort to get this girl to date me.

Maybe.

I still didn't understand what Mark had meant with his bizarre statement about Bailey being a dude, but I had extensive evidence to the contrary. I chose to ignore him and chalk it up to him being love-drunk and a general idiot. I also knew he and Bailey were thick as thieves, so it was probably some inside joke or something.

I used the key Mark had given me and let myself in. Rocco's bus was scheduled to arrive in fifteen minutes so I had time to spare.

Evidently, Bailey had asked Mark to get Rocco off the bus today because she had a previously scheduled meeting she couldn't get out of. Mark, in turn, had decided to play matchmaker and sent me in his place. We'd see how Bailey chose to take that little surprise.

I couldn't resist checking in on the gecko while I waited. The more I looked at him the more I thought the name Rocco had picked was perfect. This thing's tail looked like a pickle—it really did.

Growing up, I'd always wanted a snake or any kind of reptilian creature for that matter. I'd figured it would make me look like a bad-ass if I had a snake or something creepy. But there was no way my dad was going to allow that. And, besides, it would have been irresponsible to bring any living thing I cared about around the old man, as he didn't exactly treat those around him with kindness.

We did have a dog, Daisy, who'd wandered onto our property one day and decided never to leave. If we'd been able to convince her to find another home, it probably would have been the conscionable thing to do. But that dog was loyal, and at least the old man hadn't hit her, as far as I knew. But neglect was almost a worse type of abuse. Without my mom to hold things together, we all would have fallen victim to that.

When I'd left for the Marines, it had somehow made me feel better that Daisy was there for my mom and Mark. Solidarity in numbers, I suppose. But it had just been an easy tool to soothe my conscience.

Through the bedroom window, I heard the unmistakable rumble of the school bus engine. I headed out to meet Rocco.

"Can Aiden come play in the Fart Fortress?" was the first thing out of his mouth when he bounded off the bus steps.

Through a series of phone calls, I'd been added to the non-child-molester list of approved adults to retrieve Rocco from school and/or the bus. Someone had apparently notified the kid that I'd be the one meeting him at the bus stop today because he didn't blink an eye when he saw it was me and not his aunt waiting for him.

However, this did not explain the mention of a "Fart Fortress."

"Uhhhh…yes?" I asked more than said.

What did I know?

"Don't worry, hun," said a thickly accented voice from behind me.

I turned and immediately spotted a pretty, stacked redhead standing there amongst the small group of parents collecting their offspring from the bus. I couldn't believe I hadn't noticed her before she'd spoken.

"He's talkin' about his treehouse," she explained. Then she held her hand out to me. "I'm Charlotte Baker. You must be Jake."

I took her hand, curious as to how she had any knowledge of my identity.

Seeing my confusion, she enlightened me, once again. "I'm Laney's neighbor and friend. Our sons are good pals."

"Oh," I replied, still coming up to speed. Then, "The Fart Fortress? Really?"

She laughed. "I know. It's awful, but probably pretty apt, after all."

I returned her laugh. "I suppose so."

"How is Fiona doin'?" she asked.

Was this woman a witch? How did she know everything?

She giggled again. "You should see the look on your face, hun. Laney's been textin' me updates." She put her hand to the side of her mouth as if divulging a secret. "She wanted me to keep an eye on Bailey in case she needed any help."

"Ah, gotcha." Now it made sense. "Fiona's on the mend and, well, other than fainting at the sight of a small animal, I think Bailey's doing pretty well," I informed Charlotte.

She looked alarmed, so I quickly followed that up with, "Not to worry—it was just a funny incident."

"Okay," she said, but didn't look fully convinced. "If you say so."

I figured I'd better head back to the house before I did more damage. "I'm gonna check on the boys in the…farting place," I finished lamely.

She pressed her lips together momentarily, attempting not to laugh. "Okay, Jake. It was nice to meet you. And, if you don't mind, can you send Aiden my way in a bit?"

"Sure thing," I said and turned to head up the driveway.

It wasn't until I'd closed the front door behind me that I realized I hadn't even checked the redhead's ass out as she'd walked away.

Curious.

☘☘☘

"We need to go to the pet store!" Rocco exclaimed as he and Aiden burst through the patio door twenty minutes later.

Ha! Like I was falling for that trick—I wasn't about to make the same rookie mistake Bailey had made.

"You're not getting another pet. Tears may have worked on your aunt, but I'm immune," I informed him.

"No, seriously," the Aiden kid interjected. I noticed for the first time that he was wearing some kind of harness that held an assortment of (hopefully) fake weapons. He was nodding his blond head at me and looking deadly serious. Who was this kid?

"Okay, what now?"

"You need worms," Aiden informed me.

Both boys nodded enthusiastically.

Say what?

"Worms?" I asked, still sure I was being duped somehow.

"Totally," said the armed one. "Pickles needs mealworms and probably some roaches, but I don't think the pet store will have those."

I was suddenly not so sad that I hadn't gotten a pet reptile as a child.

I gave them both a look that said I didn't trust them as far as I could throw them, but I did pull out my phone. "We'll see about that."

Aiden crossed his arms over his stockpile of weapons and Rocco mimicked him while I consulted the internet.

"Huh. Well, it looks like I owe you boys an apology. I guess we're going to the pet store."

They both high-fived.

"You're going home, kid. Rocco and I are going to the pet store."

I'd never had the pleasure of being called a "party-pooper" until that moment.

Chapter Seven

IRISH

BAILEY

Now, where in the hell were they?

I'd just gotten "home" from my afternoon meeting with a new architect on an upcoming project. I had not gotten a good vibe from the guy and was dreading working with him on this build. There was something about his demeanor that didn't sit right with me, but I couldn't put my finger on it. Or maybe it was just me and my cloudy mood lately.

I'd been so distracted when I pulled into the driveway I missed the fact that Mark's truck was absent. I was fairly confident I would have gotten a call if something had happened, but I checked my phone just in case. Nothing.

Maybe they'd gone out to eat. That would save me from making dinner, so I was counting it as a win. I grabbed a soda from the fridge and plunked my ass down on the recliner just as I heard Mark's truck pull into the drive.

The front door opened and I yelled out, “You better have brought me leftovers or dessert! I’m starving!”

Rocco’s little head poked around the corner to the living room. He had wide eyes and a big smile. He really was all kinds of cute —no wonder he got away with murder. “Wanna watch Pickles eat some worms?”

My appetite suddenly left me altogether. Did I say “cute”?

“Um, no.”

“I’m afraid the only food we brought home is not going to be all that palatable to you, Irish,” came a deep voice that did not belong to Mark.

Goddamn—shit—mother…

How did he keep doing this to me?

I felt my face light on fire as Jake rounded the corner and descended the two steps to the living room. Despite my best efforts, other parts of me also warmed at the sight of him.

“Wh…What are *you* doing here?” I practically accused. He’d thrown me with the “Irish” moniker—that brought up some memories I’d been trying and failing to purge from all parts of my psyche.

He shrugged and put his hands in his pockets. “Mark asked me to come.”

I was going to murder Mark in his sleep. It didn’t matter that I was fond of Fiona—she’d get over it eventually.

“I’ll bet he did, the asshole,” I mused aloud.

Jake cocked his head to the side, feigning innocence. Those two were in on this together. I was sure of it.

“I thought we were going to be friends.”

Ugh. I sighed and concentrated on returning my face to its original color.

"Right," I finally said. "Um, I'm gonna change out of my work clothes. Be right back."

I escaped to the hall and made my way to the guest room. I had to pass by Rocco's room on the way.

"Eat those suckers, Pickles!" was the comment that caused me to sprint the last few feet to the guest room. I was now sharing a house with a child, a lizard, a box of crickets, and some worms. Terrific. I'd finally achieved my life goals.

I peeled off my company polo and looked down at my sensible cotton bra. I had a momentary pang of regret that I had nothing the least bit sexy or girly to change into. Then I mentally slapped myself.

Don't even think about him! This is not going to happen!

But one stubborn part of my brain couldn't help but remind me that, once upon a time, it had.

♣ ♣ ♣

After practically choking to death on my champagne—and my embarrassment—I'd wandered around the reception hall saying hello to some of our relatives and then stopped to chat with my parents.

My mother wrapped me up in a big hug. She was on some kind of contact high from Nate and Laney, and she'd been flitting around like a drunk person, telling everyone she ran into how much she loved them. It was hilarious.

"I love you too, Mom," I told her for the third time while patting her blond head.

"Oh, Bailey, I can't wait to do this all over again when it's your turn. Isn't it wonderful?"

It took all my inner strength to keep the smile plastered on my face.

My turn? I wasn't holding my breath.

My dad cut in, grabbing me for his own hug. "Leave the poor girl alone, Erin. Nobody is good enough for my girl!"

Oh God—this was almost worse.

He held me to his chest as he often did. "Ah, no man ever wore a scarf as warm as his daughter's arms around his neck." Another of my dad's famous Irish sayings. I was usually a sucker for them but could hardly bear it tonight. I squeezed him one more time and extracted myself from the hug, insisting I had a need for the ladies' room.

My turbulent musings were temporarily abated by the sight of Laney and Fiona performing some ridiculously funny dance that had them getting down and dirty. It looked like Mark was about to pop an artery as he delivered death glares to every male in the room who dared hoot or holler at the pair. I was finally starting to relax and enjoy myself.

I made my way to the stage where the band was playing. Seeing Mark go all caveman reminded me that I wanted to request a song for him as an inside joke. He was going to love this, and I congratulated myself for not being a complete asshole to him, for once.

Having completed my duties as an awesome friend, I threw caution to the wind and grab another glass of champagne from the bar. It was my brother's wedding after all. My consolation drink and I settled at a high-top table away from my meddling relatives and any other people who might want to talk to me about love. My ass took its place on a stool and planned to remain there for the duration.

My little private bubble remained intact until Mark's song

started playing and I got to see the look on his face. Aww. He met my eye and pulled Fiona in for a dance. Even I had to admit the two of them looked utterly adorable. Who would have thought?

I sighed for the gazillionth time of the evening.

"Why so sullen?" a deep rumble sounded from my right.

Startled, I turned quickly in the direction of the voice and was met by the intense, sexy, hazel eyes of none other than Mr. Tall, Dark, and Smartass.

Before I could think to keep my freaking mouth shut, I blurted, "Hot damn."

He laughed as I wished for one of those infamous sinkholes to suddenly appear beneath the hotel. "I was just thinking the same thing," he said, extending his hand. "I'm Jake."

My jaw dropped. "As in, Beckett?"

This was Mark's brother?

"The very same." One side of his mouth quirked up in a very naughty grin.

I'd been so shocked to discover his identity that it was just now registering that he'd basically called me hot! This guy—the one with the cheekbones.

It appeared Fiona had more than outdone herself that morning and had somehow miraculously transformed me into Bailey 2.0 (a.k.a. The Hot Bridesmaid). I probably owed her my first born.

Jake moved his hand a bit and I realized I still hadn't accepted his handshake. Ugh. He leaned in a bit too close for a stranger and whispered, "This is the part where you tell me your name."

I snatched his hand—there was really no other way to describe it—and shook it enthusiastically like some fan-girl.

Kill me now.

"Bailey Murphy," I answered and then dropped his hand like it had burned me.

It was official. I was not fit for human interaction.

He continued to grin. “I thought that might be who you were… Bailey Murphy.” He seemed to be tasting my name on his tongue. I felt everything in me clench in response. I was in deep trouble.

Then he tilted his head to the side and said, “So nice to meet you, Irish.”

It was a wonder I didn’t fall off my stool in a dead faint.

☘ ☘ ☘

I shook my head, banishing the memory. I took another look down at my cotton bra and granny panties and sighed. Well, there was no point in putting lipstick on a pig, so I donned my UNC t-shirt and a pair of gym shorts and went to rejoin Jake in the kitchen. He was peering into the fridge and mumbling to himself.

“Um, I’m pretty sure Fiona left some dinners in the freezer. All you’ll find in there are eggs and some leftover pizza.” I put my hands in my pockets, not knowing what else to do with them.

His eyes found me over the open fridge door.

“Ah, I should have guessed.”

He gave me a once over and, again, I could not for the life of me discern his expression.

“So, since we’re friends, is it okay if I stay for dinner? I’ll even do the defrosting.” He closed the door and gave a little bow of his head.

What could I say? I just nodded and let him get on with it.

While he was distracted with dinner prep, I couldn’t help but look him over again. Well-worn jeans, navy t-shirt that fit way too well, and work boots. How was it fair that he made casual look like that while I made it look like I’d been dumpster diving?

I had to think about something else.

"So, how are things going with the new business?" I sat on a barstool at the kitchen island.

He turned and gave me another lopsided smile. "It's actually going pretty well so far. I booked my first client and I think I've almost got my crew nailed down. It's going to be a total backyard re-design based around an event the family is hosting. It'll be kick-ass if I can convince the couple to go with the theme I have in mind."

"Oh yeah?" I asked, genuinely interested now. I waited for him to continue as he tried to figure out the microwave.

"Yeah. I've got this whole vision—kind of a modern interpretation of a French cloister garden with white tree roses and low hedges to form the quadrangle shape." He pushed a few more buttons and the appliance obeyed.

Dear God, why was it hot hearing a man talk about hedges and quadrangles? And why did he have to be interested in design? That meant we had something in common.

"Sounds beautiful," I said.

"Well, let's hope it turns out that way." He raised his eyebrows and approached the other side of the island.

"So," he said.

I narrowed my eyes. "So."

He gave it another minute, no doubt waiting for me to cry uncle and let go with the verbal diarrhea that was sure to follow. I steeled myself and kept my lips sealed, although it took great effort.

He gave up and twisted his lips to one side. "I guess it's still a no on the dating thing, huh?"

If only he knew how much I wanted to jump across that island and climb him like a human jungle gym.

I just shook my head and reminded myself that my fragile heart would thank me later.

♣♣♣

After dinner had been consumed and Jake was gone, my phone rang.

"I am pleased to announce that my fever is officially gone and I'm feeling tons better," came Fiona's cheerful voice over the line. There was hardly a trace of a rasp. "I'm still coughing a little and not feeling one hundred percent, but I'm not contagious anymore. Yay!"

"That's awesome," I replied.

"So, tell the truth. How has it been going?"

I didn't know how much to confess.

"Well, I hardly had to do a thing for Rocco today, so I'm batting a thousand right now. Not sure I can say that for the other days, but he's alive so that's something, right?"

She laughed. "I'm sure you did fine." She paused before adding, "I'm assuming a thousand is a good thing?"

"Yeah, but this shit is exhausting," I confessed. Although the exhaustion I was feeling at the moment probably had more to do with the stress of resisting Jake's many charms for a couple hours.

"Oh, girl, you should have seen Laney when Rocco was a baby. She had bigger bags under her eyes than some of my Louis Vuittons."

I desperately wanted to ask when she could relieve me of my duties, but I knew that wasn't fair since she was still a bit sick. So, I just responded, "I can imagine."

"Anyway, I wanted to tell you that if you can get Rocco on the bus tomorrow I'll be there to take over babysitting duties when he gets home in the afternoon. I miss the little guy."

YES!

I reigned in my excitement a bit. "Are you sure? You don't have to do that if you're not feeling up to it." *Please be feeling up to it.*

"Positive. There is one little thing, though."

"What?" I was afraid to ask.

"I thought I would be nice and forewarn you." She paused and my stomach sank. "Laney is going to kick your freaking ass for buying that kid a lizard! Sweet dreams." She cackled and hung up on me.

Chapter Eight

GIVING IT UP

JAKE

Even I knew when to give up.

I'd done my best, but Bailey was having none of it. She'd even purposely dressed like a guy to get her message across. It was time to move on.

It was probably for the best. I had work to focus on, and besides, I also had to figure out how to get my own place without having sufficient proof of income. That wasn't going to be easy.

I had a decent nest egg in the bank, and I was confident I'd get this business up and running, but nobody cares about that when you're applying for a lease or a mortgage loan. And there was no way I was having my mother or brother co-sign anything. I'm thirty-three, not eighteen. I'd just have to figure it out.

I'd become adept at figuring things out—I faced challenges head-on now. I was no longer that punk-ass kid who ran away when things got tough. And I'll never be him again.

I walked in the front door of Precision Lawns and Landscaping, my laptop tucked under one arm and a tray of coffees in hand. I was surprised to see Fiona's bright smile and green eyes greeting me.

"Hey, you!" I said. "You look like you're feeling much better."

"I am, thanks," she replied. "In case you were considering it, I don't recommend getting strep throat. It sucks." I detected a touch of gravel still in her voice.

"Note taken." I held out the tray of coffees. "Take your pick. I got an assortment."

"Oooh, thanks!" She inspected the selections and grabbed one from the tray, popping the lid for a deep inhale of coffee goodness. "If you're looking for Jax, he's in a meeting with Ollie." She tilted her head toward the closed door behind her.

I nodded and could feel a smile of eagerness on my face. "I'll wait. Just have some sketches to show him."

"Well, look at you all bright-eyed and bushy-tailed," Fiona teased with a mocking swirling motion of her free hand.

I scowled at her and she laughed in my face.

Yeah, she and Mark were a perfect match.

"Whatever. Please say you're giving my brother as much of this smart-ass shit as you're dishing out to me?"

"Oh, your brother's definitely getting as much of my smart ass as he can handle."

I nearly choked on my coffee, but she didn't bat an eye.

"Hey," she interjected suddenly. "I forgot! I'm planning a night out when the honeymooners return this weekend—you up for it?"

"Sure, just let me know when and where, and I'll be there. I'll bet Bailey can't wait to be off the hook, huh?"

I just had to go there, didn't I?

Fiona smiled. "Bailey has officially been relieved of her duties as of this afternoon. I wouldn't be surprised if she had her own party in celebration." She laughed.

"Yeah, it did seem to be a bit of a struggle for her, not that I get what the big deal is. He's just a kid." Well, and a lizard.

"I know, right? I'm sure she did fine, though." Fiona cocked her head. "Speaking of our tall, blond drink of water…"

"Oh, no." I threw my hands up. "Mark already tried, and I'll confess to you and you alone that I got shot down not once, but twice. I can take a hint."

Her bottom lip jutted out in a pout. It made her look about twelve, which went with the rest of her tiny person. "Why?"

"Why what? Why did I get shot down or why am I done trying?"

"Both." She propped her elbow on her desk and sank her chin into her palm.

"She's just not into me, so what's the point?"

Fiona sat up straight again, pursing her lips and raising her eyebrows to the ceiling. "Uh-huh."

Wait, that was my line.

"What is that supposed to mean?"

She continued to give me the eye. Damn, she was good at this.

"What?!" I demanded.

"Just wondering what color Bailey's panties were the night of the wedding."

Shit.

I stuttered, "I-I-I wouldn't know. Why would you think I'd know that?"

"Can it, Casanova. Fiona knows all." She dismissed me with a wave of her hand.

"Who told you?!" I slammed down the coffee cups, spraying the desk with a splash or two.

She did a little dance in her chair and smiled from ear to ear. "You just did! Sucker!!"

Double shit.

I did a face palm and said a little prayer for my baby brother that he'd survive a lifetime with this little she-devil.

☘☘☘

The rest of the week flew by, and by the time Saturday rolled around, I'd not only had a second meeting with the Vaughns but I'd also managed to secure another client. This new one was a wealthy young couple who'd just purchased a home and wanted to start from scratch on the whole property. I was on cloud nine and completely in my element. Jax was pleased as well. We had a lot to get done before the cold weather hit.

I'd told Mark I'd meet the group at M'coul's, where they were all gathered to welcome the happy couple home. It was really just an excuse to go out, not that we needed one. I knew Bailey would most likely be there, but I was doing my best to ignore the knot in my chest and keep things casual. However, the irony was not lost on me that I would be meeting up with her at an Irish pub.

My best apparently wasn't very good, as I found myself immediately scanning the crowd for her face as soon as I crossed the threshold of the bar. I gave myself an internal lecture and went in search of the party.

"There he is!" Nate called out from my left.

"Hey, man, welcome home." I smacked his back in greeting since his hands were holding full beers. "So, how was the honeymoon? Did you knock Laney up yet?"

He laughed. "You're the third person to ask me that since we got here." He shook his dark head as if this were somehow surprising.

"We're all on the upstairs patio. C'mon." He handed me one of the beers and gestured for me to follow. It hadn't occurred to me until that point that he and Bailey really didn't share any physical characteristics. She was all light and sunshine while Nate was dark like me. Maybe they had the same eyes? Not that I was about to check out my buddy's eyes.

What was I doing? I had to let this go. No matter what had happened between Bailey and me, this group of people had become my friends and I wasn't about to stop hanging out with them just because I'd been given the Heisman.

Stepping out on the patio, I wasn't at all surprised to see the guys standing in a group to one side while the girls sat around a table on the other end of the space. And, yes, there she was.

She had her back to me, but I could see she was wearing a pair of dark jeans and a sky-blue, sleeveless top. Her hair was in a ponytail, exposing the long curve of her neck. I wanted to go over and kiss the spot right behind her ear.

Dammit.

I forced myself to turn my back to the ladies and focus on the male contingent. Just about every guy I knew in this city was gathered here tonight. Gavin was in some kind of argument with Brett, his best friend. It was probably about baseball, as the playoffs were around the corner and Gavin was a former player. Then there was Mark, of course, and a couple guys who work with him at Built by Murphy—Trey, Court, and some dude whose name I always forgot. And Nate, looking tan and completely smug, as well he should.

I couldn't help but bring him back down to earth—I'm a giver that way.

"So, how's Pickles?"

Yup, that did it.

He scowled. "Did you have anything to do with that, asshole?"

I laughed. "Not a thing—that was all your sister. I was just there to witness the aftermath."

He leaned in conspiratorially. "I think it's kind of cool myself, but Laney is creeped out by the insects. If I want to continue getting laid, I figure I'd better toe the line and pretend to be annoyed."

"You're a smart man, Nate Murphy." I toasted him.

"That I am," he responded, and it wasn't lost on me that his eyes sought out Laney as he said it.

Without my permission, my head turned to the table of women as well, and my eyes zeroed right in on Bailey's smooth, ivory neck. My sensory memory kicked into overdrive.

☘ ☘ ☘

My earlier silent interaction with the hot bridesmaid had, unfortunately, been interrupted by my mother. She'd pulled me aside wanting to see pictures from the ceremony and I couldn't really refuse. She hadn't been able to make it to the church since she was catering the reception and Fiona was the maid of honor.

My mom sighed and awwed through the assortment of photos I'd managed to collect on my phone. If there were a few too many of a particular blonde, my mother certainly didn't mention it.

By the time she'd gotten her fill and had to return to her duties, I'd lost sight of my conquest. However, a half hour later I spotted the gorgeous bridesmaid sitting alone at a high table on the far side of the room.

Perfect.

I was able to openly appreciate the view as I approached her from the side. She was nothing short of breathtaking, with her long hair pulled up into an artful arrangement and her make-up just subtle enough to let her natural beauty shine through. And that body in that dress. I had to bite the inside of my cheek.

I heard her sigh loudly and took my moment.

Bailey Murphy.

I'd had a hunch she was Nate's sister, but that couldn't be helped. If everything went according to plan, I'd either get a date or a taste of her before the night was through. Although, with her opening line and the way she was looking at me after I'd just called her "Irish," I was beginning to think I was going to get lucky —pun completely intended.

She turned to face me full-on and I could see her pupils dilate and hear her breath hitch. Then, she did the one thing no man can resist. She bit her bottom lip and stared at mine.

Holy shit.

It was on.

It didn't matter that we were in the middle of a crowded wedding reception. It didn't matter that we'd just introduced ourselves. This girl was primed and I was pretty sure I was about to get jumped. Hell, yes.

I couldn't help but lift my hand and touch the side of her long neck with my fingertips. Bailey turned right into my touch and then, yup, sliding off the stool she grasped the front of my dress shirt and started pushing me backward toward the wall behind us.

Hoping like hell I wasn't on some kind of hidden camera show, I went with it, and when my back hit the wall I spun her around so I was pressing her into it instead.

I heard her gasp before her mouth sought mine and we were kissing like two horny teenagers. Her tongue ran along my lower lip and I growled before slanting my head and invading her mouth with my own tongue. She tasted like champagne and I was about to get drunk on her.

I felt the nails of one hand bite into the skin of my chest through my shirt while the other made its way under my suit coat and explored the muscles of my back. A shiver ran through my entire body and I couldn't help but pull her even closer and grasp the back of one of her thighs through her dress.

Perfection.

I had to get more. Completely forgetting where we were, I shimmied the material of her dress up a bit on the side until I felt the top of a stocking. That sent my cock into a state of rigor mortis I didn't think could ever be relieved.

And that's when I heard my blond goddess gasp again, but this one sounded different. It was followed by the words no man ever wants to hear when he's about to get lucky.

"Shit—your brother!"

Chapter Nine

THE SEX ELEPHANT AND THE ASSHOLE

BAILEY

Shit.

I'd known Jake would probably be here at M'coul's, but a tiny part of me was still holding out hope that he'd somehow caught Fiona's strep throat.

What? This guy was like catnip to me and this kitty needed to back away!

"Bailey, hun, your face just turned as white as a hillbilly's ass in winter," Charlotte said in her characteristic drawl.

Every face at the table turned to me. My pale skin subsequently transitioned to blazing red, I was sure. I scoffed at her. "Yeah, right. Have another drink, Baker." This is why I didn't do girl talk. What's wrong with keeping yourself to yourself?

"Oooh, am I missin' somethin'?" she asked, obviously not fooled by my flippant response. Charlotte was Texas born-and-bred and we all loved how she peppered every conversation with her thick accent and, more often than not, some odd-ball saying her "grand-daddy" had come up with. I was guessing the hillbilly with the white ass had come from his collected pearls of wisdom.

I'd gotten to know her a bit this past spring when Fiona had been refusing to submit to the inevitable and put poor Mark out of his misery by admitting she loved the asshat. Charlotte and I had both been recruited to distract Fiona while she worked her shit out. I'd been relieved for the couple when they'd finally gotten their act together, but truthfully, I hadn't been confident I could handle any more of Fiona's decreed GNOs ("Girls' Night Out," or, "Got No Orgasms," as I liked to call them). Don't get me wrong—I like these women—but gabbing about men and fashion isn't exactly my thing.

Now that Fiona and Mark had worked everything out, it was just fun seeing them together—it was like watching a well-dressed flea buzzing around a big dumb dog.

And the GNOs had slowed to a trickle, thank God. What was wrong with watching a movie or going for a run? Did it always have to be gab, gab, giggle all the time? Yuck.

"No, Charlotte," I answered at the exact same time that Laney and Fiona said, "Yes, Charlotte."

I gave them both a look intended to invoke terror in their tiny hearts. It had no effect.

Charlotte laughed and Laney continued, "There's something going on between Bailey and Jake." She looked like the cat who'd eaten a whole cageful of canaries.

I gasped. "There is not! Don't listen to them," I told the southern redhead. She ignored me and kept her eyes on Laney. I sank down in my chair.

"I can't believe you didn't see them at the wedding! They were about ten seconds away from putting on their own how-to sex demo at the reception."

Oh God. Had everybody seen us? I sank further into the chair until I was practically under the table.

"How in holy hell did I miss that?" Charlotte asked, clearly disappointed.

Was no one on my side here?

"It was awesome!" Fiona piped up. "You should have seen Nate. He was calling Jake all sorts of names and was about to go hunt him down and kill him to defend Bailey's honor. We had to physically restrain him while Mark went to throw water on them. At least, that's what I assumed he did." She winked at me with absolutely zero subtlety.

Shit.

"Come to think of it," said Laney, playing with her long, dark hair. "I don't recall seeing either one of you at the reception after that. Mark came back and I saw him give Nate a thumbs-up but… wait one damn minute! He was totally lying!" She leaned in suddenly.

"And don't think I didn't make him pay for it when I found out," said Fiona as she lifted her martini glass.

This was clearly the wrong thing to say. Laney rounded on Fiona and pointed a finger right in her face. "You knew and didn't tell me?! What kind of best friend are you?"

Fiona set the glass down with a bit too much force. "I just found out this week! What did you want me to do, call you on your honeymoon and interrupt your tropical twat tangle to tell you Bailey and Jake had sex!"

The last sentence was, unfortunately, spoken at a volume that carried across the entire patio. There was no need to look around to know that every single eye was directed at our table. The only good piece of news was that I was already three-quarters of the way to the floor so I really didn't have far to go to literally hit rock bottom. I was already there, figuratively.

Fiona's voice sounded again from across the table, but this time it was much quieter. "Oops."

♣♣♣

To escape the complete and utter humiliation that seemed to be my general lot in life, I eventually excused myself to the restroom. I kept my gaze on my shoes to avoid everyone's eyes as I exited the patio, but I could feel them on me anyway.

I splashed water on my face, took a few deep breaths, and then decided that a little alone time was in order. I slipped out the front door of the pub and leaned against the wall outside.

It wasn't long before Fiona found me.

I should have hidden better.

"I am so so so sorry, Bailey. I can't believe I did that. I mean, I *can* believe it because that's the type of thing I always seem to be doing, but I'm so sorry I did it to you. I promise nobody is going to talk about it anymore, and the guys have moved on, I'm sure—that is, if they even heard it in the first place." She squeezed my arm.

I gave her a look to let her know I was not born yesterday.

"Alright, alright. They probably heard it. But they're guys—pshhh—their attention spans only last a few seconds before they're thinking about their own penises again, instead of someone else's." She paused and closed one eye. "Wait, that didn't come out right."

I ended her misery with a pat to her hand.

"It's fine. Don't worry about it."

She leaned against the wall next to me. "So, um, you wanna tell me what's going on?"

I raised an eyebrow and looked at her sideways.

"It's just that I know you turned Jake down when he asked you out this week. Don't you like him? I mean, the air practically sizzled up there."

I laughed, but it held no humor. "I like him too much. That's the problem."

"That's great! How is that a problem? He obviously likes you."

I couldn't believe I was participating in chick talk with the girliest girl in the entire Triad. Instinct told me to shut my mouth, that I'd already said too much, but I pushed off the wall and faced her. She was dressed in some kind of silky top with a printed skirt and fuck-me heels. Her hair was practically floating around her head like a halo and her make-up was flawless. I threw a hand out and waved it up and down in reference to her ensemble and general adorableness.

"Have you seen him? Have you seen you? You're much more his type than I could ever be."

"What in the hell are you talking about, you crazy bitch?"

"Look at me! If you hadn't intervened, I would have shown up tonight wearing a Panthers t-shirt and my oldest sneakers. Even with this outfit, which you know is the dressiest thing in my closet, I'm still band-camp to his quarterback."

Her face scrunched up in obvious confusion. I couldn't really expect her to understand. And it was far from the whole story, anyway. "Forget it. It's not something you could understand."

That got me a look—one that said she did not like to be underestimated.

"Listen here, Bailey Murphy!" Oh no. Out came the wagging finger and the fist on the hip. It was time to get comfortable because it was gonna be a while.

"Despite what you may think, you are no fascinating enigma. It's an old story, as in, really old."

I was trying to decide if I should be insulted when she continued—without needing any invitation, I might add. "You may think you're fooling everybody but you can't fool me. You're self-conscious and insecure around people—hot guys especially. You play down your looks and you amp up the snark and sarcasm in some kind of attempt to cover your insecurities." Oh great. Now her head was weaving back and forth too.

And she was not wrong.

"If I had to guess, you probably even used to dress in all black and spout off about being a non-conformist and not wanting to be held down by 'the man,' whoever that is. And then you became an actual adult and realized if you wanted to eat and live in anything other than a cardboard box, you'd need 'the man' to pay you."

I tried to cut in but her other hand shot out to stop me.

"And don't even get me started on that job you hate."

I tried again but was intercepted once more.

"And I know you're aware of all this, so don't try to play dumb with me, chica! You're a fucking porcupine and you know it!"

I finally got a word in. "May I speak now?"

She nodded, having finally lowered her finger from my face. "You may."

"How the fuck did you just do that? Are you a profiler for the FBI in your spare time?"

She started giggling.

"Porcupine? Really?" I asked and, what can I say? It was contagious. Despite everything in me that resisted by habit, we were both a laughing, teary mess when Laney and Charlotte came to find us and coax us back to the patio.

I had to hand it to Fiona—the girl was sharp. But she'd missed the part where my prickly outer nature also served to protect my heart from collecting scars. That was still my secret to keep.

☘☘☘

I managed to survive the rest of the evening, and everyone was extremely gracious about the giant sex elephant in the room, or patio, I should say. Even Mark managed to keep his mouth shut about it, which was shocking to a degree where I was almost worried for the state of our friendship.

Another week began with me attending more boring-ass meetings and pretending I was elsewhere. Without Rocco to worry about, I was able to resume my normal schedule. I ran in the mornings, binged on junk food, sketched at night, and made my weekly stop at the Shearwater.

I chose to go on Wednesday this week, as I needed a mid-week boost. The paper arts exhibit was due to close this weekend so it was my last chance to experience my snowflake and all the other divine paper creations. I intended to get my fill since I had no other obligations for the evening.

Alone in the gallery, I'd reached a perfect state of quiet calm when a familiar voice caught my ear.

"I assume you'll have the front gallery cleared by Sunday," the voice demanded. It wasn't a question.

"Certainly," came the curt response.

"And don't forget we need a few of the alcoves as well, Paul."

Two sets of footsteps sounded across the wood floor, coming closer than I would have liked. One was swift and sure while the other shuffled.

Dammit.

I turned quickly so my back was to the two men who'd just entered the space holding the paper sculptures.

Please don't see me. Please don't see me.

"Ah, I see the recycling hasn't been taken out yet," said the first voice, followed by a chuckle.

I held in my gasp of indignation. Asshole!

The second man, who I now knew to be Paul, the assistant to the curator, let out a nervous titter.

Oh, get a backbone, Paul!

Perhaps I should have told myself the same thing.

I shifted to the left, hoping one particularly large sculpture would obscure me.

No such luck.

"Bailey?"

I froze.

"Bailey, is that you?" the asshole asked again, the intonation at the end of his question rising, almost assuming a British lilt.

You're from Virginia, douchebag!

I turned around, feigning surprise.

"Anton! I didn't see you there!" Two could play at this fake-ass game. My smile was so artificial it could outlast a Twinkie.

"Hello, beautiful," he said as he leaned his blond head toward mine and kissed my cheek. His voice held too much weight, too much intimacy. His hand skimmed my waist as he bent.

My stomach dropped and I couldn't decide if the cause was butterflies or good old-fashioned bile. I half-heartedly returned his kiss, mine hitting only the air. My lips would never touch his skin again if I had anything to say about it.

"You are a sight for sore eyes," Anton said, taking in my face. Then his gaze moved down to my work attire and his expression almost turned to a sneer. "Although, I see some things never change."

Okay, we were done here.

I forced my smile to remain in place as I boldly looked him

over as well. Skinny jeans, ivory sweater—even though it was seventy-five freaking degrees outside—and black hipster glasses I had once found both terribly genuine and endearing. "No, indeed they don't," I challenged, feeling proud of myself for not letting my voice wobble.

He exhaled through his nose and assumed a familiar expression —one that was probably meant to seem patient but felt only patronizing.

Asshole.

"Come now, let's not squabble."

Again, dude, you're from Virginia!

"I don't know what you mean?" He still wanted to play this game? Fine. "But I really do have to run." I made a move to sweep past him.

"Wait," he said and grabbed my arm.

I had to take a slow breath to keep from yanking it back.

"Here." He held a postcard out to me with his other hand. "Come to my show. I'd love it if you were there. If you remember, you did help inspire some of it."

My chest caught fire. I snatched the card out of his hand and he released my arm. I attempted a casual pace as I walked by Paul, wanting to sprint instead.

"We'll see you there, yes?" Anton called after me.

I didn't answer. I burst through the doors of the gallery and ran to my car. It was only a small relief that I managed to make it to the driver's seat before the tears came.

Chapter Ten

THE GREAT WALL

BAILEY

The first time I had my heart broken I was six years old. The object of my true love was none other than Andy Pulaski, the only boy in the first grade with red hair and the only boy who would ever hold my heart—or so I swore to myself at the time. I could see it all laid out before us. We'd get married as soon as we were eighteen and we'd live in the house right next to my parents. I wasn't sure how one kept the stork away, so I figured he would deliver a baby boy and then a baby girl, and both would have red hair just like their daddy.

Unfortunately, Andy and I weren't exactly on the same page. Two things stood in the way of our happily-ever-after. The first was my theretofore unknown case of cooties. The second, and more troublesome, was the regrettable fact that his heart already belonged to Brittany Taggart and could not be swayed. Yes, Brittany Taggart of the shiny black curls and rainbow-striped tights—

not Bailey Murphy of the sloppy blond ponytail and skinned-up knees.

Upon discovering this news about both the cooties and Brittany, I marched up to Andy's lunch table in the cafeteria and proceeded to spit right in his applesauce.

To this day, I insist it was the other way around—that it had been Andy who'd been hopelessly in love with me and had chosen to show his affection by picking on me, as young boys will do. I'm the only one who knows the real story. Well, me and my parents. And, of course, Andy. And his parents. And the elementary school principal. And probably the secretary who'd arranged the parent conference. The point is, I had my little heart broken and I did not like it one bit.

You'd think I would have learned from my first experience, and, indeed, I thought I had. The next time I chose to give my heart away, I selected a more mature candidate. Surely, an older boy would be more careful with my heart.

But, again, it was not to be, as I learned in the course of another parent conference when Mr. Adler explained to my parents that declaring one's love to one's science teacher was not appropriate third-grade behavior and he'd truly appreciate it if they would instruct me to cease my attempts to kiss him after class.

My dad had consoled me by taking me out for ice cream and telling me that Mr. Adler wasn't good enough for me anyway. To his credit, my father did also tell me to cut the kissing shit out. But he assured me my love was a gift to be earned by the right candidate—that candidate not being a thirty-two-year-old elementary school teacher.

It was quite a while before cupid's arrow struck again, but his aim was true when I lost my heart to Corey Snodgrass (*I know, I should have expected bad things given the unfortunate last name*).

We held hands at a junior varsity football game and shared our first kiss outside a smelly men's restroom by the snack counter. Neither the stench nor Corey's Dorito breath could dampen my thrill at the monumental milestone.

Shortly thereafter, an ill-fated meeting between a car and Corey's bike resulted in a compound fracture of his leg and hip, causing him to miss two weeks of school. My fourteen-year-old soul longed to be by his bedside nursing him back to health. But having both a newfound fear of bike-riding and no driver's license prevented me from wiping my love's brow and whispering soothing words in his ear.

These obstacles did not, however, hinder Jennifer Shelton, and upon Corey's return to school, the two were joined at the hip—one recently healed and the other clad in skirts that were way too short, in my opinion. Slut.

I vowed to protect my heart at all costs from there on out. Never would I let myself be so vulnerable again.

That was, until I was sixteen and Jacob Silverstein told me he loved me. I handed my virginity over to him on a silver platter and invited him to take all he wanted and come back for seconds. Predictably, all Jacob had been after was a certain cherry and not the whole sundae.

I cried into my dad's neck, cursing Jacob's name while my father told me once again that there was nobody good enough for his girl. He even quoted Yeats, because being Irish made Yeats an expert on all things, including love. "Hearts are not to be had as gifts, hearts are to be earned," my dad advised. I assumed the same went for virginities but didn't ask for confirmation. My dad assured me I'd always have him, but that didn't soothe the sixteen-year-old heart as much as it had the six-year-old one.

I did not confess the extent to which Jacob had taken advantage of me, of course. But boys will be boys, so it wasn't too surprising when, a week later, some locker room talk ended with Jacob sporting a pair of shiners and my brother some bloody knuckles.

I'd learned my lesson for good. Love was for suckers. Sex, on the other hand, was not.

I maintained a reasonably healthy sex life throughout my college years and my twenties, preferring short, casual relationships with my fellow art nerds, carefully selecting my partners so as not to risk more damage to my most vital organ. A vague mutual attraction was all I required, but anyone who made my pulse quicken and my palms sweat was immediately taken out of the running. Fool me once and all that.

After a time, I fancied myself impermeable, and I eventually let my guard down. That, of course, was when Anton Germaine spotted me sketching on a park bench in the Tanger Family Bicentennial Garden. He was so slick, I hadn't even realized I'd agreed to go out with him until it was too late.

I convinced myself I could handle it—I was a grown woman, after all. Twenty-nine, in fact, and surely I could control my emotions. I'd had enough practice by that point.

But the thing I'd forgotten was that love doesn't care about your plans or your barriers. It doesn't care that you've built a virtual Great Wall of China around your heart to keep the scars to a minimum. All defenses are useless in the face of a quickened heartbeat, an offered hand, and a devilish smile.

And for a girl who'd always been critical of her abilities as an artist, Anton wielded the most powerful weapon to break down any and every wall. He praised my artwork and assured me I had limitless potential.

☘ ☘ ☘

The evening I ran into Anton at the Shearwater, I did something I seldom do. I got shit-faced.

Around the third beer, the brilliant thought (because all notions born of alcohol are brilliant) occurred to me that I should invite someone to drink with me. After all, everyone knows that only alcoholics drink alone. Pshhh.

I texted Mark first, but when he failed to respond I moved on to Laney. She was my new sister-in-law—surely, that fact alone was worth a celebratory drink or two. My text to Laney went unanswered as well and I was starting to get a little miffed. What good are friends if they won't come over and drink with you after you run into your asshole ex-boyfriend?! The fact that none of them knew about the asshole ex-boyfriend seemed unimportant.

I decided to start sketching while I waited for someone to respond—yet another fantastic idea. I amazed even myself at the success of that endeavor. Best sketches ever. Time for another beer.

The next morning, I awoke to not just a giant headache and cotton mouth, but several text messages and a mirror image of a graphite rendering of something resembling Daffy Duck tattooed on my cheek. Good lord.

I brushed my teeth and tried to ignore my reflection in the bathroom mirror. I figured it was time to read the texts.

*8:06 pm **Bailey:** Marl, come get shit on my face!!!!!!*
*9:42 pm **Mark:** Put the beer down and walk away!*
*10:02 pm **Mark:** Are you still alive?*
*10:03 pm **Bailey:** I'm sooooo goof at drawing!!!! Hellllooo?*

*10:05 pm **Fiona:** Hey, girl! I'll call you tomorrow to schedule a GNO! No is not an option.*

8:11 pm ***Bailey:*** *Hey Sis! I have deer—yah!!!! Partay!!!!*
9:34 pm ***Laney:*** *Aww—take some pictures of the deer!*

10:23 pm ***Bailey:*** *I no you no your sexy as fuck*
10:25 pm ***Jake:*** *call me*

Notification: 10:45 pm Missed call from ***Jake Beckett***

Shit.

Oh, shit.

I remembered nothing after I'd started sketching! I didn't even remember sending Mark another text, much less Jake! Why did I have to be such an idiot?

I debated throwing myself out the window, but what good would that do when I lived in a one-story condo? Then I looked to see if Jake had left a voice-mail.

Nothing.

Was that good or bad? I couldn't decide.

My phone rang and I cringed as I picked it up and looked at the number.

Mark.

"Hello?" I covered my eyes and answered.

"Hey there, Amy Winehouse! How's the headache?"

I growled in response.

"Just thought you might want to come in sometime today. You remember work—that pesky thing that gets in the way of drinking." He chuckled and I checked the time.

Holy shit! It was 10:15. I'd missed half the morning!

"Don't worry," Mark said. "I called Ruiz and pushed your meeting back to this afternoon. Ibuprofen and Gatorade are your friends today. Remember that."

"Thanks, Mark."

"Crap. You didn't even call me Buffy. You must be in bad shape."

I cringed again.

"Take your time," he said. Then he cleared his throat. "Call me later, okay?"

This must be way worse than I thought if Mark was using his concerned voice.

"Okay," I managed to say before hanging up and dragging my hungover ass to the shower.

Chapter Eleven

IT'S ALL FRENCH TO ME

JAKE

Well, I guess you could say the cat was out of the bag. I was doing my best to avoid Nate since he had plans to ensure I'd never father a child in this lifetime. I was mostly laying low and sticking with my plan to focus on work.

I hadn't seen Bailey since the disastrous night at M'coul's when she'd practically sprinted out of the bar. As soon as Fiona and her giant mouth had announced our private business to the entire patio full of patrons, I'd known the night would be an early one.

I saw Laney give Fiona a swat and bury her own face in her hands over the whole "tropical twat tangle" comment. I had to admit, that was fucking hilarious. However, my smile over that masterpiece of alliteration died on my face as soon as I'd seen Nate's expression.

Yeah, the dude was not pleased.

I threw my hands up in a defensive motion and opened my

mouth to speak. I'd been about to say something to the effect of, "Don't blame *me*, man. *She* jumped *me*," when I remembered I actually liked being alive. So, I wisely kept my mouth shut and just nodded in agreement as Nate called me every name in the book.

I don't have a sister, but I thought about what I'd say to any asshole who thought to put a hand on my mother and figured I deserved what I got and more.

Gavin finally intervened. "Nate, shut the fuck up. You just married my sister."

That did the trick and Nate went to go sit with Laney to cool down.

I decided to call it a night and snuck out the side entrance before Bailey came back. Seeing just how much she regretted our night together managed to pretty much kill my mood. I also didn't want to make her feel any more uncomfortable than she clearly already was. Since when was I a pariah to women?

Despite my resolution to focus on other things, I continued to have the same damn dream about Bailey. This caused my lousy mood to bleed over into the work week and I'd even groused at my mom on Monday morning. Completely ignoring my comments, she'd just kissed my cheek and gotten on with her day, her mother's intuition no doubt telling her I was lost in my own pity party.

I decided then and there to grow a pair and snap out of it.

And I'd been doing well until that text message.

I no you no your sexy as fuck

I'd been watching TV and almost choked on my beer when that unexpected, and obviously alcohol-inspired, text popped up on my phone. I texted Bailey to call me and immediately retreated to my bedroom to wait. The call never came and my follow-up went unanswered.

What the hell was I supposed to do now?

A soft female voice brought me out of my reverie. "So, we're going to need to leave room for a nice play area with a swing set and playhouse."

I was meeting with Tag and Tessa McGuire—*I know, you don't need to say it*—and we were discussing the preliminary layout of their new backyard. If anything had the power to bring me out of my head, it was this huge new project.

I smiled and nodded while I noted her request on my list.

"I know we don't have any children yet," Mrs. McGuire crooned, taking her husband's hand into hers, "but I'm hoping we will one day soon."

Mr. McGuire bent down and kissed her cheek. "I can't wait, love muffin." She ducked her head of dark curls coyly.

I was suddenly feeling more like myself. It took everything in me not to either choke or laugh. Who were these people?

Oh, yeah, that's right. Rich people. Carry on.

I wasn't used to dealing with young people with money. Most of my high-end clients in Florida had been older couples wanting to be surrounded by beautiful things as they enjoyed their retirement. But a client was a client, and this was a crucial one—and a damn entertaining one at that.

"That sounds great," I managed to say.

My comment brought their attention back to me. Mr. McGuire loosened his tie a fraction but didn't remove his jacket. I was sweating just looking at him. "I also like the idea of adding a game area for when we entertain. What about a French bowling court?"

Huh?

Mrs. McGuire clapped. "Oh, boules! That would be wonderful!" The sheer material of her sleeves shimmered as she brought her hands together in excitement.

I scratched my head. "Uh, I'm afraid you're gonna have to

explain what that is, Mr. McGuire. This southern boy is not familiar with that one," I grinned and went with the "aw, shucks" routine.

"It's Tag and Tessa," Mrs. McGuire patted my arm. "How many times do I have to tell you?" She smiled and gave me one last pat.

Okay, this woman was probably twenty-five and she was patting my arm like I was a misguided child. I suppressed both my grin and my eye-roll.

We were sitting at a large glass-topped table on the deck of their new home—a deck that I thought was perfectly nice but they'd deemed inadequate. Oh well, their money. They'd have to hire another contractor for that one, however, as I wasn't licensed in that area. Maybe I'd send Nate their way. I did kind of owe him for nailing his sister.

Tag laughed and I wasn't sure if it was meant to be patronizing or not. I decided to give him the benefit of the doubt. "You may know it as Bocci," he explained.

Well, why hadn't he just said so? I didn't understand why you would need a "court" just to play bocci ball, though. That would be like having an entire part of your backyard designated specifically for cornhole. Whatever. I took a long drink of my iced tea and watched as the condensation dripped onto the tabletop.

"I will certainly put that on my list to research for you. Now, what are your thoughts on the garden dimensions?"

We continued to discuss specifics so I could come up with more detailed sketches for our next meeting. Tag's phone rang toward the end of the conversation and he excused himself while Tessa walked with me to the front of the house.

"You're welcome to park in the driveway, you know," she said, gesturing to my truck which I'd parked on the street in front of their property.

"No, ma'am," I returned. "That's not how I work. I like to keep your driveway clear as much as I'm able to."

Instead of patting my arm again, she settled her hand on it this time, her eyes rising to meet mine. "It's Tessa," she reminded me in a soft voice and then, I shit you not, she swept her bottom lip with the tip of her tongue.

Dammit all to hell.

♣ ♣ ♣

"Oh, you're in it up to your eyeballs on this one!" Jax hollered and continued laughing. He finally rested his arms on the table and sunk his chin into his chest to keep himself from completely losing it, I assumed.

I didn't see what was so damn funny. Of course, if the shoe had been on the other foot I can't say I wouldn't have reacted similarly. Okay, I probably would have been worse.

Still, this was going to be a problem if I didn't nip it in the bud. And this situation was way too delicate to fuck it up.

Jax must have sensed the degree of my concern because he cut into my thoughts. "Relax, it happens. We'll just make sure to have crew around whenever you think you might have to be alone with her—piece of cake." He pointed at me and continued, "Whatever you do, though, use text messages and e-mail for any communications that aren't in person. You do not want this woman calling you for a chat. She calls, you let it go to voicemail and text her back. Or arrange a time to meet if you can't get it done over text."

I nodded my head. It wasn't as if I'd never been hit on by a client, but they'd always been older and had been a breeze to brush off without hurting anyone's feelings—or anyone's project. But I had a bad feeling about Tessa McGuire.

Jax took a drink of his soda as the waitress placed our lunches in front of us. He gave her a wink. "Thank you, darlin'." She blushed and sashayed away from our table.

I gave him a look. "Seriously?"

"What?" he asked, a french fry hanging out of his mouth.

I just shook my head at him. "Nothing."

He threw his chin out at me. "My crew is wrapping up our fall lawn applications so we'll be available to help with anything you need coming up. First frost won't be for about two months so you've got time to get things in the ground."

We continued to make plans for the two new jobs, and the waitress made several more appearances at our table. Either she was in the running for the Most Attentive Waitress Ever competition or she was developing a big old crush on my partner. She couldn't have been more than twenty-one and I'd put Jax somewhere in his late thirties. She hardly gave me a second glance and I tried not to take it personally.

We left the restaurant a half hour later, and to Jax's credit, the only things left on the table were a big old tip and the receipt she'd written her number on.

☘☘☘

I gave Mark a call to see if he wanted to go out for a beer. I figured giving him a hard time and checking out some eye candy would brighten my day. Unfortunately, Fiona had declared it to be TV night on their couch so my presence was demanded there instead. It wasn't like I had invitations piling up, so I headed over to Mark's place after dinner.

Fiona opened the door wearing her usual heels and fancy duds.

"You're watching TV," I told her. "You can at least lose the shoes."

She just stuck her tongue out at me and pulled me into the house. "I can't afford to be any shorter around you. Are you sure you don't have that disease Abraham Lincoln had? You know, the one that made him freakishly tall."

I barked out a laugh. "I'm pretty sure being 6'4" doesn't make me diseased."

"Well, whatever." She waved me away with her hand. "Unless you're willing to crouch down all evening, the heels are staying on. Go find your brother."

And, with that, I was dismissed.

An hour later, Fiona and Mark were fighting over the remote and squabbling over which show to watch next. In an attempt to change the subject, I brought up the story about Jax and the jailbait waitress.

"That doesn't surprise me one bit," said Mark. "I'll bet that dude gets tons of tail." I was thinking he wasn't wrong.

Fiona scowled. "How do you know she wasn't just gunning for his big tip?"

Mark and I glanced at each other briefly, but there was no helping it. We both choked out a laugh and it all just descended from there, as it often does.

"What?! Waitresses do it all the time. They schmooze the customers to make more money. You don't really think all waitresses find you that charming, do you?" She looked like she felt sorry for us.

By this point, Mark was slapping his knee and I was trying to keep tears at bay.

Now Fiona just looked baffled. “What is so goddamn funny, assholes?”

“Nothing, Shortcake,” Mark choked out. “We’re actually in complete agreement with you.”

I just nodded my head and managed, “Yup. Big tip.”

“Does insanity run in your family? I’m calling your mother.” Fiona smacked Mark on the back of the head and she and her high heels left the room.

None of us ever had the heart to tell Fiona when her mouth got in the way of her brain. That girl had a dirty mouth on a normal day, but it was always worse when her intentions were pure.

“Oh, God.” Mark finally said when we’d calmed down a bit. “I swear I should just marry that girl. The entertainment value alone is worth the cost of a wedding.”

I just nodded, knowing that while he was making a joke, he really would marry her in a second.

He turned to me. “Speaking of weddings…”

I put my head in my hands. Here we go.

“I guess you and Bailey are big lying slutbags, huh?”

I flipped him off. He just laughed.

“Yeah, I guess so,” I admitted. “But she wants nothing to do with me.”

“Aw, poor Jake. Not used to the word ‘no,’ are you? Sounds like you failed to impress.”

I brought my head back up and threw a glare at him.

Fiona re-entered the room, phone in hand. “Well, Kelly confirmed that insanity does not run in the family but idiocy does.” She sat back on the couch and grabbed her glass of wine from the coffee table.

Mark pulled her in with an arm and dropped a kiss on her head.

"We were just talking about Jake getting his first ever fuck-off from a girl."

"Really?" I gave him the look of a betrayed man. Why had I wanted to reconnect with my brother again?

Fiona waved her hand. "Oh, I already know all there is to know. For some reason, both you and Bailey trust me. I have no idea why."

This piqued my curiosity. "Oh?"

"Yeah—must be that idiocy thing," she teased.

"You're not going to tell me anything, are you?"

She put a finger to the side of her mouth like she was considering it. "Let me ask you this. Do you actually want to date her or just get laid?"

I guess that was a fair question. "I thought I wanted to date her, but she definitely doesn't want to date me. Not that I'd turn down getting laid," I tried to joke but Fiona glared at me.

I switched to contrite and her expression evened again.

"All I'll say is nothing is quite as it seems."

"Thank you, oh wise one." What was I supposed to do with that? All that confirmed was what I already knew—women are confusing as shit.

"But if all you're looking for is a piece of ass, look elsewhere."

Chapter Twelve

SOMETIMES THE FALL GOETH WITHOUT THE PRIDE

BAILEY

I spent the day after the Anton encounter/drunk-texting debacle trying to avoid Mark while also searching the internet for a phone app that would require me to take a breathalyzer test before calling or texting anyone. I was successful at the first but failed at the second. I barely made it through the afternoon and put myself to bed right after dinner. I was going to start fresh in the morning.

I was determined to permanently block all thoughts of Anton Fucking Germaine from my mind, and the best way to begin was with a morning run. There was a reason I liked to start every morning with a run—it always helped clear my head. And if it could help clear that asshole from my head, all the better.

Until the cocksucker sighting at the gallery the other day, I'd thought I'd done a stellar job of purging his existence from my mind. Based on my reaction and the aftermath, however, I'd not been as successful as I'd thought. How could he still affect me like that?

I wanted to hit something, throw something, stab someone. Okay, well, that was a bit much—unless, of course, I could stab Anton. I might find that quite satisfying.

My footsteps pounded the dirt path in a perfect rhythm as my arms pumped in a matching dance of athletic precision. Each intake of fresh air was a new thought; each exhale was an old one leaving my body. In, out, in, out, in—"Oh shit!" The expletive shot from my mouth along with the last exhale. My limbs lost their perfect rhythm as I crashed forward into the dirt.

Fabulous. Could things get any worse?

A piece of advice: never ask that question.

"I think that tree root had it in for you."

I didn't need to look up to know whose voice that was.

I no you no your sexy as fuck—Gah!

I chose to create a nice little bed for myself out of the newly fallen leaves that had, no doubt, obscured the offending tree root. I closed my eyes and let my head drop to the ground.

"Oh, come on. It can't be that bad. I have to say, though, I'm beginning to think it a bit odd that every time I see you you're horizontal."

He must have realized how that sounded because he quickly followed up with, "Oh, sorry." He didn't really sound very sorry, though.

I sighed. It seemed he wasn't going to leave me there to die in peace. "It's fine. Want to help me up?" I finally opened my eyes and looked up.

Jake was silhouetted against the cloudless autumn sky, but there was no mistaking the angles of his face or the flawless cut of his build. He reached a hand out and I took it, allowing him to pull me upright. My stomach lurched a bit.

"Anything broken?"

I paused to get my bearings, then dusted my knees off and ran my hands over my hair, liberating a few leaves that had tangled in the strands.

"Just my pride, thanks," I mumbled, finally taking a good look at him now that the bright sky wasn't behind him.

Yup, just as I'd suspected. Male perfection. Okay, well maybe that was going too far. I'm sure he wasn't every single woman on earth's cup of tea, but he hit all of my buttons. Yes, sir.

His shirt had a dark V from sweat, and there were beads of perspiration dotting the olive-toned skin of his brow. He had clearly been on a morning run just like I had. The only difference being his fortunate ability to remain upright during his.

"I didn't know you ran here?" I tried to cover my discomfort.

"This is actually my first day," he replied, looking around him at the lush lawn and trees. "I usually run in my mom's neighborhood, but I'm looking into renting a condo around the corner from here so I thought I'd check out the park this morning."

Oh God. *I* lived in a condo around the corner from here. This was *my* park. The universe had better have a damn good explanation for this! Was it wrong to wish for a plague of locusts to come down on his potential condo? *No, seriously, was that wrong?*

He must have seen the horrified look on my face. "Bailey, hey, are you okay?"

I opened my mouth to reassure him, or apologize for the text, or maybe yell at him—I don't know. And then something completely unexpected, completely humiliating, and completely revolting happened instead.

I vomited all over Jake Beckett's running shoes.

☘☘☘

"Okay, that should do it," Jake said as he tossed the empty water bottle into the recycling can.

"I can't believe I puked on you," I said for what was probably the tenth time.

He just chuckled. Why did he have to be so nice about this? He'd just rinsed my breakfast off his shoes and he was laughing about it! If Dante had a tenth circle of hell it would surely involve some horrifying combination of my humiliation and regurgitated Fruit Loops (*yes, I eat kids' cereal—suck it*).

"Your incredulity has been noted." He approached me where I sat on the tailgate of his truck in the parking lot. I couldn't look him in the eye, but I sensed him studying me before I felt his finger tuck a wayward strand of hair behind my ear.

My belly swarmed with butterflies and heat, and I prayed I wouldn't upchuck again. I gripped the bottle of water I'd been drinking from and ordered my heartbeat to slow way the hell down.

"You okay?" Jake asked quietly, his hand now holding the side of my neck. He crouched down so I had no choice but to meet his eyes. They were warm hazel pools of concern.

I just nodded, afraid I'd squeak if I tried to utter a single word.

"Let me drive you home. I don't want you getting sick again." He released my neck only to grasp my hand and help me down to the pavement.

I was going to have to let him drive me home. I didn't want to risk puking again until I was within safe distance of a bathroom—where God intended all crazy women to puke.

Either I'd eaten a bad batch of chalupas the night before, or I was letting the stress of my humiliation and the return of all my

Anton-fueled emotions worry me to the point where I'd made myself ill. I could now add that to the list of reasons I hated Anton. It would probably fall somewhere between his making me try raw oysters and his breaking my heart.

Jake opened the passenger door and helped me up before crossing over to the driver's side. "Which way?"

I pointed left and hoped that he'd say his potential new place was in the opposite direction on Lawndale, but he said nothing. The truck pulled out onto the street.

"My turn is coming up just there on the left," I instructed and then continued directing him to my place.

I loved my condo. It was nestled in the back of a neighborhood consisting of larger homes, with tons of mature trees to provide privacy. My unit had three bedrooms, two baths, and a walk-out patio. It was way more space than one person needed, but I'd gotten it for a steal when the housing market had been in the dumpster. One of my dad's favorite lessons was on the value of a dollar and how to use it wisely. "As we Irish say, a fool and his money are easily parted. Don't be a fool, Bailey." I took his advice seriously and had gotten myself a sweet deal.

I had one half of a brick duplex and my neighbor was this nice older Korean couple who didn't seem to mind my music and the sometimes-odd hours I kept. They undoubtedly felt sorry for the single old maid living next to them because I often came home to a plastic container of homemade dinner waiting on my porch.

Whenever I returned the container, I'd chat with Mrs. Kwon —usually about her daughter, Soo-jin, who lived in DC and insisted on going by the name "Susan," much to her mother's displeasure. I generally tried to stay out of it by nodding my head and making small sounds of agreement. But I'm sometimes tempted to comment something along the lines of, "That bitch!"

just to see how Mrs. Kwon would react. I feared I'd lose out on my free dinners if I let go of my impulse control like that, though. And Mrs. Kwon's kimchi was not worth fucking around over.

Jake pulled into my driveway and got out to walk me in. Crap. I opened the garage with my code and continued through the inside door. I didn't stop at the kitchen and I didn't check to see if Jake had followed me inside. I had only one thing on my mind and that was finding a toothbrush as soon as humanly possible. There was no way I was hanging out with this man for one more minute while I still had puke-breath.

After I finished in the bathroom, I came back out to find Jake examining the paintings I had hung on my living room wall. The back of his t-shirt was darkened with sweat in the center. I wanted to reach under the hem and remove his shirt entirely.

My mind wandered back to Fiona's frighteningly accurate analysis of my behavior, and I was thrown into an internal battle with myself. Why let my insecurities rule? Why let the Antons of the world win? And, besides, it was clear to both Jake and me that I wanted him. But then I remembered that men like Jake are made to break hearts like mine.

Jake must have sensed my presence because he turned around to address me. "These are beautiful. Did you paint these?"

"Um, yeah," I admitted and joined my hands together behind my back to keep them occupied.

He moved on to the other wall. Okay, yes, my place is completely covered in my own work. At one point, I had been confident enough to put myself out there.

"Wow," he said. "I'm really impressed."

I let out a mirthless laugh. "Well, you'd be the only one, then."

His brow creased in confusion. "What do you mean?" He

pointed to one particular oil of a street kid tucking money into his shoe. I liked to call it *Staying on His Feet*. "This is incredible."

I felt my face color, as it just loved to do around this man.

"Mark said you were an artist, but I just assumed he meant the design work you do for your company."

I had to laugh at that. "There's not a whole lot of art to that, let me tell you." I passed by him to grab some water from the kitchen. "Drink?" I asked.

"Sure. Water, if you don't mind."

I got us each a bottle from the fridge, hoping mine would tame the color in my cheeks. I turned around and there he was, standing way too close. What was he, a freaking panther? I handed him his bottle and our fingers brushed. I fought a shiver at the frisson of electricity that passed between us.

"So, what are you doing working for a construction company when you could be doing this?" he asked, gesturing toward the living room and the paintings displayed there.

I bit my lip. That was way too difficult to explain, and I didn't even know if I wanted to try. "It's complicated," I finally settled on.

He nodded and then said, "Ah, family."

"That's definitely part of it." I raised the bottle to my lips just as he did the same. I watched his throat work as he swallowed, and my knees sent an S.O.S. signal to the rest of my body. *We're going down!*

Jake finished his entire bottle in one go. "Are these 'complicated' things part of the reason you won't go out with me?"

He was really going there, wasn't he? I couldn't seem to catch a break.

I stuttered in my response. "I-I-It's hard to explain that."

He studied me and then nodded, his expression turning knowing. "Question." He moved a step closer. "Are you attracted to me?"

Ha! Like my horny text and my jumping him at the wedding hadn't been clear enough! Add in my skin's propensity to mimic a pomegranate and I may as well just take out a billboard—*Take me now, Jake Beckett, you sexy beast!*

I felt like my entire body was about to combust. "Um," was all I could manage.

"I'll take that as a yes." His lips quirked up in a cocky, lopsided grin.

Jerk.

Correction: hot jerk.

"I gotta tell you, Irish. You sure do know how to send a guy mixed signals."

Like he had to tell me.

☘ ☘ ☘

Mark was approaching with a speed that flustered me completely. What was I doing? I'd just physically attacked a stranger and stuck my tongue down his throat!

But, God, could he kiss.

I didn't have time to think. I grasped Jake's sleeve and pulled him in the direction of the hotel hallway.

In all the times I'd practiced in my heels, I'd never attempted running and I'd certainly never attempted doing so while dragging another human behind me. I wobbled a few times but finally managed to pull Jake into an alcove in a closed-off bar area. We were both breathing hard from not just the physical exertion of our escape but from our hot-as-hell groping session in the reception hall. I couldn't even let myself consider that my parents may have seen me. My breasts were practically heaving and I was worried they might spontaneously jump out of my strapless dress.

I heard quick footsteps and the sound of Mark's voice mumbling something. There was no way he could see us in our current hiding spot, but Jake pressed me further into the wall anyway. And I didn't mind one bit. Even fully clothed, his body was doing things to mine I didn't even know were possible. And the feel of his sizable erection against my thigh was making my brain a fuzzy mess.

Why shouldn't I have this? What was so wrong with taking advantage of this situation where a super-hot guy had mistaken me for a super-hot girl and wanted to get with me? I assumed this happened to gorgeous girls all the time—it had just never happened to me. I could be this girl for one night, right? And I didn't have to invite my pesky heart to the party.

"If we don't find a room, I'm stripping your dress off right here," Jake growled in my ear, making everything south of the border clench tight. He nipped my earlobe and I let out a whimper.

Summoning all the courage I had, I announced, "I have a room upstairs and it will be *me* stripping *you* down, Jake Beckett." Oh my God! I really said that!

He groaned and pressed in closer while one hand grabbed my ass and the other held the back of my neck for the searing kiss he delivered. I was lost in our tangle of tongues and arms when he finally pulled back a touch. "I think Mark's gone. Do you have your keycard?"

I silently thanked Fiona once again for showing me how nifty thigh-high stockings can be for storing all sorts of things, including room keys. I reached down, boldly lifting the hem of my dress to reveal the lacy top of the stocking and its contents.

"Clever," was all Jake said before sliding his hand up my silk-covered leg to retrieve the card. His fingers danced a path toward my inner thigh on their way back. I might have moaned.

At this point, the wall was eighty percent responsible for keeping me standing. But I was all in and I had to remember who I was tonight—strong, confident, sexy. I took Jake's hand and gave him a wink. "Follow me."

We moved to the elevators as one, and once we were inside and the button for my floor had been selected, I found myself pressed against the wall again. He loved doing that, didn't he? I decided it was time to turn the tables so I pushed him across the floor and pinned him to the other side of the elevator. I settled with my thigh between his legs. That got me a naughty grin.

"So, that's how it's gonna be, huh, Irish?"

I didn't answer. I just grazed my fingernails down the front of his shirt until my hands rested on his belt. I could feel his cock twitch in his pants and I reveled in the power I had over him. It was a heady feeling.

The elevator dinged and he was back in control again. He spun me and put his arms around me from behind, settling his lips on my neck and marching us down the hall. My eyes wanted to close from the delicious assault to my skin. We almost missed my room but I caught the room numbers through slitted eyes and stopped our forward motion. Jake's hands made quick work of the door lock and then we were alone. Alone in a hotel room while the rest of our families celebrated, drank, and danced just floors beneath us.

I'd made my bed and, dammit, I couldn't wait to lie in it.

Chapter Thirteen

SEX AND CONSPIRACIES

JAKE

Her pupils were almost completely dilated and I hadn't even touched her yet. She was incredibly bad at hiding her emotions, and no words were needed to understand her answer to my question. Hell, yes, she was attracted to me.

And despite the fact that she was a sweaty, dirty mess and had just thrown up on me, I felt my attraction to her down to my bones—one bone in particular letting me know his feelings on the subject loud and clear. I wanted to shake my head or burst out laughing, this situation was so ludicrous.

So, I did what any person with common sense and a penis would do in that moment. "Shower?" I asked.

Her head jerked slightly as if I'd just brought her out of her thoughts and back into her kitchen. "What?" she whispered.

I assumed a confident grin that usually got me what I wanted. "Do you want to take a shower?"

"T-t-together?" she asked as if I'd just suggested we murder a litter of puppies.

I cocked my head. "What's so wrong with that idea?" I ran a finger down her arm.

That seemed to set off some kind of trigger because she backed up quickly, smacking her head on the refrigerator. Jesus, I hoped to hell she had good insurance with her propensity to injure herself at every turn.

"Ow." She held the back of her head and retreated to the living room.

I followed, not willing to let her get out of this so easily. I did not understand this woman. She ran so hot and cold.

I knew Fiona said not to pursue her if all I wanted was a piece of ass, but when Bailey undressed me with her eyes—well, I'm only human. And, besides, she'd turned me down when I'd tried to ask her out on a normal date. I guess it couldn't hurt to try again.

"Okay, forget the shower."

She made a sound I couldn't decipher and kept her back to me.

"Let me take you out to dinner tomorrow night."

She turned around then, and I was sure she'd balk at the idea so I cut her off before she could open her mouth.

"You owe it to me for puking on me." Yeah, I went there. It was pretty low, but I needed her to see that we should explore this thing between us.

She opened and closed her mouth a few times before she seemed to come to a decision. "Fine."

I smiled.

She put a hand out to stop me from approaching. "But nowhere fancy, and I'm going to meet you there."

Well, that sucked. I was kind of hoping for a repeat of the high heels and stockings. Not to mention, meeting her at the restaurant would preclude the chance of any form of intimacy. But beggars can't be choosers, and I'd already gone way beyond my normal capacity for begging where this girl was concerned. What was a bit more?

"Deal. How about Freeman's at 7:30?"

She nodded. "Fine."

Why did I get the feeling she was looking forward to this about as much as a beheading?

☘ ☘ ☘

I waited outside the small restaurant for Bailey to arrive. I couldn't remember ever feeling this nervous for a date—which was particularly ironic since I'd already had sex with her. Everything about this was backward.

"Hi, Jake."

I'd been so caught up in my head that I'd missed her walking right up to me. I took in her flawless skin, gorgeous blue eyes and cautious smile before giving the rest of her a once-over. She wore skin-tight jeans, a fitted green t-shirt, and tennis shoes. At my perusal, she looked down self-consciously, as if regretting her choice of attire.

Truthfully, it didn't matter what she wore; she was stunning. I was beginning to understand she preferred casual clothes, but that didn't bother me. I'd opted for a button down rolled up at the sleeves and a pair of jeans myself.

I gave her a grin. "Nice shirt, Irish."

She looked from her green top to me and wrinkled her nose. "I promise you, it wasn't on purpose. It was the only clean shirt I could find."

I laughed at that. "Well, I approve. You ready?" I gestured to the door and she nodded.

I opened the front door to Freeman's and placed my hand on the small of her back to lead her in. I could swear I felt her tremble. I was taking this as a good sign.

Once we were seated and had our drinks, I offered a toast. "To first dates." I raised my glass.

She tried to purse her lips at me but a shy little smile escaped and she clinked her glass to mine. I winked at her.

"All right," she said, shaking her head. "Sorry I made this so difficult for you. I have to say, though, I'm surprised you hung in there for so long."

"What can I say? I'm tenacious." I took a sip of my beer.

"That's one word for it." The corner of her mouth quirked up, which made me laugh again. She was damn cute.

The waiter returned to take our dinner orders. I hadn't even glanced at the menu so I just asked him to recommend something.

"I would say that was brave of you, but everything here is delicious," she said, taking a sip of her drink.

"Well, I'm glad I picked a place that meets with your approval." I gave a mock bow of my head.

"It's really the only reason I agreed to go out with you." She tried to hide her grin but did a poor job of it.

I pointed at her. "Ha! Totally untrue. You agreed before I said where we were going."

"Touché." She tucked her hair behind her ear. I could tell she was barely resisting rolling her eyes at me. She changed the subject instead.

"So, did the clients like your design?"

For a moment, that took my thoughts straight to the awkward-as-shit situation with the McGuires, but I realized she was asking about the Vaughns.

"Oh, yeah, they did! We made a few adjustments, of course, but they went for it."

"That's awesome. It must feel great to have them like your vision." She smiled.

"Definitely."

Then I told her about the McGuires and their French bowling court. I left out the part about Tessa and the driveway.

Bailey laughed, as I'd known she would. "Oh God, that is so ridiculous. You should recommend adding a putting green and a cricket pitch so they can round out the pretentiousness and make it truly international."

"Excellent point," I nodded. "But you must deal with pretentious people all the time with the whole art scene, right? I mean, maybe it's a stereotype but…" I trailed off.

A dejected look briefly overtook her face and I regretted bringing it up. But she then cleared her expression and finally responded, "Yeah, I guess. Back when I was trying to break into the local scene there was definitely some of that." Then she let out a sharp mirthless laugh.

Uh oh. I'd treaded on touchy ground.

"What happened?" I ventured.

Her eyes were on the table but she finally raised them to mine. They explored my face as if determining whether or not I could be trusted. Then she spoke again. "Let's just say I put myself in the wrong hands and let my naiveté get the best of me."

I had the sudden urge to punch someone in the face. All I needed was a name. But the waiter chose that moment to arrive with our dinners and the tension of the conversation was broken.

Bailey gave him a smile and then took a deep breath. That was my sign that the subject was closed.

"Thank you. This looks terrific," she told him.

☘☘☘

The rest of the dinner went better than I ever hoped or expected. Bailey showed me her sharp wit and dry sense of humor, but she also let some of her softer side emerge—although, that seemed to be unintentional.

I shared a couple stories about Mark and she cackled evilly over them. I feared I may have earned myself a beating from my not-so-little brother if Bailey ever chose to repeat anything I said.

Bailey, in turn, shared stories from work and some funny moments with her family—especially those involving her dad and his devotion to everything Irish.

We were standing at her car when she told a particularly funny anecdote involving her father's conspiracy theory about Notre Dame football.

"That's something I've never understood," I told her.

"What? You mean you're not a conspiracy theorist?" She grinned.

"No. What I don't get is why Notre Dame is the 'Fighting Irish' when the name of the school is French."

She put her hand over my mouth as if to silence me from said conspirators lurking around Freeman's. She even looked around furtively. "Don't ever let my dad hear you say that. If he says it's Irish, it's Irish. No arguments," she stated emphatically before she lifted her hand from my face. "And, besides, it's all about us Catholics—you know, the downtrodden Irish."

I had to laugh. "So, basically you're saying that my little nickname for you was fated."

"No, I'm saying my dad is insane. Pay attention."

I was really getting turned on by her sass and I was more than disappointed I'd have to end the night here at her car.

"Well, I was recently told idiocy runs in my family. It sounds like maybe insanity runs in yours. Should I be afraid?"

She mock-glared at me and gave a dismissive huff.

I couldn't help it. I reached out for her arm and pulled her into me. "If you don't stop sassing me, I can't be held responsible for what I might do to you," I whispered.

Her face instantly pinked, and I could just imagine the mental picture my words had conjured.

Great, now the semi I'd been sporting all evening turned into a level-five hard-on.

I thought she'd pull away, but then she surprised me again.

"Oh? Do tell," she boldly returned, despite her look of embarrassment at my comment.

Ah, there was the girl from the wedding.

The one who was audacious and eager. No holds barred.

☘☘☘

I found myself in real-life fantasy. I was in a hotel room with an unbelievably sexy woman who kept looking at me like she was starving and I was a Vegas buffet. I sent a small thank you to Mark for insisting I come to the wedding and then swiftly purged all thoughts of my brother from my mind. I was going to fully enjoy this moment, this night, this…whatever it was.

I'd just closed the door and Bailey had taken that opportunity to pull ahead of me into the room. The lights were still out, but the moonlight coming through the far windows silhouetted her and I could see the movements of her body as she took quick, shallow breaths. Then I noticed one of her hands going behind her back and I realized she was pulling down her zipper.

Thank Christ.

There was no way I was missing one bit of this show. My hand groped blindly along the wall while my eyes remained pinned to this gorgeous creature. I found the switch and the lights flashed on.

A look of surprise and…something else crossed her face when the light first came on, but it was quickly masked with a knowing grin. Oh yeah, she knew exactly what she was doing to me.

"God, you're sexy," I told her as I remained frozen in place.

The zipper continued its slow decent and she began to shimmy out of the dress, wiggling her hips back and forth. I set my jaw and stayed where I was until the dress dropped in a pool of blue at her feet and she stepped out of it.

Holy mother of…

A lacy strapless bra exposed dark pebbled nipples while a pair of incredibly tiny matching panties barely covered her pubis. The lace-topped stockings that had been driving me mad encased some of the longest and most beautiful legs I'd seen in my life, and it was all set off perfectly by the glimmering heels on her feet.

I almost wanted to take a picture so I'd have something to remember this vision, but I was pretty sure it would be burned on my brain for an eternity.

She'd struck me immobile and I stared at her stupidly, completely caught up in the image she presented. She took pity on me and approached.

"Your turn," she whispered.

I immediately snapped out of it and began removing my clothes like they were on fire.

I almost tackled her in my zeal, but I had to get my hands and mouth on that flawless skin. I quickly disposed of her bra and backed her up to the bed. Her knees hit the king-size bed and she fell on her back, her breasts bobbing with the motion. I climbed on after her and straddled her thighs. The backs of both hands caressed gently over her pert nipples and she whimpered in response so I replaced one hand with my mouth, causing her to squirm under me.

I slowly removed her thong panties and got my first feel of her exquisitely bare ass. I was definitely going to get my mouth on it later. I'd get my mouth everywhere on this woman's body before the night was through.

My cock was rubbing against her thigh and she put a hand between us, drawing her fingers down from my sternum to my aching cock. I ran my tongue up her neck until I reached the underside of her ear where I placed a kiss. "I need you." I almost begged.

She must have found my tone amusing because I could feel her smile against the skin of my shoulder right before she gave it a nip. "I need you too." Her voice sounded between panting breaths.

I covered her mouth with mine again and our tongues explored each other as our hands did the same. When I couldn't stand it any longer, I reluctantly retreated from her body so I could get a condom from my wallet. When I turned back to the bed I was treated to the same miraculous sight as before, only this time she was horizontal with just the stockings on. Those were most definitely staying.

I rolled on the condom and approached. Bailey lifted her arms above her head like a complete wanton and licked her lips.

Holy Christ.

I kissed up her body from her thatch of blond curls to her chin before hovering over her completely and placing a slow kiss on her lips. Her thighs parted in invitation and I entered her slowly, allowing her to get accustomed to the feel of me. We groaned in unison as I pulled out just once before thrusting in fully. She gasped and then curled her legs around my waist.

After that, it was a frenzy.

Sweat-slicked skin and wet tongues danced over one another as she met my thrusts beautifully and moaned my name into my mouth. Her fingernails scored the muscles of my back as they worked to move my body over hers.

At one point, I adjusted our position and she made a sound I didn't think I'd ever heard a human make before. I felt her begin to pulse around my cock and I continued thrusting through her climax. She whimpered in my ear and I just moved us again so her calves rested against my shoulders, allowing her no reprieve.

Her head was thrown back and her mouth had dropped open to allow her cries to sound throughout the room. It was sexy as fuck.

It was a wonder we didn't break the bed or at least provoke a call to the front desk.

I managed to hold out while she reached her peak again, but that was the last straw. With a succession of frantic thrusts and groans, I finally gave in to my release and then narrowly avoided collapsing on top of her in sheer exhaustion. We both fell back into the bed in a tangle of sweaty limbs and heaving chests.

"Holy shit," she panted.

"You can say that again." My heart was beating out of my chest and despite the exhaustion, I'd never felt more alive.

☘ ☘ ☘

My body remembered the feel of her as I leaned in and kissed her outside Freeman's. She didn't hesitate to return the kiss, so I pressed her into the passenger door of her car and wrapped my arms around her. I needed this woman like my next breath.

But I knew it was not going to happen tonight. It had taken everything in my arsenal to get her to agree to this date and I wasn't about to fuck it up by molesting her on the street.

I pulled away and put my forehead to hers. Her eyes were soft and lazy. "Bailey Murphy, will you go out with me again?"

That got a full smile out of her and then she looked to the side as if trying to come up with an answer.

"I suppose I could manage that," she replied and then backed up and rocked on the heels of her sneakers. "So, um, you wouldn't be interested in coming to an art show with me, would you?"

I'd go pretty much anywhere she asked me to go. "Sounds perfect. When?"

Her smile got even brighter. "Next Friday night? Eightish?"

I gave her another light kiss on the lips and got the details. I'd scored another date and was feeling like my luck was finally turning around.

Chapter Fourteen

GIRL SHIT

BAILEY

I couldn't believe I'd asked Jake to Anton's opening! What had I been thinking? My initial instinct when Anton had first handed me the invitation was to burn it and maybe roast a good marshmallow or two over it. But the more I'd thought about it, the more determined I'd become to show him that he couldn't intimidate me. He was probably expecting me to either chicken out or show up with my head bent and shuffle around for a few minutes before fleeing. So I'd decided to show up, head high, and get the closure I needed to stop letting thoughts of him make me vomit.

Inviting Jake to go with me would either prove to be the best idea I've ever had, or it would end in complete and utter humiliation. It was really a toss-up. But if I was going to explore this self-confidence thing, I'd have to take a few risks. And, yes, maybe part of me wanted Anton to see that there was a hot man who wanted me. I could admit it, as petty as that may be. *Don't pretend you wouldn't parade some man-candy around your ex!*

But, apart from anything involving Anton, the biggest part of me just wanted to see Jake again. I ignored the pounding of my heart at the thought of him. I knew I should take it as a warning, but I just couldn't.

With the decision made and the date with Jake on the books, I was feeling ridiculously happy and positive—so much so that I could hardly even come up with any snide comments to throw at Mark when he called over the weekend to check on me. And I even agreed to one of Fiona's dreaded GNOs, but I managed to put her off for a week, citing my busy schedule. *Cough.*

This new attitude had a surprising side effect as well. It was standard for me to do some sketching in the evenings; however, I hadn't touched my paints in months. Since Anton, in fact. But I found myself preparing a couple new canvases early in the week and I began a new painting by mid-week. It was all a bit nerve-racking, but I felt excited about my art for the first time in too long.

Over the course of the week, Jake and I exchanged some flirty text messages—I found it much easier to be outgoing and brave when I didn't have to look at him. He tried to sneak in a dinner date early in the week, but I didn't want to press my luck. I needed to pace myself to let this newer, more confident Bailey gain a foothold.

I kept reassuring myself that I could do this. I just needed to keep that pesky warning voice at bay and everything would be fine. After all, it had worked since the very beginning with Jake. There was no reason it couldn't continue.

☘☘☘

"Holy shit," I repeated as we both panted on the king-size bed.

I was in a state of shock. I had no earthly idea sex could be like that. So nerve-tingling, so toe-curling, so all-encompassing, so… everything. Every cell in my body was wide awake as if Starbucks was throwing a two-for-one special and all my cells developed a sudden taste for espresso. But, at the same time, I was completely exhausted from the physical exertion and, I was afraid to admit, the emotional upheaval of the ridiculously fucking awesome sex we'd just had!

Jake chuckled in the bed next to me and then rolled over to place a kiss on my naked shoulder.

"The last thing I want to do right now is move, but I've got to take care of this condom. Don't move a muscle."

"Mmm," was the only response I was capable of as he rose from the bed and I got the full view of naked Jake. Naked was a damn good look on him. He was fit and well-built with muscular arms and a toned upper body from the physical work he did, I imagined. He was naturally a big guy, so there was lots of territory to go over in my little visual survey of his body. I sighed when I lost sight of him as he entered the bathroom.

I heard the toilet flush and the sink turn on and I waited motionless for him to return. I finally understood what the word "sated" really meant. I could happily die here and now, feeling fully satisfied. Well, maybe not. One more round wouldn't go unappreciated.

When the door to the bathroom opened and Jake emerged, he was carrying a washcloth. I looked at him in question, but he proceeded to the bed where he parted my legs and gently cleaned me with the warm cloth. I couldn't stop staring at him as he went about his task. Did guys do this? I never knew that. I was so mesmerized, I forgot to be embarrassed.

Once he deemed the job finished, he placed a sweet kiss on my inner thigh which caused my pelvis to jerk up. This made him laugh out loud and repeat it on the other thigh while I let out a little whimper.

He finally raised his head. "You'll have to give me a bit. I'm not as young as I used to be." He dropped the cloth and used his arms to pull himself on top of me again so we were nose to nose. His eyes were soft and smoky, and I guessed mine were a mirror image.

I wrapped my arms around his neck and we both settled on our sides, legs intertwined. His hand wandered to my hip and stroked me there.

An urge to explain, to defend myself suddenly overcame me now that the afterglow was receding a bit. I fixed my eyes on his stubbled chin. "I don't normally…I mean, this isn't usually how I…" I began, but he cut me off.

"Me neither. Honestly, I was thinking the best I'd get tonight was your number and maybe a promise for a date."

"Oh, God." That caused me to cover my eyes with my hand.

He seemed to realize what his comment implied about my degree of sluttiness and quickly tried to repair the damage. "That's not what I meant! Shit. I didn't mean to imply anything. Believe me, I couldn't possibly be more pleased with this evening's turn of events."

I peeked out between two fingers, still feeling like the biggest ho-bag in the Triad.

"Where's your phone?" Jake asked, seemingly out of nowhere.

"Why?" I responded warily.

"Just give me your phone," he insisted, propping himself up on an elbow.

I decided to hand it over but then remembered it had been confiscated by Fiona when she'd seen my phone-holder/wallet I usually carry with me. I'd been given a lecture about sparkly clutches and weddings and there was some threat about a personal search for my ovaries before she'd shoved my things in her own little bag. I'd been lucky she'd allowed me to keep my room key and some lip balm.

"Um, Jake, I think you're overestimating the magical powers of these stockings. A keycard was about all they were going to hold."

That, of course, brought his eyes back down to the silk that still covered my legs. The smoky look to his eyes turned hungry again. I squirmed.

He seemed to shake himself out of it, unfortunately, and stood abruptly, walking his naked ass over to his pants and returning with his phone. He settled himself alongside me once again and tapped at his phone.

What in the hell was he doing?

"What's your number?"

Seriously?

"Seriously?"

"Yes. What's your number? Come on." He gestured impatiently.

I rattled off my number and watched as he entered it into his contacts.

"There. Now I can call and ask you for that date."

I shook my head. "Jake, you really don't need to do that. I'm a big girl," I began, but he shook his head at me in return.

"No way. You're not getting out of this. I delivered my best goods just now. You owe me at least one date."

I laughed at that and let him take that as my acquiescence. And

I almost managed to block out the inner voice that told me this follow-up date was just a pipe dream.

"Damn, you're beautiful when you laugh."

His comment sent my skin into a full-body blush.

I was thinking he was beautiful when he did anything at all. I didn't know how to respond, so I leaned over and kissed him. He returned my kiss and was soon pushing me onto my back again.

♣ ♣ ♣

"Help!" I cried into the phone.

"Calm down and tell me what's wrong," said Laney.

I knew I'd called the right person. She's a parent, which places her in my newly designated top category of people I admire the most. She'd know what to do.

I had stupidly let the entire week go by without giving any thought to what I would wear to the damn gallery. I'd never had to worry about such things before, but even I, the queen of casual, knew that I couldn't show up at Anton's opening looking like a bag lady. Especially with Jake and his smoking hot "I don't even have to try—I was born this way" aura on my arm!

I explained the situation to Laney. She made appropriate noises as I spoke, but then went silent when I finished my panicked tirade about my utter stupidity and lack of forethought.

"Are you still there?" I asked.

"Yeah?" It came out as a question. Shit. What did this mean?

"What?!"

"I'm afraid I'm going to have to call Fiona on this one."

"No way! Not this time. If God didn't intend for me to have hair on my body I wouldn't have it! All I need is a dress or something. Surely, you can help me without calling *her*." I think I whined.

"Bailey, calm down. It won't be that bad."

Said a woman who'd never been pinned down by a real-life fairy and forced to wear a shoestring masquerading as underwear.

I whimpered while she continued, "I'll make sure she knows your boundaries. What time is Jake picking you up? Oh, God—I love saying that! Jake is picking you up!" she squealed.

"Yeah, yeah. I'm happy to give you a lady boner." I rolled my eyes like a freaking teenager. Would I ever be a real adult? Wait, I had to stop thinking like that. Confident Bailey doesn't think things like that.

"Oh, shut up and let me have my fun!"

"Whatever. He's picking me up at 7:30."

"Perfect. We'll be over at 6:00."

"Wait, what? Why on earth would we need that much time?" But she'd already hung up.

Shit.

The cavalcade of two (*yes, in this case, two is still a cavalcade —you didn't see everything they brought*) arrived at six on the dot and marched right into my bedroom without invitation.

"Do come in and make yourselves at home," I muttered.

Fiona patted my cheek, damn her. "Oh, is somebody nervous about her big date?"

"I'm more nervous about what body part you're going to amputate."

She just smiled in return. Oh, hell.

"First," said Laney, "let's pick out a dress." She swept her hand out like a *Price Is Right* model and gestured to the array of colorful outfits now adorning my bed.

I gulped. "I think we're gonna need a bigger bed."

❧❧❧

"Wow," we both said in unison when I opened my condo door and saw Jake and his cheekbones on my front porch. He was all done up in a gray dress shirt, black tie, and black dress pants that fit him way, way too well. It took me a moment to collect myself and register that he'd "wow"ed me too. Thank God!

With Laney's help, I'd managed to hold Fiona off to a certain extent. But I was, in fact, wearing a dress and heels for the second time in my adult life—and all within a month. I'd drawn the line at the assortment of lacy undergarments I'd been presented with, though. Apparently, the information hub Fiona calls a phone housed a list dedicated to the sizes and measurements of all her friends. You know, in case she happened to be out somewhere and felt a compulsive need to use her credit card on girl shit. Unbeknownst to me until tonight, I was on that list.

But I was nervous enough as it was. I didn't need a thong to push me even farther outside my comfort zone. And, besides, if I stuck with my granny panties I'd be less likely to jump Jake.

I looked down at my black silky dress and snakeskin heels. I'd really only agreed to the heels because, knowing Fiona, they were real and that meant there was one less snake in the world.

What? We've already established reptiles are not my thing.

Spurred by the smoldering look in Jake's eyes, I even worked up the nerve to do a little turn so he could see the high slit up the side. Yeah, he liked that. I felt emboldened and was loving this new me, even if my stomach was still swirling with nerves.

Just don't throw up on him again.

He leaned in and kissed me briefly on the lips.

"Aww," came a little chorus from behind me. I'd almost forgotten Cinderella's little mice were still here. (*And, no, I've never seen that movie. I have, however, been told all about it. Apparently, I was playing the part of a housekeeper who likes to talk to rodents and ride around in a pumpkin. And girls think guys are weird.*)

Jake's gaze darted past my shoulder. Taking it all in stride, he winked at them. Because it wasn't like Fiona and Laney didn't have their own testosterone-laden man-persons waiting at home to melt *their* panties. *Oh, yuck.* I suddenly realized the way Jake made me feel was the same way my annoying brother and moronic friend made these two feel. Gag.

"Ladies," Jake said. "Are you joining us this evening?" He was smiling, but he shot me a quick questioning glance.

I shook my head furiously. The last thing I needed was Tina and Amy following us around all night offering commentary on our date.

They slipped past us, Laney blowing us a kiss and Fiona smacking my ass on their way out. Bitch! "We were just stopping by. Have fun, kids!" And then they were gone.

"You look stunning, as usual," said Jake, ushering me toward his waiting truck. I stumbled a bit on the "as usual" part of his comment, but regained my balance and even allowed him to help me up into the passenger seat. Look at me being all girly and shit!

This date was off to a promising start.

Chapter Fifteen

ONLY SLIGHTLY BETTER THAN A BEHEADING

JAKE

I'd never been to the Shearwater Gallery before, and now I knew why.

Sure, my job title had the word "designer" in it, but landscape design involves dirt, thorns, sweat, and physical exertion. It certainly doesn't involve anything remotely related to the scene that lay before me.

Crisply-dressed servers passed trays of hors d'oeuvres and champagne while guests mingled and perused the artwork adorning the gallery walls. That in itself was not off-putting in the least. It was the rest of it that left me feeling like I wanted to simultaneously laugh and turn right around and find a burger joint for our date.

I'd seen what Bailey had on the walls in her condo. *That* was art. This? *This* shit was not art. I'm sorry, I know it's subjective, but this was a bunch of pretentious bullshit.

A large canvas, probably eight feet tall, hung as the only piece on the far wall. There were six black lines crossing each other over a white background. That was it. We approached, surrounded by a throng of guests, and I caught sight of the price tag.

$12,000.

Twelve thousand fucking dollars for something Bailey could have done in five minutes, probably while shit-faced drunk like she'd undoubtedly been the night of her text.

I no you no your sexy as fuck.

My dick twitched at the memory. I told it to calm the hell down and remember where we were. My eyes went back to the painting —that did the trick.

I looked beside me to see if Bailey's reaction was the same as mine. She was frowning. Then she swung her head around, taking in the entire space as if looking for something.

"Huh," she said absently. She walked away without a backward glance so I followed her. We walked past several similar paintings and crossed into a smaller gallery space behind the one we'd first entered.

The work here was much different from the shit in the main gallery. Most of it still wasn't my taste, but at least this qualified as art. I'm no expert, but it was plain to see that this work was a collection from a variety of artists, as opposed to the first exhibit.

Bailey zeroed in on one piece in particular and approached it quickly, stopping on her heel when she was a few feet in front of it.

The painting was small and colorful, and even I could identify its style as abstract. It had clearly captured her attention so I gave it a longer look, trying to see what had her arrested. Then I saw it. The shock of blond hair, the naked breast, the curve of a feminine hip. Holy shit. Was this her?

"Is that…you?" I asked.

Her eyes snapped to mine, startled. “What?! No.” She shook her head vehemently. “Of course not.” She gave a nervous laugh.

I looked at the tag next to the canvas.

Ma Rose Irlandais Sauvage by Anton Germaine

$2,000

Part of me wanted to snatch the canvas from the wall so no one else could see Bailey laid out like that. There was no doubt in my mind she was the subject of this painting. I didn’t need to know French to understand this reference. An urge to punch someone surfaced, and that someone went by the name of Anton Germaine. He’d been with Bailey, that was certain from the intimacy of the image. This was no model/painter set-up. This was post-coital. This was fucked up.

She’d brought me to an ex-lover’s exhibit, knowing there would be a nude painting of her at the event. What the hell kind of game was she playing?! My mind raced. How could I even be sure he was an ex? Maybe she’d been saying no to me because she was fucking him.

“Yeah,” I huffed out. Then I turned on my heel to leave.

“Jake, wait,” she said and I heard her heels on the wood floor following me. I had to weave through a few groups of people on my way to the main gallery so she managed to catch up to me. I felt a tug on my shirt. “Jake, please.”

I took her arm and quickly escorted her to a quiet corner of the room, not wanting to cause a scene. We stopped short. Her cheeks were flushed as she looked up at me, her brows drawn together.

“What, Bailey? Are you serious with this shit?” She looked taken aback and her mouth gaped as she quickly shook her head. I continued before she could answer, “You’ve been driving me crazy with how hot and cold you run. Then we finally have a great date and you decide to follow that up by bringing me to the art show of one of your boyfriends? And don't even try to deny it." I pointed behind us to the painting of her. "That painting is of you. That painting is of you, in bed, right after that Anton guy fucked you."

She winced. "I…I," she attempted to speak but just stuttered.

"Why would you bring me here?" I squeezed her arm in some attempt to force out an answer I could live with.

"Jake..." She shook her head again. "I…It's not like that…I didn't know…"

"You made it!" came a loud voice from behind me. My eyes were still locked on Bailey and I saw her visibly pale. I released my hold on her.

Even through my anger and confusion, a wave of protectiveness surged. Before I could turn to see what had her so addled, I felt an arm brush mine. Two hands grasped Bailey's bare upper arms and a fedora swooped down alongside her face. The fedora sat atop the blond head of a man just shorter than me. He kissed Bailey's right cheek and followed with the left. Her eyes found mine and all I saw was panic.

WTF?

The man stood back, still holding her arms. His eyes swept over her form and my fists clenched. He had yet to even acknowledge my presence, even though Bailey and I had clearly been involved in an intimate conversation when he'd approached.

I took the brief opportunity to look him over, trying to determine who he could be. Skinny black pants and pointed-toed shoes were topped off by a tailored leather jacket and that dumb-ass hat. There was a ring on his pinky finger and the t-shirt he wore under his jacket swept down in a V too low for any straight guy. Black hipster glasses rested on his nose and he reeked of patchouli. Ah, this must be one of the artists exhibiting along with the "boyfriend." But if that was the case, why the deer-in-the-headlights look on Bailey's face?

"Beautiful, I'm so pleased to see you," the man said with a smile and a hint of an accent I couldn't quite place.

I did not get a good feeling.

He released her arms and swept his hands out in a dramatic gesture. "What do you think?" The dude let his eyes take in the room around him, not even pausing to acknowledge me.

Bailey stammered, "I-It's really wonderful, Anton."

Anton? *Anton.*

This motherfucker was going down.

"I knew you'd think so," he said and reached for her hand just as a slender black-haired woman slithered up to Anton's side and placed a perfectly manicured hand on his shoulder.

With the distraction provided by the woman, I noticed Bailey was able to pull her hand back from this douchebag. At least that was something.

Anton turned to the new arrival and then back to Bailey. "Ah, you remember Sloane, don't you?"

Bailey took a step back as if she were about to retreat, but the wall stopped her and she wobbled a bit on her heels. I instinctively reached out to steady her. She looked up briefly into my eyes and I could see a hint of relief.

There was something going on here and I did not like it one bit.

With one hand still holding Bailey's arm, I turned abruptly to this asshole and stuck out my other hand. "Jake Beckett."

He looked first at my face and then my hand as if I'd suddenly materialized before him in that very moment. Then he looked back at Bailey, ignoring my hand.

She seemed to recover somewhat and attempted introductions. "Of course. Anton, this is Jake. Jake, this is Anton." She gestured awkwardly to her side with one hand. "This is his show."

Anton begrudgingly accepted my hand then, as there was no graceful way out of it. His eyes stayed on Bailey. "Well, my dear, it's not *entirely* my show, as you can see." He released my hand as quickly as possible and brought it to the side of his mouth for a stage whisper. "Just the good parts." He and Sloane both cackled at this.

"And what do you do, Jake?" asked Sloane, her hand caressing Anton's shoulder. She was all sharp angles, from her nails to her hairstyle, right down her bony body to her black heels.

I didn't need to impress these people. "I'm in landscaping," I answered, rocking back on my heels and putting my hands in my pockets.

The couple glanced at each other and Anton nodded. "Well, that's just fascinating." His patronizing smile flashed from Bailey to me and back again.

I felt Bailey's hand on my arm as she stepped closer to me. "It is, in fact," she said.

"I'll have to take your word for it," Anton replied. "So, what do you think of your piece?"

Bailey colored and I watched her face, trying to decipher her reaction.

"Oh, well…Anton. It's not exactly what I expected." She ducked her head.

"It's quite a nice little painting," interjected Sloane. "It's amazing what Anton can do given any subject, no matter how…raw."

Oh, wow. These people were good. Good at being complete dicks.

"Come now, Sloane." Anton patted her hand. "I seem to

remember you being quite…enthusiastic…about our little subject once upon a time."

Um, what the hell did *that* mean?

She waved him off. "Yes, well, we're all entitled to lapses in judgment now and then, aren't we? Anyway, come get some champagne with me." She turned on her heel and slithered off, leaving Anton with me and a trembling Bailey. She looked like she might go down, so I snaked an arm around her waist in support. Her eyes were still on the floor.

"Well, it was wonderful to see you, especially looking so stunning. I quite miss our little…talks." Anton's eyes traced Bailey's body. "Until next time." He began to follow Sloane and then turned, almost as an afterthought. "Jack." He nodded at me.

"Andy." I nodded at him. This wasn't my first day.

He gave a dismissive chuckle and continued on his way.

If I thought punching him in the middle of this party would do any good, I wouldn't have hesitated. But it would only have embarrassed Bailey and proven to these assholes that I was the uncultured hick they thought me to be.

Instead, I pulled Bailey forward and steered her toward the door, grabbing two champagne flutes in my free hand on our way out and not bothering to stop when the server protested.

☘ ☘ ☘

I popped the cork on the bottle of champagne I'd ordered from room service. The attendant had offered to open the bottle for us, but there was no way he was getting even a small peek at my blond goddess.

Bailey held the two flutes in her hands while I poured.

"To weddings," I said, taking one from her.

She grinned and clinked glasses with me before taking a sip from hers. "Oh, that's not half bad. You know, I'm usually a beer girl, but the champagne has been going down smoothly tonight." She started to bring the glass back to her lips and then stopped, her smile faltering a bit.

"What's wrong?"

She shook her head. "Nothing. I mean, I actually don't really like beer all that much. I don't know why I said that."

I grinned and took a sip of my champagne. "Well, that's a shame, cuz I'm a beer guy all the way." I lifted my glass. "This fancy stuff is okay now and then, but give me a good IPA any day."

She looked down at the bed and rearranged the sheets around her, a half-smile on her face. Her eyes came back to me where I stood at the edge of the bed dressed in just my boxer briefs.

"So, Jake, I hear you're going to be working with Fiona's boss. Landscape design?"

I sat down and stroked her leg through the bedsheet. "That's the plan. I apprenticed in it several years back and then got my certification. It took a while to figure out what I wanted to do, but I finally found it." I traced a finger along her thigh. "How about you?"

She seemed surprised I asked. "Oh. Um, I went to school for interior design and space planning. You know, so I could pitch in with the family business." She grinned. "Wielding a hammer wasn't really for me."

I laughed. I couldn't see this sexy, feminine siren wearing a hard hat. "I would think the stockings might look strange with work boots," I joked.

She smiled and looked earnestly at me, tilting her head to the side. She opened her mouth to say something and then seemed to think better of it.

"And besides," I leaned in for a kiss, "you'd distract the hell out of every male there. They'd have to depend on the female crew members to get all the work done. Doesn't sound very fair to me." I kissed her again, lingering this time.

"Not fair at all," she responded distractedly, letting her fingers run down my arm.

"I think it's cool that your whole family works together. The loyalty you all have is really something. I'm afraid I can't say I've always put my family first, to put it mildly," I admitted.

She stopped the movement of her fingers and looked me. "You mean because you've been away?"

"Yeah, it's kind of a long story…" I trailed off.

"I may have heard a little something about that." I was pretty sure everybody had heard a lot of something about it. "But, you know, all family is complicated." She looked down at the sheet again and I tucked a lock of wayward hair behind her ear.

She smiled and resumed her tactile exploration of my arm. Her fingers stopped on my tattoo. "What's this?"

I glanced at it out of reflex—not that I didn't know exactly what was there. "It's just from the Marines. We all got them. Everyone in my unit."

She traced it with her index finger. "Did you have to go overseas?" Her eyes found mine again, concern clouding her features.

"I did, but not to Iraq or Afghanistan. I ended up in Indonesia, aiding after the tsunamis. Then they brought me back stateside to help after Katrina."

"God, that must have been so hard. Seeing all those people lose everything—their families and homes." She shook her head.

I stroked the inside of her arm. "It was tragic, you're right, but you can't let yourself get lost in that when you have a job to do. It would end up paralyzing you, and then what good would you be to anybody?"

She shook her head. "I don't know how you did that."

"Well," I responded, "don't start hero-worshipping me or anything. I got out after my four years were up. Other guys are still in there, plugging away. They're the ones who deserve the respect."

I looked up and her eyes were pinned on me. "I admire anyone who fights for what they believe in—anybody who is strong in character, who knows what they want and doesn't let anything stop them."

"Sounds like you're thinking of someone in particular." I raised an eyebrow at her.

She lost her intense expression and laughed lightly, shaking her head again. "No, just wishful thinking."

I gave her a puzzled look, but she cut me off with a kiss.

Chapter Sixteen

RULE: MALE BEST FRIENDS SHOULD NOT WEAR PANTIES

BAILEY

"So, you care to explain any of that?"

Jake hoisted himself up onto the tailgate of his truck and sat next to me. We were in the parking lot of the gallery with the hitch down and the pilfered champagne flutes sitting on the truck bed between us. He'd rushed me out of the gallery when I'd been lost in my flummoxed state and I'd hardly noticed where we were going. My mind had been a swirling mess of panic, anger, and humiliation. Turned out my risk had come back to bite me in the ass.

Goddamn that asshole, Anton. This whole evening had been one giant mistake. This whole "experiment" with Jake had been a mistake. What had I been thinking? That I could use sheer will to redirect my fate, to change my entire personality and lot in life? I was so stupid. One crazy night of hot sex with a stranger, coupled with some flirting and a shared meal would not change anything. I was out of my depth. Again.

It was probably for the best that I'd come to my senses before my emotions could run any deeper into all that was Jake Beckett. I heard my heart whimper at the thought and ignored what that might mean.

I looked down at my silky black dress and snakeskin heels and let out a mirthless laugh. They were mocking me. I shook my head and kept my eyes down.

"No," I said, "I can't really explain anything."

"Bailey, you've got to give me something here. Anything."

I just shook my head again.

"Are you still dating that asshole?"

What? After that awful scene, *that* was what he wanted to know?

"What? No. Oh, God." I covered my face with my hands, horrified that Jake knew I'd ever been with Anton at all. That goddamn painting! Worse yet, how could Jake think I'd be dating Anton and have sex with *him* at the same time?

"Oh, God," I repeated as the thought dawned on me that Jake was probably having sex with all sorts of women. I was way out of my league. I needed to go home.

"Talk to me." He tried to hand me one of the glasses of champagne as some kind of peace offering. "I'm trying to understand this."

I brushed his offer aside and slid down off the truck and onto the concrete, almost falling as my heels awkwardly hit the pavement. He reached out to steady me but I righted myself and took a step back.

"There's nothing to understand. I'd like to go home now if that's okay." My stomach churned and I feared we'd repeat the shoe-puking scene.

"Bailey…" he started, but I cut him off.

"Please." I could feel tears welling in my eyes.

My tone must have been quite pathetic because, after a pause, he hopped off the truck and went to the passenger side to open my door. I got in and put on my seatbelt, keeping my eyes glued to the floor mat the entire time.

I heard Jake sigh before he closed my door and rounded to the driver's side to take me home.

I don't know what became of the stolen champagne glasses.

♣ ♣ ♣

"Open the damn door, Bailey. I know you're in there!"

No. Not now.

I was minding my own business, all snuggled up on my couch with my blanket and my giant box of tissues. I even had an Indiana Jones marathon going on the TV. I felt a new kinship with Indy now that I'd experienced reptile-induced terror first hand.

A fist pounded on the door. I did not need to deal with humans right now. Especially one in the form of a pussy-whipped gym rat.

"Go away!" I shouted before reaching for another tissue. On top of the giant hit to my personal life, the universe had decided to throw me another bonus and grace me with a damn cold. I was congested, exhausted, and snotty on top of everything else.

"I have a key and I'm not afraid to use it!"

"I have a baseball bat and I'm not afraid to use it either!"

"Why do you think I haven't used my key yet?"

Wuss. "I thought you said you weren't afraid, Buffy!"

"Bailey, just open the damn door! I forgot my key and your neighbors are coming out!"

Well, shit. I peeled myself off the couch and went to let the big lug in.

"What do you want?" I didn't even spare him a glance. I just retreated to my blanket fortress and un-paused the TV. The bad dude's face was about to melt off and I didn't want to miss it.

Mark stood silently in front of the couch for several minutes. I finally started feeling unnerved so I paused the show again and looked up at him. He had some short scruff on his face to match his buzz cut and his brown eyes were creased in a look I didn't see very often from him. Worry.

Shit.

I set down the remote.

"Fine. You want to know what happened, I take it?"

"You could say that." He shoved his hands in his pockets. "Last I heard, you and my brother were attempting to date. Then I get a call from him that some asshole ambushed you at a party and you turned mute and froze Jake out. And, worse yet, you let that douchebag from the party get to you."

I scoffed and tried to brush it off. It didn't work.

"That doesn't sound like you at all. What the hell happened? You've been acting odd for months now, and every time I try to pin you down about it, you suddenly return to your usual snarky self and I let it go."

I sneered at him and tried to stand up. Mark stopped me by dropping down next to me and physically holding my legs down.

"Not this time. Spill it. What the fuck is going on?"

I let out a breath and tried to tamp down my annoyance at his nosiness. "It just didn't work out with Jake, that's all."

"Nice try. You just met him like a month ago. This goes back way before that. Truth time. Go." He reinforced his grip on my legs and I shot him a death glare. What, was he going to water-board me next?

"Fine. The asshole at the party was this guy named Anton. He's pretty big in the local art scene. We used to have a thing."

"A thing?" Mark's forehead furrowed.

"Yes, Mark, a thing. You know, boys have penises, girls have vaginas…" That got me my own death glare.

"Go on." Damn, he was pushy today.

I went for flippant. "It ended and I moved on."

"Ha, not so fast. What aren't you telling me?"

I tried to get up again, but the damn idiot's arms were made of steel. "Get off me!" I smacked his beefy arm.

"Not until you tell me what happened." He was cool as a cucumber while I was starting to burn up. Why couldn't he just let this go? We never talked about my "feelings," and I preferred it that way. It was the whole purpose of having a guy as a best friend! Vaginas gossip and share; penises watch football and fist bump—or something like that.

"Nothing, Nancy Drew! We just broke up. It happens."

"Why didn't I know about this guy? I'm your best friend."

"And have you and Nate go 'vet' him for me? I don't think so." I gave him a sharp look which he chose to ignore. I'd have to go full-on bitch. "And contrary to what you might think, I don't tell you everything, you conceited ass." I tried my best but it didn't change his course.

"Uh, uh. Not falling for that. How long did you date this guy?" I was becoming increasingly uncomfortable and ticked off under his scrutiny.

I looked away. "Why does it matter?"

"It just does. How long?" God, he should take up a second career as an FBI interrogator.

I tried shifting away again, but Mark maintained his firm grip. "Four months. Are you happy now?"

"Four months?!"

My eyes flew back to him in challenge. I was officially pissed off. "Yes, four months. Are you hearing impaired?"

"Stop trying to bait me. It's not going to work, Bailey."

I delivered a fake-ass smile. "Mark, as much as I love this little heart-to-heart chat, I'd really like to get back to my show. I'll lend you a crowbar if you'd like to pull your panties out."

"No."

Did he just tell me I couldn't watch TV in my own home? Or maybe he just liked his panties where they were.

"No? This is *my* house, you ass."

"And you're *my* friend." Well, shit. This was even worse than I thought. I couldn't do this.

"Well, *friend*. I'd really like you to leave now." I pushed again at his arms and thought for a moment that he was releasing me. Instead, he readjusted so he was kneeling on the floor in front of me, our faces only a foot or so apart.

"Not until you tell me what I want to know!" Mark's eyes blazed.

"God, you're a pain in the ass!"

"And I'm okay with that. What did this Anton guy do to you and why wouldn't you tell your friends and family about him after four months?"

I was about to remind him what my mother was likely capable of given the barest wind of a man in my life when I realized Mark thought Anton had done something to physically hurt me. Shit. I couldn't let him think that—it would be cruel. I drove my fists into the couch on either side of my trapped legs. "He didn't do anything! He was helping me."

Mark's expression turned surprised. "Helping you? With what?"

I sighed in defeat. "With getting into the Master of Fine Arts program at UNCT. Or so I thought." There, the cat was out of the bag. It had been extracted painfully by its mangy tail, but it was out.

Mark suddenly loosened his grip and sat back on his heels. "Why wouldn't you tell any of us about that? That's awesome!" He started to smile but it fell when he continued, "Jesus, you almost had me thinking…wait, what do you mean, 'or so I thought'?"

I looked to the ceiling and let out a mirthless laugh. Now that I was free to move, all I actually wanted to do was pull my blanket over my head and lie down. I sank back into the couch while Mark remained perched on the floor in front of me. If he wanted the story so badly, I'd give it to him. I already felt flayed open so why not twist the knife myself. "Well, Buffy, it turns out that while my pussy might be grade-A material, my paintings are not."

"What the fuck?" Any relief he'd expressed moments before was long gone. I could feel the vibration from his growled response.

He'd been the one to push for an answer, so he'd just have to deal with it now. I tilted my head and looked at him again. "Oh, come on, Mark. You're a smart guy." I knew I was being unfair.

"Enlighten me, Bailey." His jaw was so tight I worried it might crack.

I sighed, feigning a carefree air. "It's an old story, Mark. Lure the girl in with promises of a bright future, convince her she's a diamond in the rough. All she needs is a little polish." I framed my face with my hands sardonically.

"If only she'd shed that pesky day job that's getting in the way of her potential." I barked out another laugh and it tasted bitter on my tongue. "Not to worry, though—that day job doesn't get in the way of fucking her at night. That is, when there aren't any other ingénues that need a good screwing." My eyes refused to meet Mark's, not wanting to see my hurt and humiliation reflected there.

"But, you know, in the end, she's just not sophisticated enough for the high-brow artist and his shit-hot friends." I raised a finger as if just remembering the rest of the story. "Oh, and about that Master's program? Mr. High-Brow just doesn't feel comfortable recommending her at this time; she isn't ready. In fact, her work is really quite pedestrian—just like her."

"Bailey, Jesus, what…" I finally worked up the nerve to look at Mark again. His face was ashen.

I waved a dismissive hand. "It's fine, Mark. It's over. Has been for months now."

"That night," he interjected, furrowing his brow, "the night of that party at Laney's when I was supposed to pick you up. I *knew* something was wrong. Shit. I should have stayed. You looked like you'd been crying. *Shit*."

I scoffed again. "As if. I don't cry." I curled my lip, fooling no one. "And anyway, there was nothing you could have done. I learned a hard lesson. One I should have already known. My mistake."

"Bailey." His voice was soft.

I pulled the blanket up to my chin. "And one I almost forgot, yet again. So, really, it was a good thing Anton was such an asshole the other night. I needed a reminder. Fool me once and all that."

"Bailey." His voice was firmer this time.

"So, if I've answered all your questions, I'd really like to finish watching my movie. You can stay if you want, but I'm done talking about this, Mark."

"Bailey!" he shouted.

"What?! What else could you possibly want?!" I shouted back. And then, to my utter horror, I burst into tears.

Chapter Seventeen

SIGNS YOU MIGHT BE A GIRL

BAILEY

"Oh no." Mark's voice lost its intensity and fell completely flat. My chest began to heave with a torrent of sobbing, the likes of which I'd never experienced. I felt Mark's hand awkwardly pat my back, although it felt more like he was trying to dislodge something that had become stuck in my windpipe than actually provide comfort.

An even bigger wave of tears and snot began to flow and I was helpless to stop it. What was happening to me?

"Hey, um, it'll be okay," Mark attempted to soothe while I reached blindly for my box of tissues. "Hang on. I'll be right back."

I heard him head toward the kitchen, presumably to get me a glass of water, or perhaps a giant bottle of tequila. I continued to lose my ever-loving shit and tried to figure out where everything had all gone wrong.

Mark returned a few minutes later and, as I'd suspected, he

handed me a glass. It didn't smell like tequila. Damn. He sat next to me again while I chugged the water down, suddenly desperately parched from my uncharacteristic bout of dramatic girl-tears. This, in turn, made me start hiccupping, and that was when Mark finally gave in to the inevitable and wrapped me up in a big burly man-hug, complete with back and forth rocking motions. We stayed like that for a good long while, neither of us saying a word.

Then, once my tears finally abated and his shirt was sufficiently soaked, he grabbed the remote and we watched Indiana Jones kick some Nazi ass.

Twenty minutes later, the doorbell rang.

You've got to be fucking kidding me.

I felt Mark stiffen beside me.

"Huh, are you expecting anyone?" he asked in an incredibly poor attempt at ignorance.

"You just had to do it, didn't you?"

"I don't know what you're talking about." He scampered off the couch before I could physically assault him. I was feeling too shitty to even attempt chasing him.

"Fine. Just let them in. What do I care?" I could only imagine the pathetic scene I presented with my tear-drenched face and the pile of snotty tissues forming a moat around me.

I heard the sound of the door opening followed by two feminine voices laced with equal parts caution and concern. "Hi, Bailey," they both said hesitantly. Great, I was a real live freak show.

Before I could even glance at Fiona and Laney, I heard Mark say, "Well, I'm out of here," followed immediately by the sound of my front door latching shut. Coward!

I sighed and prepared myself. I hadn't shared this much

personal info in, well…ever. Leave it to the male species to be the cause of my descent into the gossip vortex.

"Hi." *Sniff.*

One syllable was apparently all they needed as invitation to deliver boob-crushing hugs and settle in on either side of me. They didn't even seem to mind my tissue collection.

"Mark told us all about it. Well, at least his version, so you may have to backtrack a bit," said Laney.

I actually managed a genuine laugh at that. I could only imagine what Mark had said. It was probably something along the lines of, "Bailey's vagina got run over by some artist at a pedestrian crossing and there's snot coming out of her nose. Get over here now."

"We're worried about you, babe. We've never seen you like this," Fiona chimed in, grabbing my hand and giving it a squeeze.

"That makes four of us," I joked lamely.

"Can you tell us what happened?" Laney grabbed my other hand, and for the first time in my adult life, I actually felt that strength in numbers thing that women were always talking about—that feeling of sharing the load making it lighter somehow. So, I took a deep breath and spilled my guts about Anton, revealing the whole awful truth.

☘☘☘

The day I had my heart broken by Anton Germaine had actually started out as a good day—a great one, in fact. I'd taken some of his constructive criticism on a work-in-progress and was feeling proud of the result I was achieving. The piece was one in a series of oils I'd conceived of weeks earlier when I'd found myself mesmerized by a TV program about the America's Cup. I'd been obsessively poring over photos and videos of sailboats since, determined to capture their majestic beauty and quiet power on canvas. Anton had been a great help, and I felt my work had elevated under his tutelage over the last several months.

I rushed up the steps of his rental house just north of downtown. I'd skipped out of work early and was eager to show Anton the progress I'd made on the painting. Careful not to damage the canvas, I used my foot to push the front door open while I balanced my things in my arms.

"Hey, Anton! Wait till you see this!" I shouted excitedly into the quiet space. I set down my bag and took the canvas with me to go in search of my boyfriend. When I didn't find him in the kitchen, I jogged up the stairs, thinking he was probably in the shower. Being a painter was dirty work—wonderful, but dirty.

"I finally figured out how to manage the glare off the water—" I stopped dead in my tracks at the threshold of the bedroom. A dark-haired and very naked woman was grinding on top of my equally naked boyfriend. They both turned to look at me as I stood dumbfounded in the doorway. My breath froze in my lungs and I dropped the canvas to the floor.

Anton's expression morphed from exhilaration to disappointment, his lips pursing. The woman's expression was a combination of smugness and irritation. She didn't bother to slow her motions.

What the fuck?

"Anton, what the fuck is going on here?" I managed to whisper.

"Bailey," was all Anton said.

What?! That was it?! Where was the remorse? The panic? Where was the desperate attempt at an explanation? *And why in the hell was she still on top of him?!* He couldn't even seem to muster a look of embarrassment, for God's sake.

I turned to get the hell out of this place and I heard the woman say, "You're free to join us if you like. I do love blondes."

My foot caught on the top step and I narrowly escaped a tumble down the stairs. My hands grasped at the railing, the edge digging painfully into my side in the process.

"Sloane, you're not helping," I heard Anton say, his voice getting nearer.

I needed to get out of there before he caught up with me. I almost made it to the front door before remembering that my keys were in my bag I'd discarded earlier. Shit. I turned to the living room and was stopped abruptly by Anton's hand on my arm. I shook it off violently, refusing to look at him.

"Bailey, beautiful, don't be so angry."

Don't be what?!

I rounded on him, forgetting my resolve. "What the hell is that supposed to mean?!" I shouted. "How am I supposed to feel when I walk in on my boyfriend in bed with another woman?!"

This was like some Lifetime movie. I was even having trouble resisting the urge to slap him across the face.

He held his hands out to the side. "I'm not built to be monogamous. I figured you knew that. I'm sorry if this comes as a shock."

"I don't even know how that's possible," I put my hands in my hair. "All those things you said to me. All the time we've been together—I thought we were *together*." I kept shaking my head as if that would somehow help explain this complete clusterfuck.

He approached, still naked. I wanted to run but he was between me and the door. "We've had our bit of fun and it's run its course. It's nothing personal."

Except it was. To me, it was as personal as it got. I'd fallen in love with him, and worse yet, I'd trusted him.

"And besides, I just see myself with someone a bit more…

sophisticated, more self-actualized. You understand." And then Anton honest-to-God chucked my chin. "I really need to surround myself with people who take their work seriously and are willing to fully dedicate themselves." He gave me a knowing look.

This wasn't the first time he had doubted my dedication to my craft. He'd told me countless times that if I was truly serious about being an artist I needed to quit the "establishment" and immerse myself in a less restrictive existence.

I'd tried numerous times to explain to him about my family and my obligations to them. But he always had a response to everything, even my arguments regarding my mortgage and my preference to eat on a daily basis.

"Come now," he said, "we can still be friends." He reached for my hand and I snatched it away before he could make contact.

How could I have fallen for this man and his lies? I knew better!

I picked up my bag and rushed past him, not bothering to respond. It wasn't until later that night that I remembered the painting. I was wrapped up in a blanket with a cold beer and a heartbreak soundtrack on my headphones when I decided I never wanted to see that canvas again. Surely, Anton and Sloane were having a good laugh over it. Stupid, naïve Bailey Murphy and her pathetic attempts at painting and love.

☘☘☘

"What a dick," Fiona said, her lip curling in disgust.

"A *pretentious* dick," Laney added. "Yuck."

That got a little smile out of me. I'd managed to deliver the entire saga without crying, and I did feel a touch better having gotten it off my chest.

"Well, ladies, Anton may be the reason God created the middle finger, but at least I can thank him for one thing."

They looked at me expectantly.

"He taught me a valuable lesson about where to put my trust and to always know my place." I pushed off the couch and headed to the kitchen for more water.

"Hold on a minute, woman!" Fiona demanded. "Your *place* is any-damn-where you choose. Don't let that asshole win."

I turned around again and saw them both standing with hands on their hips. Twin pillars of indignation with attitude.

"Look, I appreciate the pep talk, but it's just not meant to be. I'm destined to sit at that desk moving drywall and countertops around on a page until I die." Okay, perhaps I was throwing myself a bit of a pity party.

Fiona tilted her head. "Says who?"

"Um, common sense?" I replied.

"Who says you can't be an artist?" she rebutted while Laney nodded in support.

"Are you kidding? There's a reason the word 'starving' always precedes the word 'artist.' And, besides, I can't even stand up to my own father about this and you know what a marshmallow he is."

Fiona wasn't done. "Surely you can find a way. Look at me. I never thought I'd get to do something I love for a living and now I get to cook and plan parties."

I turned back around and headed for the fridge. She couldn't understand, as sweet as it was of her to try. She's a kick-ass cook, and she comes from a shitload of money. I was about as likely to make a living from my art as I was to be an astronaut. Or Gwen Stefani. All scenarios were equally unlikely.

"Oh, come on," said Laney, following me. "I've seen your work. It's incredible! And your dad would understand."

I set my glass down hard on the counter and then stomped my foot in frustration. Like a child. I was sinking to an all-new low. "Look, I've tried!" I stalked back out to the living room. I was an aimless mess. "They said I wasn't good enough!"

Fiona's head snapped back. Oh, shit. The finger was surely not far behind. "Who is 'they'?"

"The goddamn MFA board! Anton Fucking Germaine! That's who!"

Their brows formed identical creases and they turned to each other in confusion. If I hadn't been so worked up I might have laughed.

"Who the hell cares what that shithead says?"

"The board, that's who! I got a letter a week after Sloane and Anton's bull-rider show. They rejected my application and wished me the best of luck in my future endeavors," I mocked.

"Well, shit," was Fiona's response.

Laney approached and hugged me again. I sagged in her arms, exhaustion threatening to overtake me. "I'm so sorry," she whispered in my ear.

"This calls for ice cream and a chick movie," Fiona declared.

I groaned. "Please, no more girl stuff."

She regarded me and then relented. "Fine, but just this once."

Chapter Eighteen

INSURANCE

JAKE

"What do you know about this Anton guy?" Mark's voice boomed over the phone and I had to pull it away from my ear for a second. Although I'd been expecting his call, I hadn't quite anticipated a punctured eardrum.

After spending my entire Saturday alternately feeling sorry for myself and trying not to call Bailey, I'd finally broken down and tracked down Mark instead. I told him about our experience at the gallery and Bailey's subsequent shut-down. I was at a complete loss and I hoped that, as her best friend, he might have some insight. Instead, he'd responded with a bunch of swearing and said he'd take care of it. Who the hell knew what that meant.

It was now Sunday and I was looking around a local nursery at some potential options for the McGuire's garden. I had an online supplier that was surprisingly good, but I wanted to source as much as I could locally.

At the tone of Mark's voice and the mention of Anton, however, all thoughts of work were banished.

"I know he's an entitled prick if that helps. Why? What did you find out from Bailey?"

"Later. Right now, we need to find that Anton asshole. Did you get a last name?"

My back stiffened. "What did you find out, Mark?"

"Nothing good, I can tell you that. Now, how about that last name?"

"Germaine. Anton Germaine."

"Okay, I'll call you back in a bit. Head on over my way. We've got a meeting with this dickhead today." With that, he hung up.

Shit.

☘☘☘

"This is becoming a regular thing with us," I observed as I sat in the passenger seat of Mark's truck while we staked out a campus building at UNCT. Months back, he and I had spent a similar day staking out the local hospital for some loan sharks (*I know—I can't make this shit up*) who'd been after our parents. Well, really our piece-of-shit dad, but our mom had gotten caught up in the resulting shitstorm.

"Huh, you're right. What does that say about us?"

"I'd rather not think about it," I replied, eyes on the door of the Fine Arts building. Mark's snooping around had revealed that Anton was participating in a workshop on campus today and it was scheduled to end any minute now. All we had to do was wait until he emerged so we could have a little talk with him.

I'd quizzed Mark about his visit with Bailey this morning, but he hadn't given me the whole story, I knew. What he did tell me, though, was enough to refuel my desire to give that pompous asshole a taste of my fist.

This Anton guy had taken advantage of Bailey. He'd promised to help in her career as a painter and then discarded her in a hurtful manner. There was more to it, but Mark said it wasn't his to tell. I determined I'd hear it from Bailey one way or another. But first, someone deserved an ass-kicking from a couple of hick good-old-boys.

"That's him," I said fifteen minutes later, pointing out the window toward the double doors of the building.

"Which one?" Mark sat forward in his seat, following my finger.

"The one who looks like a walking penis with glasses."

He reached for his door. "Let's go."

We both got out and headed toward the sidewalk where Anton now stood talking with two very young co-eds. Both were gazing up at him with something resembling hero-worship.

"Yo, Germaine!" Mark called out as we neared their position.

Anton turned briefly, a look of confusion on his face, before turning back to the girls and excusing himself. He faced us as we approached. I saw the exact second recognition dawned because it was the same moment his expression shifted from confusion to smugness.

"Ah, the gardener." He looked me over from head to toe, clearly unimpressed. I gave not one shit. Then he treated Mark to the same once-over. "And who do we have here? A lumberjack?"

Mark let out a fake laugh. "You hear that, Jake? This asshole thinks he's funny."

Before I could respond, Anton cut in, "Look, *guys*, I really don't have time for this. Say what you need to say and be on your way. I'm sure there are holes needing to be dug somewhere." He hitched his messenger bag up on his shoulder and raised his eyebrows in expectation.

How had this dude made it this far in life without having his face rearranged?

My hands were clenched in fists at my sides but I forced my voice to remain as casual as possible. “I don’t know, Mark, he may have something there. I’m thinking digging a hole might not be a bad idea—maybe a six-foot-deep one? What do you think?”

Mark turned to me, pretending to completely ignore Anton. “You know, you’d think it was a six-foot hole, but these days they actually only excavate four feet. Has to do with the use of concrete to prevent sinkholes. There’s also something about bodies rising to the surface in flood conditions. I dunno. I saw it on TV.” He shook his head.

I nodded in return, feigning interest. “Hmm, fascinating.”

“Okay, gentlemen. While I find this little threat terribly amusing, we’re done here.” Anton brushed past us, “accidentally” plowing his shoulder into Mark’s. Given the sheer mass of my brother, the assclown just ricocheted off him. I almost wanted to laugh at the utter stupidity of that move. Anton steadied himself and chose to leave a wider berth this time. Mark stopped him with a hand to the chest.

“Oh, we’re just getting started, Germaine.” Mark rocked his neck from side to side, eliciting a popping sound. If I were Anton, I’d be mentally drafting my will.

He finally seemed to grasp that he was not the one in control of this situation. His hands rose in a defensive position. “Look, I don’t know what Bailey told you, but I’m not to blame for anything here. We dated, it ended, and that’s it. If she’s still sensitive about it, that’s not my problem. We’re all adults here, so there’s no reason for you two to play big brother.”

"Now you see," I said, "that's where we'll have to agree to disagree. I've only spent ten minutes in your presence, and you've been rude, patronizing, and a general asshole. I can't imagine how much damage you managed to cause our girl in the amount of time she wasted with you."

Mark still had a hand to his chest, keeping him still, and I stood close with my arms crossed to keep myself in check.

"You have no idea how much I tried to help that girl. She was hopeless. She'd never make it in the art world. I was doing her a favor."

At that, Mark shoved him and Anton almost lost his footing before righting himself and pointing a finger at Mark. "You touch me again and I'm calling the police." He hitched his bag back up on his shoulder and backed away a step.

Mark and I took another step toward him, narrowing the gap. "We must have very different ideas of what constitutes help," I began before Mark cut in.

"Treating her like shit and cheating on her sound like pretty shitty favors to me. Not to mention sabotaging her with the board and using her for sex."

I stepped back on my boot. "What the fuck?!"

Mark tore his gaze from Anton and looked to me. Clearly, he'd revealed more than he'd meant to. His face was tight with tension and I was guessing mine looked the same. We simultaneously turned our attention back to Anton, who now had a sheen of sweat on his brow. A panicked, chicken-shit expression overtook his face and it was clear he was about to run.

"Hey, Anton," I growled. "Does your insurance cover vision?"

The unexpected question caused him to pause and his expression morphed to one of confusion. "What? Why?"

"No reason," Mark replied just before his fist connected with the side of Anton's face, sending his glasses flying and knocking the douchebag to the ground.

He lay on the sidewalk holding his cheek and cowering in fear as I crouched down beside him. He flinched when I spoke in a low tone. "You ever talk to her, touch her, or even think about her again, and we're gonna have a problem. Understand?" He just nodded slowly and I stood back up.

Mark was already walking away, and a few students had started to gather around, one of them bending down to help Anton and a couple others raising their voices to us as we walked toward the truck. We didn't acknowledge anyone and we didn't look back. We did, however, make sure the black-framed glasses that had fallen in our path made solid contact with the bottoms of our work boots.

♣♣♣

"Do I even want to know what happened here?"

I chuckled as our mom crossed her arms and raised her eyebrows at Mark. He and I were lounging on her couch watching football while Mark iced his hand down.

He threw a glare at me before answering her. "Probably not."

She bent down, her "mom face" firmly set, and held out her hand. "Let me see."

Mark sighed and removed the ice pack. I cringed a little, but our mom took it in stride, lifting Mark's large hand for inspection. His knuckles were swollen and turning a nice shade of purple. Two were split, probably from the glasses, but the blood was mostly dry.

Our mom tsked and then released his hand. "I'm getting some bandages and then you're telling me what happened." We both got the stink-eye. "And I want the whole story so I can decide if you're just irresponsible or downright stupid."

I laughed again but Mark cut me off. "Shut up, asshole. If I hadn't gotten in there first, you would be the one getting a lecture." He was not wrong. "Damn." He stretched his fingers out and winced. "I didn't realize punching a guy could do so much damage. I need to work with this thing tomorrow."

"Speaking of work, you'd better avoid Bailey—she's probably not going to be too impressed."

"Yeah, good point."

Our mother returned and knelt in front of the couch, her hair falling in her face as she inspected the damage again. Mark jerked his hand back when she touched a knuckle. "Stop being a baby. If you're going to get in a fight, you have to deal with the consequences."

Again, I failed to hold in my laugh, which earned me another glare from my little brother.

"I'm guessing you weren't just an innocent bystander, Jake, so you'd better watch yourself," our mom warned.

That shut me up.

"I have a feeling I know what this is about but I'm really hoping I'm wrong," our mom said as she applied antibiotic ointment to Mark's torn hand.

Mark and I looked at each other, identical frowns on our faces.

"Um, what do you think this is about?" Mark ventured.

She raised her eyes from her task and pinned us both. "Bailey."

Shit, news traveled fast.

"How in the hell…"

Mark cut me off, "Shortcake. Dammit!" He punched the couch with his uninjured fist.

"Easy there, Rocky," our mom replied. "I had her on the phone earlier about a work thing and you know Fiona. She said you and Bailey had a heart-to-heart this morning and she's going through some stuff. There was mention of some guy followed by a string of cuss words, so I put two and two together." Then she turned to me. "I was hoping things were going well between you and Bailey. What's with this other guy?"

I explained the gallery disaster, eliciting several frowns and head shakes from her while she finished her job on Mark's hand. She then sat back on her heels and crossed her arms.

"This sounds very strange. I can't see Bailey associating with those types of people."

"That's what I was thinking too," I responded.

Finally, Mark spoke up. "It's more complicated than that."

This was already clear to me, given the few comments he'd unwittingly let slip during our confrontation with Anton. I wondered what he was doing right now and if it involved a trip to the doctor. I should have felt bad, but I was having a hard time mustering up any remorse.

"So, you punched him in the face, I'm guessing?" our mom asked, turning a stern look in Mark's direction.

"Yup," he said, leaning back into the couch, a big old smile on his face. "Just trust me, he had it coming."

I nodded my head in agreement.

"Well, I can't say I condone violence as an answer to anything, but you're grown men. I'll have to trust that you used relatively decent judgment. I imagine it would take a lot for either one of you to actually punch another person, even if you do spend a lot of time practicing at the gym." She gave a half-smile. "Bailey is lucky to have the two of you in her corner."

I huffed despondently and she shot me a curious look. "Mom,

I'm thinking she's done with me. You should have seen her face on Friday night."

An affectionate expression crossed her features and she winked at me. "I wouldn't throw in the towel just yet, sweetie. I have a feeling this whole thing had very little to do with you and a whole lot to do with her."

"Huh?"

She patted my hand. "Trust me. It's a girl thing."

Mark suddenly chuckled, apparently recalling something. "Uh, yeah. If all the tears I had to witness this morning proved anything, it's that Bailey's a girl after all. Color me surprised."

I smacked the back of his head and he tried to fend me off, forgetting about his injured hand for a moment. "Ow! Shit!"

That got him another smack to the head, this time from our mom. "Stop cussing!"

"What happened to violence never being the answer?! Everybody, stop hitting me! I'm a damn hero!" he cried, laughing and shielding himself from further assault.

"That rule doesn't extend to family," I said, and my mom laughed. I gave Mark one more pop. "Especially when that family member is still keeping secrets!"

"I plead the fifth based on the best-friend code. And besides, just grow a pair and stalk her like you did before. It seemed to work the first time."

At that, our mom just shook her head and stood up, gathering her medical supplies. "I'll leave you to it. And don't eat all my food." She walked to the kitchen.

"I didn't stalk her. I merely won her over with my charms." Well, perhaps that was pushing it.

"Yeah, right," Mark replied, grin still firmly in place. "So, how are things going with that new condo you're renting *right near Bailey's*?"

Shit. Totally busted.

I glared at him. "Okay, fine, there's no condo. But I had to figure out some way to run into her. You practically sent me an engraved invitation when you told me about her morning runs!"

He furrowed his brow. "God, you're whipped."

"Speak for yourself, asshole!"

He punched my arm with his good hand. "I'm just giving you shit, Nancy."

"Well, then you're gonna to love this one. The morning I conveniently ran into Bailey, I ended up with puke on my shoes. I guess Karma didn't like my sneaking around. Happy now?"

He guffawed just as my mom's head popped sharply around the corner from the kitchen.

"Bailey threw up on you?" She didn't look disgusted like one might expect. Instead, her expression was uneasy.

"Yes, if you can believe it. But you'd be proud of me—I drove her home and made sure she was okay. I remembered my lessons from childhood and was a perfect gentleman," I joked.

She didn't smile back but ducked back into the kitchen instead.

Mark and I looked at each other in question. Then we shrugged simultaneously and turned our attention back to the game.

Chapter Nineteen

SIGNS YOU'RE DEFINITELY A GIRL

BAILEY

Normally, having people hanging around my place all day would have me itching for a little privacy and some one-on-one time with my sketchbook. I had to admit, though, having Fiona and Laney park themselves on my couch for the majority of the day actually felt great. It helped soothe my injured spirit—and Fiona's ability to take the paltry contents of my refrigerator and turn them into actual food was a bonus I hadn't anticipated.

"I still don't understand how I've never seen this movie before," Laney said, forking another bite of frittata into her mouth and gawping at the television.

"Jesus, it's like a man-candy muscle buffet," Fiona added. She sipped her wine and it practically dribbled down her chin as she stared at a bare-chested Chris Hemsworth and the rest of the cast of the latest Avengers movie.

I felt a bit smug. "Now aren't you glad I nixed the chick flick?"

I took a bite of my own slice of frittata, moaning at its deliciousness. "Damn, Fiona. I need you to move in with me so I can eat like this every day," I mumbled over my mouthful of food.

"It's just eggs." She grinned, eyes still glued to the men on screen, none of whom appeared able to afford shirts with sleeves.

I had to smile at that. What I got at the McDonald's drive-thru was "just eggs." It was no wonder her catering business with Kelly was taking off.

"Hey, I'm surprised you don't have any catering gigs today," I told her.

She finally tore her eyes from the TV and shrugged. "We had two yesterday, and Kelly and I still have our other jobs so it's nice to have a day off."

"Aww, and you decided to spend it with pathetic old me." I flashed her a self-deprecating smile.

"Hey, none of that!" Laney chimed in. "Girl time is a valuable commodity and it's high time you recognized that." She elbowed me playfully.

"Yeah, well, I'm new to this so you have to cut me some slack."

Fiona paused the TV and I immediately regretted my interruption of the man parade. They were going to make me do more talking—I could feel it.

"So, now that we have some food and a couple movies under our belts, it's time to spill some more," Fiona declared.

I knew it! I tried to pull the blanket over my head but it was snatched out of my grip—quite aggressively, I felt.

"No. It's somebody else's turn."

Fiona put a mocking finger to her chin and turned to Laney. "Oh, I'm sorry. Laney, did you happen to run into a cocksucking ex recently and let him make you feel like shit?" Laney pretended to think about it and then slowly shook her head. "And I don't suppose you blew off a hot Beckett brother for reasons you have yet to share?"

Laney shook her head again. "Still no. Sorry."

They both pinned me with their stupid eyes.

"Whatever." I know, I'm brilliant.

Their expressions did not change.

"Look, it's complicated."

"So? We like complicated," Laney said while Fiona nodded her agreement.

I sighed. Then I sighed again just to make sure they knew how put out I was. "Fine."

Fiona folded her legs under her butt and cradled her wine glass like she was settling in for story hour. I glared at her before attempting my explanation.

"So, remember the wedding?" I asked like an idiot. Of course they remembered the wedding. But they just nodded as if my question was perfectly reasonable. Wow, they were good at this girl shit. "Anyway, I was all dressed up and I was feeling a bit…off. You know, with the weird clothes and my brother getting married." I looked to Laney then. "Not that I'm not really happy for you guys!"

She waved me off. "No, I totally get it. Weddings can do that."

I nodded. "So, Jake shows up at the reception, and I mean, I just…wow." I squirmed at the memory. "He was looking at me like I was lunch and, I don't know, something in me just snapped. I had totally sworn off men since the whole Anton thing, but there was something about the way Jake looked at me—and then there was my mood, and the way I was dressed…I totally climbed him like a giant, manly Sequoia!" I covered my face in embarrassment and I heard Fiona choke on her wine. Laney erupted in laughter. Oh God, this was humiliating. Why did people share this stuff?

They both grabbed at my hands, prying them from my face. Fiona giggled. "Girl, I'd be worried if you'd never jumped a man—especially one looking as hot as a Beckett brother in a suit."

"Oh my God. I know. That suit—and those cheekbones. It was like somebody dangled an entire testosterone-laden pot of chocolate fondue under my nose. I was powerless."

They both giggled at that. "I don't get what the problem is, then," said Laney.

I wanted to cover my face again but I resisted. "I guess that night, in itself, wasn't a problem. My plan, if I actually had one, was just to have that one night with him and that would be it."

"But why?" asked Fiona.

This was where it got hard.

"Well, first, I acted completely out of character. I mean, I was dressed all fancy and I was totally forward with him. You did hear the part about me jumping him, right?" They nodded. "That is *so* not me."

Fiona shrugged. "I guess, but it sounds totally hot and he clearly dug it."

"Yeah, but it's like false advertising. I mean, look at me." I gestured down to my men's boxers and *Pig Pounder* t-shirt. "And, besides, I'm not the kind of person who can have casual sex with someone like Jake Beckett and keep things from getting messy. I mean, look what happened with Anton. And he was never half as tempting and addictive as Jake! Jesus, you should have seen me—I was like some sex-crazed stripper on a Beckett-induced high."

They were both smiling. Shit, I'd shared too much.

Retreat!

"I think I'm gonna grab a drink. I'm feeling a bit parched." I started to get up and they both pushed me back down. What was it with people trying to fuse me to the couch today?!

"Not so fast!"

I delivered a few more glares and then sighed in defeat. "I'm an idiot."

"No, you're not."

"It's just that I should have known better. I should never have accepted another date—a first date, actually. I just got so caught up in him that I threw caution to the wind."

"And what's wrong with that? You think Fiona and I weren't scared to take a chance on our guys? If you recall, Fiona flipped the hell out before she and Mark got their shit together."

I smiled a little at that. Fiona really had lost her shit. But then, we were talking about Mark so it's understandable.

"I'm really happy things worked out for you guys, but it's not going to happen for me. And, besides, I'm sure Jake doesn't have any real feelings for me. He's just looking for a good time with a sexually confident girl. Like I said, it was false advertising."

"Okay, first, how do you know Jake doesn't have feelings for you? Do you have any actual evidence that he's just looking for a casual fling? And second, what the fuck is wrong with you?!" Fiona hit me with a couch pillow.

"Jesus, what's wrong with *me*? What's wrong with *you*?!"

"You're totally hot, and you're a complete catch! Why would you sell yourself short?"

"Correction. I was hot and a catch on the night of the wedding. Not in my real life."

This time it was Laney who hit me with a pillow.

"I'm gonna start fighting back soon, and I've got more muscle than you two put together—just sayin'." Laney scoffed and Fiona started in on me again.

"Jake has been practically stalking you! And by 'you' I mean the t-shirt wearing, prickly, stabby Bailey. Not just the one in a dress! What do you want him to do, rent out a billboard saying, 'Yo, Bailey Murphy, I've got a huge boner for you!'?"

Laney laughed, but I felt my eyes welling with tears—*again*. My next words came out in a whisper. "He's going to get bored with me and break my heart, and I can't take that again. Especially from someone like him."

Laney grabbed my hand. "What exactly do you mean, 'someone like him'?"

"Someone who'd be so easy to fall in love with. Someone so exactly everything I've ever wanted," I confessed gravely.

Remember that Great Wall? The one that love laughed in the face of? Well, it had one crucial design flaw. One that would inevitably bring the whole thing crashing down in a pile of dust and bricks time and time again. I was beginning to understand that I could re-erect it all I wanted, but it would never be impenetrable. It could only ever offer brief periods of protection until my traitorous heart threw a damn rope ladder over the side along with an engraved invitation to come on over and steal it.

I sniffled and Fiona handed me a tissue. "Oh, sweetie."

"I know," I gave a pitiful laugh. "I'm half in love with the smartass already. You wouldn't know it from hanging out with me, but it doesn't take much. I'm kind of a love wimp."

That made them both grin.

I felt a couple fat tears roll down my cheeks. "And to make matters even worse, I think I'm finally turning into a girl!" Cue sobbing mess, yet again.

Shit.

♣♣♣

I watched Jake's chest rise and fall as he slept beside me. I only felt a little like a creeper, but I couldn't sleep and he really was a sight to behold. My fingers itched to stroke the contours of his well-developed arms, but mostly, I just wanted to kiss him again. There was something about his kiss that flipped a switch inside me. I knew I was in deep trouble.

After we'd finished the champagne, we made out some more and talked into the night. We joked and bantered back and forth and even had our first fight—well, I had to call it that because how could a person seriously try to argue that *Goodfellas* is better than *The Godfather*. He was clearly trying to make me mad. We quickly had make-up sex, though, so all was right with the world again when Jake finally passed out and I found myself still wide awake.

This night had been the most incredible of my life and I was ripped to shreds that things with this man couldn't last past this one night. I could feel my heart wanting to give itself to him already, and I wanted to kick myself at my stupidity. Jake had the power to utterly crush me as I'd never been hurt before. I knew it and I couldn't let it happen.

I'd just have to write a note with some made-up excuse, and sneak out before he woke up. I couldn't bear to see his face when the light of day broke whatever spell had been cast on us. To hear him make false promises and walk out the door would hurt too much. I resolved to carry out my plan just as a powerful yawn forced my eyes to close. I supposed I could just close my eyes for a moment.

Sunlight pierced through my eyelids and I blinked them open. Shit! I'd fallen asleep. I looked quickly to the side, but, apart from me, the bed was empty. I swallowed the lump in my throat that had suddenly formed.

Well, it looked like I'd gotten my wish after all. I wouldn't have to see his face when he promised to call. And I wouldn't have to fight against the urge to give in and take a chance.

I slowly sat up and stretched. My body ached in places I didn't know could ache—a bittersweet reminder of my night as Bailey 2.0. I made my way to the bathroom and caught sight of a piece of hotel stationary on the counter.

Morning, Irish. I didn't have the heart to wake you—you were sleeping like the dead so you must have needed it. I guess I did a good job wearing you out last night! My mom called and needs help transporting some supplies this morning. I'll call you later today.

—Jake

I walked back out to the bedroom, still holding the note in my hand. I read it over one more time before sinking back onto the bed, my head a confused mess.

Of course he wrote a note, I told myself. He's a great guy. Good guys write notes the morning after. But I wouldn't hold my breath for that call. And even if he did, by some miracle, follow through, I would have to steel myself to resist the temptation to take things any further. Because when Jake Beckett walked away, as I knew he would, he'd take more than I could afford to lose.

☘☘☘

It was Monday morning, and I was at my desk, staring at my phone as it sat there taunting me. I had a missed call from Jake and a voicemail I had yet to listen to.

The girls had finally left my place around dinnertime the night before, and I'd fallen asleep almost immediately thereafter. All that sharing was exhausting. I don't know how they did it on a constant basis. Before they left, I voluntarily doled out hugs instead of arm punches, which would have been my normal MO. These girls had given up their Sunday to hang out with me and try to make me feel better. I was realizing how lucky I was to finally have girlfriends. *Crazy, I know*.

I was still trying to work up the nerve to listen to Jake's voicemail when a call from Kelly came through. That was odd. We rarely spoke on the phone. I had a sudden fear that she was calling on behalf of Jake. That thought was both frightening and laughable. Before I could think too hard about it, I answered.

"Hi, Kelly."

"Bailey, hi. How are you?"

"Apart from needing a nap already, I'm good," I joked. "What's up?"

"Oh, well," she paused, her voice sounding a bit strained. "Could we meet for lunch today?"

"Uh, sure," I said, still feeling a bit wary. "Any place in particular?"

"Well, I was hoping you could come over to my house. I'll cook."

Ah, she was trying out recipes. I was always up for that. "Sure! I'd love to be your guinea pig. Fiona was over yesterday and made this awesome frittata. I didn't even know what one was until then." I laughed.

She returned my laugh before continuing, "Great. How about noonish?"

"Sounds good. I'll be over then."

I was starting to think having professional caterers as friends was one sweet deal.

When midday approached, I snuck out without telling anyone where I was going. I hadn't seen Mark all morning and I was kind of glad. Part of me was embarrassed about the previous day, but the other part just needed a break from anything remotely emotional.

Kelly answered the door wearing a yellow top that brought out the various colors in her eyes—eyes that were eerily similar to Jake's, I noted. Damn. She beckoned me in and wrapped me up in a hug, which was kind of a new thing, but I went with it. I was getting super good at this sharing stuff.

I looked around the small but tidy living room. "Is anybody else coming or is it just us?"

That's when I noticed her wringing her hands. This could not be good.

"Kelly, is something wrong?"

She gave me a pained smile. "I don't know."

I just looked at her questioningly.

"Oh God, this is none of my business." She covered her eyes with one hand and shook her head.

Jesus. Was she really going to step in on Jake's behalf? Had he asked his mommy to talk to a girl for him? What the hell? I was pretty sure using your mom as your pimp broke some sort of cosmic code of conduct.

"What's going on?" I asked quietly with a tilt of my head. I half expected Jake to pop around the corner and yell, "Surprise!" in some impossibly sexy way.

"Do you want to eat? We should eat," she said and nervously shuffled toward the kitchen.

"Kelly?"

She stopped in her tracks and then turned slowly to face me again. Inhaling deeply, she threw her hands out to the sides. "Okay, you're probably going to laugh, but something occurred to me yesterday and I can't get it out of my head."

Okay, this didn't sound so bad. I gestured for her to continue.

"Well, it's just that I know you fairly well and I heard some things."

I cut her off. "Oh God, Kelly. I know. I'm sure it's really weird for you that Jake and I went out a few times. But I'm pretty sure it's over anyway. And I'm also pretty sure you heard all about the fiasco on Friday. Really, let's just move on. You don't need to worry, and I'm sorry if we put you in an awkward position." Kill me now.

She held her hand out to stop me. "No, that's not it. Well, not really. I was actually thrilled when I heard you and Jake were dating."

I couldn't help it—a little smile escaped before I remembered we were over.

"But I'm referring to a few…other things. It's just that you've been uncharacteristically emotional lately, right? I mean, in all the time I've known you, I've never seen you shed a tear."

Huh? "Um, yeah…" Where was she going with this? "I think Fiona and Laney are on a campaign to free my inner girl," I tried to joke.

She didn't acknowledge my lame joke. "And I heard about you passing out a couple weeks ago—and then Jake said something yesterday about you throwing up."

I covered my eyes. "Seriously?! He told you about that?!"

"And you said earlier that you needed a nap." She powered right on through.

I moved my hand and looked at her again. What in the world was she getting at? "Yeah, I've been totally exhausted. I have this cold and I'm all congested. It's kicking my ass."

She folded her hands neatly in front of her and gave me an expectant look. When I didn't respond, her expression turned to one you'd give someone who insisted unicorns existed. I'm sure the look I returned fell somewhere on the scale between bat-shit crazy and utterly stupid.

I couldn't take it anymore.

"What?!"

She approached and took both of my hands in hers, leading me to the couch where we both sat. Oh, look, another person making me sit. Gah!

Finally, she spoke. "Bailey, sweetie, I know this is intensely personal, but I have to ask anyway. When was your last period?"

What. The. Fuck?

I stared at her silently. I was dumbfounded. I mean, I was the absolute *definition* of dumbfounded.

Kelly just held my hand and waited for a response.

My eyes finally fell to the side as I counted. Then I counted again. The sum was not good. My period was four weeks late—how had I not noticed this? What the hell was wrong with me?

But, no—this was impossible. There was no way I could be pregnant. The only person I'd had sex with in the last several months was Jake. We'd used protection! Not to mention, I'd just been to the hospital where they'd checked me over and declared me healthy—as in, *not pregnant*!

Wait, no. Shit. They hadn't actually done a urine test. I am completely incapable of peeing under pressure—the expectations are too intense for my poor bladder, and it always crosses its legs and refuses to cooperate.

But, regardless, I couldn't be *pregnant*.

Oh, God. Please don't let me be pregnant. Are you listening?

My panicked eyes found Kelly again. She gave me a half-smile and squeezed my hands. “I got you something,” she said before rising from the couch and retrieving a drugstore bag from her purse.

It didn’t take a genius to know what was in that bag, and I wanted no part of it. No, ma’am! I was done being a girl.

Chapter Twenty

DISCOVERY

JAKE

"Put the taller trees in the back corners," I instructed Tom, one of the crew working with me on the Vaughn project. "I don't want them potentially obstructing anyone's view if they decide to grow much taller."

I wiped the sweat from my brow with the back of my glove and surveyed the yard. We were making good progress and I was hoping to finish the planting in the next few days. Then we could focus on some of the material installations while keeping an eye on the shrubs and trees to make sure they were acclimating. Last week, the yard had been an unholy mess as we'd pulled old plants and began digging holes. I was afraid Mrs. Vaughn was going to kill me but, as promised, everything was now coming together. My vision was coming to life, and even the prim older woman was beginning to relax.

"I'm quite partial to the rose trees," a voice sounded from

behind me. I turned to see the older woman as she watched Tom settling one of the trees in its new position.

"I'm happy you like them. They'll be beautiful next summer, just in time for the wedding."

I felt my phone vibrate in my back pocket, and I quickly pulled a glove off to snatch the device before the call could go to voicemail. Jax. Damn.

"Not who you were hoping to hear from, I take it?" asked Mrs. Vaughn. I felt myself color a bit as I realized my emotions must have been written all over my face.

I shrugged sheepishly. "Not exactly."

"Well," she began, dusting some invisible lint from her skirt, "perhaps it's old fashioned of me to say, but don't you think you should call her instead of waiting around for her to call?"

I chuckled, surprised that she was delving into this. "Believe me, ma'am, I've been more than clear about my intentions. And, just for the record, I did call last night. I even left a message," I said with a grin as if divulging a secret.

She nodded and smiled shrewdly. "And you're worried she's not interested, is that it?"

I looked at my boots, trying not to smile outright. "That's not exactly the impression I've gotten."

At that, Mrs. Vaughn actually laughed. "I think I'm beginning the get the idea, Mr. Beckett. In that case, all I can tell you is that a young woman always has her reasons. Perhaps it's time you go discover hers."

She gave a nod and turned to walk back to the house. Then she paused, looking toward Tom again. "Tell your man he'd better line those trees up precisely. We're striving for perfection, Mr. Beckett."

"Yes, ma'am." I smiled and headed toward Tom while Mrs.

Vaughn walked back to the house. A return call to Jax would have to wait. We had perfection to attain this afternoon.

By the time the day was over, I was filthy, smelly, and exhausted. We'd kicked ass and accomplished more than I'd planned for the day, however, so I was feeling good on the drive home.

I gave Jax the return call I owed him and learned that a certain Tessa McGuire was not sharing my good mood.

"Man, you weren't kidding with that one," Jax said.

"What one?" I had no idea what he was talking about.

"Tessa McGuire. She stopped by today since you apparently didn't return her phone calls this weekend." I could hear the delight in his voice. Why was my pain so pleasing to him? Ass.

"Seriously? I texted her back telling her we were right on schedule! Her project isn't even starting until next week."

He chuckled at that. "Well, apparently, she was looking for a little more *personal* attention."

"Shit," I groaned into the phone.

"Relax, I got you covered. I told her you would stop by tomorrow afternoon to answer whatever questions she has. I also talked to Ollie and he's making himself available to go with you."

I sighed. "Thanks, man. I don't want to drop this project, but I do not have a good feeling. I appreciate you having my back."

"Not a problem. Apart from the money we'll make on a project this size, I gotta say the entertainment factor is making this one worth the trouble."

"Says the guy who doesn't have a stalker."

He laughed. "No. I mean, you should have seen Fiona when Mrs. McGuire came in asking for you. I thought our girl was going to claw that woman's eyes out. You've officially got yourself a five-foot bodyguard, complete with high heels and a dirty mouth."

"God, I can just imagine." I chuckled at the mental image.

"I'm thinking of installing surveillance cameras for the next time your admirer stops by," he joked. "And I'm guessing there will be a next time."

Unfortunately, I was guessing the same thing.

Thoughts of Tessa McGuire flew from my mind as soon as I pulled onto my mom's street and noticed Bailey's car parked in our driveway.

"Hey, man, I gotta go. Thanks again." I didn't even wait for a response before hanging up.

I parked my truck on the street and jogged up to the front door. I walked directly to the living room, expecting to see her on the couch, but there was no one there. An inspection of the kitchen proved the same. I'd just turned around when I was halted abruptly by my mother as she raced from the hallway.

"Jake, wait," she said in a quiet but urgent voice as she practically ran into me and put a hand on my arm. She seemed a bit panicked.

"You okay? What's wrong? Where's Bailey? I saw her car in the driveway."

"Come into the kitchen." She dragged me by the hand and I followed, trying to guess what was going on. "Sit." She gestured to one of the kitchen chairs, but I didn't feel like sitting.

"What's going on, Mom?"

She sat down and began wringing her hands.

"Did something happen?"

"No. No. I just wanted to catch you before you went bursting into your room." She paused and bit her lip before continuing. "Bailey's asleep in there."

I looked down at my mom. “Oh, is she all right?”

“Yes. Just exhausted. Let her sleep, okay? When she wakes up you can see her.”

“Okay.” I sat down, now unsure what to do with myself. “Just curious. How long has she been here?”

My mom stood up at this question and walked to the fridge. “Um, since around lunchtime?” she asked more than said. “You look like you need a drink. Water?”

“Yeah, thanks,” I responded distractedly, trying to work out why Bailey would have come over in the middle of a workday. “Didn’t she have to work today?”

Setting the water in front of me, my mother said, “Oh, I invited her over for lunch and she wasn’t feeling well. I suggested she lie down and she’s been asleep ever since. I called Mark and told him to let work know she was ill.”

“But you said she was fine.” Something wasn’t right here.

“She is.” I got a pat on my hand. “Like I said, you can talk to her when she wakes up.” My mother left the kitchen and headed quietly down the hall to her room.

Something *definitely* wasn’t right here.

Twenty minutes later, my mom emerged from her room, dressed for her evening shift at her waitressing job. I was given both a kiss on the cheek and a pointed reminder to let Sleeping Beauty rest before my mother exited the house and I heard her car pull out of the driveway.

The woman I was crazy about was lying in my bed, having completely shut me out for the last three days. There was no way I was going to stay here on the couch like a sucker. I moved directly to the bathroom where I quickly showered. I dried myself off and wrapped a towel around my waist before walking quietly to my bedroom door and slowly turning the knob.

In my bed lay my blond goddess, her cheeks pink and a blanket pulled up to her chin. She slept with a small frown marring her face and I wanted to wipe it away with a kiss. I moved to stand at the side of the bed and looked down at her for a few moments. She didn't move a muscle. My mother had been right. Bailey was completely and utterly exhausted.

As quietly as I could, I exchanged the towel for a pair of boxer briefs and then carefully climbed into the small bed next to her. Moving with painstaking care so as not to wake her, I arranged us so her head rested on my shoulder, and my arms wound around her. I closed my eyes, feeling the exhaustion from my own day hitting me. Before I knew it, I was fast asleep as well.

I was awakened by a mumbled voice and a hard chin digging into my shoulder. My eyes snapped open and I looked down to see Bailey slowly emerging from her marathon nap. The room was lit only by the waning light of dusk coming through my window, which told me I'd been out for over an hour. Bailey's cheek rubbed across my chest and she lifted her head as her eyes blinked repeatedly. The frown from earlier deepened until her eyes found my face and a beautiful smile formed on her perfect mouth.

"Jake," she said sleepily.

"Hey, Irish," I responded quietly, returning her smile. I'm sure we looked like a couple of idiots but I didn't care.

We looked at each other for one perfect moment and her expression told me everything I needed to know. She wanted to be with me. So, it was settled. I'd make it happen.

I brought my hand up to brush her hair out of her face and the movement acted as some sort of catalyst. Her smile froze and she shot to her knees on the bed. She whipped her head around, as if not recognizing her surroundings, and the motion seemed to cause her pain because she moaned and covered her head with her hands.

I sat up and pulled her to me. "Hey, easy there. You're really feeling sick, aren't you?" I stroked her back, but she was stiff in my arms.

"Oh my God," she mumbled.

"Come on, lay back down. Don't make it worse," I coaxed, but she was unmovable.

"Jake," she said into my chest, "please."

"Please what? Do you need me to get you some ibuprofen? How about some water?" I released my hold so I could pull back and look at her again.

She was looking up at me with an expression I didn't understand. It was almost a look of fear. What the hell?

"No," she replied. "I just…I just need a minute."

"Um, okay." I tilted my head because I didn't grasp what she was asking for at all.

"Can you maybe go stand over there?" She pointed vaguely to a corner of the room. "No, wait, I'll stand. Then I can think better."

"Bailey, what the hell is going on?" I seemed to be asking that question a lot lately. I was beginning to get a complex.

She got out of bed and paced to the door and back. Her shirt was untucked and her hair had fallen out of its ponytail. She looked like she'd just been ravaged on her desk at work—either that or taken a tumble in the dryer. I was hoping we could square away whatever was putting that look on her face and she'd come back to bed.

Her thumbnail was held firmly between her teeth and her eyes squinted in concentration. She took a deep breath, dropped her hand and blurted out the absolute last thing I ever expected to hear.

"I'm pregnant."

Chapter Twenty-One

THE DEAD RABBIT PITCH

BAILEY

There are moments in your life you'll never forget as long as you live. Every detail is burned into your memory and you can pull the moment out to replay it whenever you feel the urge. If the memory is particularly painful, it often comes out unbidden and you have to fight to push it back in because you never want to experience it again.

The moment I spoke those words to Jake and saw the look on his face was one of those I knew I'd have to learn to banish. Because it was the kind that would haunt me.

My words were hanging in the air when his face morphed from concern and confusion to something I can only describe as utter horror. He was the kid from *The Shining* and I was the creepy twin girls.

How had I let Kelly talk me into this? It had seemed like such a no-brainer when I'd been sobbing on her couch and she was holding me in her tight embrace. Of course I had to tell Jake. I mean, his own mother knew, for God's sake. And it wasn't like this was something I could hide—I may be the queen of junk food, but no amount of pizza rolls and mozzarella sticks was going to hide the giant belly in my near future.

Holy shit. I was going to have a giant belly! I was going to be one of those unfortunate pregnant women I see at the store, trying to reach the cereal box on the top shelf. Her ginormous belly gets in the way and she's left flailing helplessly until someone takes pity on her and grabs the damn box of Frosted Flakes. That was going to be me! *Me!*

I pushed the disturbing image aside and focused again on Jake's face—he looked like he was witnessing an autopsy. The only thing that could make this moment worse would be if I vomited on him again. Which, in my current state, was entirely within the realm of possibility.

I found that I couldn't move or speak. I was frozen in this moment as it seared itself into my memory to torture me later. Time passed—no clue how much—and we both stared.

Then, thank God, Jake's expression shifted—not to anything good, mind you, but it did change. He affected either a lost or paranoid look now. It was hard to tell. His eyes shifted around the room as if looking for an answer to some unspoken question. I'd been looking for that answer all damn day and I could assure him it lay nowhere in this house. The only answer that existed could be boiled down to one word: FUCK!

Yup, the deed had been done and we were totally fucked.

He finally spoke. "Are you sure?"

And *that* was what he said.

I sputtered, "Am…am I sure?" I shook my head, not in answer to his question, but in sheer disbelief. "Do you really think I'd say something like that if I wasn't sure, Jake?! Of course I'm sure! Jesus!"

He put his hands out. "Okay, sorry. Sorry. I just…I'm just trying to process this." His hands went to his hair where they scrubbed furiously, making a giant mess of things. If I hadn't been so preoccupied with the minor issue of my *pregnancy*, I might have found it rather sexy.

All right, I had to cut him a break here. I'd had several hours to digest this information and I was still a shell-shocked ball of emotions. He'd had a couple of minutes. I needed to reign in the crazy. "Sorry. I didn't mean to yell at you. I know this is an absolute shock."

He nodded with wide eyes, his hands now dropping to his sides. "We used a condom. We used several condoms."

If I detected even the barest hint of a smile after that comment I was going to stab him. "Yes, I'm aware. Congratulations. Your sperm are overachievers."

Of course they were. I mean, look at him. It should have come as no surprise that Jake Beckett had super-hero sperm that could leap tall buildings in a single bound. A mere bit of latex was no match for Jake's super-sperm. They scoffed at such pathetic obstacles. Hell, he'd probably knocked me up with triplets!

He gave a mirthless laugh, apparently oblivious to the fact that I was on the verge of a nervous breakdown. His spine lost the ability to keep him vertical and he collapsed back on the bed, covering his eyes with one arm.

I was left standing awkwardly in the middle of the floor with my heart racing. Well, at least he hadn't asked me if I was sure the baby was his. That was something, right?

I didn't know what to do. Should I tell him not to worry about it—that I'd figure it out on my own? No. That was ridiculous.

Should I ask him what he wanted to do? What if he wanted me to have an abortion? As terrifying as the mere thought of a baby was, I knew I couldn't do that. And it wasn't as if I were destitute or physically unable to care for a child. If I had to do it on my own, I would. My family would surely pitch in, right?

I was having this baby one way or another.

The words hit me squarely in the chest. It was the first time I'd let that concrete thought run through me. *I was having a baby*. This was one hell of a cosmic joke.

Despite my resolve to cut Jake some slack, I found my eyes becoming wet once again as I watched him lay there, no doubt begging God or the devil to make this go away. Didn't he understand I felt the exact same way? The same fear and helplessness? I suddenly wanted to punch him and his stupid supersperm.

Instead, I decided to leave before I did or said something I couldn't take back. I had just turned to the door when I heard Jake's voice.

"Where do you think you're going?" His tone was gentle.

I turned back to him, still absolutely out of my element. He'd removed the arm from his face and was up on one elbow in the bed. The man had just heard the most shocking news of his life, and he looked like he was in the middle of a photo shoot for Calvin Klein underwear. Despite the dire circumstances, I wanted to roll my eyes.

"Get your knocked-up ass over here, Irish." And then he gave me a sheepish smile.

A giant sob welled from my body, and I collapsed on top of Jake, eliciting a grunt of surprise. He put his arms around me and stroked my back while I let go a torrent of hormonally and emotionally driven tears. He whispered soothing words in my ear while every drop of moisture in my body deposited itself on his chest and pillow.

"Hey, it's gonna be okay," he murmured. "We'll figure this out together. You're not alone in this, okay?"

His words were a balm to my tortured heart and mind—and uterus, apparently.

We stayed wrapped up together until I ran out of tears, and then Jake covered me with a blanket and went to get some water. When he came back, I gratefully accepted the bottle, draining it as he resumed his position on the bed. I was soon tucked into his side as I'd been when I'd awoken.

"Look, I obviously don't have anything figured out yet, and I'm sure you don't either, but we'll make a plan together. Okay?"

I nodded into his shoulder. "I need to make a doctor's appointment. I'm sure there's a ton of stuff I need to find out."

"You tell me when and I'll take you."

I couldn't believe how calm he seemed about all of this.

"Okay. I'll call them tomorrow and let you know."

I wondered if he was having the same out-of-body sensation I was experiencing. We were having a baby. A small human was growing inside of me at that very moment, made up of half cheekbones and half tomboy.

"I know there's some rule about not telling people you're pregnant until a certain amount of time passes. Are you past that point?" He pulled back and looked down at me.

"I have no earthly idea what you're talking about."

He uttered a small laugh. "We'll get a book."

"Probably a good idea to get several," I replied.

"Regardless, we're going to have to tell Mark since I'll need his help moving my stuff into your place. Although, then Fiona will find out and there's no point trying to hide it after that."

I hardly heard the end of his thought because my brain had arrested at the part about him moving into my place. “Um, what?”

“Come on, you don’t really think Fiona could keep something this big to herself, do you?”

“No, I mean the part about you moving your things into my condo.”

“Well, yeah.” He shrugged as if this was some foregone conclusion. “It’s not like you can move in here. I’m sure my mom would love that, but not a chance in hell. If you think your family would feel better if the wedding came first, though, I suppose we could do a courthouse thing. I just figured you’d want a real wedding—but it’s totally up to you.”

It took a moment for all of that to sink in.

“It’s up to me,” I repeated.

“Yeah. I mean, no offense, but guys don’t really care all that much about weddings.”

I stared at him, wondering if the pod people had taken over. He was lying there, casually talking about marrying me in the same way one might chat about what to watch on TV. “Okay,” I began. “If it’s up to me, I choose no wedding and no moving in together.”

His mouth turned down and a huge crease appeared on his forehead. “What are you talking about? We’re having a baby. We need to get married and move in together. I don’t care which order that comes in, but we’re doing it.”

I sat up in the bed, pulling away from him. “Did you just order me to marry you?!”

He grunted and rubbed a hand over his face. “Look, you’re taking this the wrong way. There’s a baby involved. It’s not about you and me anymore. It’s about that baby.” He pointed to my still-flat stomach.

I winced inwardly at his words. *It’s not about you and me…it’s about that baby.* Ouch. “It seems entirely about you and me when we’re discussing living arrangements and life-long contracts, Jake!”

“Are you saying you don’t want our baby to have both his parents living with him?”

“That’s not what I’m saying.” My hands clenched into fists. “Among other things, I don’t understand why we have to decide all of this right now! I mean, the rabbit just died!”

“What? What rabbit?”

I shooed him, “You know—the pregnancy-test rabbit.” I shook my head. “Never mind. I was watching some documentary on Discovery Health—forget it.”

“Is this some hormonal thing?”

If he finished this conversation with his balls still attached, it would be a miracle.

“No, Jake.” My voice was steel and he appeared to understand the unspoken threat.

“Sorry. I shouldn’t have said that.”

I felt a tiny bit of relief wash over me. “Great. I’m glad you’re coming to your senses. We’ll just play this by ear. You can come with me to doctor’s appointments and we’ll worry about the rest down the road.”

He shot me a quizzical look. “I meant I shouldn’t have said you were hormonal. We’re still getting hitched and living together.”

“No, we are not!”

Logically, I knew this baby changed everything. Regardless, I was not going to be some obligation or a consolation prize. We could raise this baby without being together. People did it all the time. I wasn’t about to offer myself up for the part of the albatross.

“Why are you so against this? Does this have to do with that

Anton guy? Because you are never laying eyes on that asshole again." A vein popped out in Jake's neck.

"What the hell? How could you ask me that?"

"From what I've learned the last couple days, I think he's the reason you wouldn't give me a chance in the first place!" I didn't even want to think about what he might have heard from Mark and the girls.

"Well, Jake, if a chance is what you've been looking for, you certainly have one now. A screaming, pooping, eighteen-year-long relationship is right around the corner. Enjoy!"

"Exactly—that's why we're getting married."

"No!"

"Why not?"

"Oh my God. Let's hope the baby doesn't get your intellect."

And, with that, I stormed out of the room, desperate to get out of this house. I could not bear to look at Jake for one more second.

Chapter Twenty-Two

ALERT: IMMINENT ALIEN INVASION

JAKE

I had absolutely no idea what just happened.

I mean, Jesus, I'd gotten Bailey pregnant. That fact alone completely blew my mind. We'd been careful, I was sure of it. But I guess we were one of the unlucky couples who fell in the two percent error margin.

Unlucky. Was that the right word?

I mean, I was in no way prepared to be a father, but I'm thirty-three. I always figured I'd have kids at some point. I guess that point was now.

And, sure, the order of events was not ideal, but I'd had that gut feeling about Bailey for weeks. Of any girl I'd ever dated, my feelings ran the deepest for her—which had to say something, given that we'd only been out on two and a half dates.

Unlucky was not the right word. Scary as shit? Yes. Unlucky? Not really. *I know, I'm shocked too.*

I didn't know how to categorize my feelings for Bailey at this point. There was lust, affection, and a general desire to just be around her—all the time. That, and a compulsion to touch her and take care of her. I had no idea if that was love or not. I'd never been in love before.

We had time to find all the right words down the line. We'd just move in together, get married, and have this baby—because he was coming either way. The rest would work itself out, and the thought of waking up next to Bailey for the rest of my life felt surprisingly un-scary. In fact, it felt pretty fucking awesome.

She was having my baby—*my* baby.

Shit, I was going to be a dad. If she thought I was going to bail on her or be a shitty husband and father, she had another thing coming. I was going to stick like glue to her and that kid, come hell or high water. She would never feel like my dad had made my mom feel, and our son would never have a single reason to doubt his father's loyalty and devotion. Never.

When I'd made the decision to come back home, it was to make up for lost time and fix what I'd broken by running away and staying gone for so long. I guess Fate wanted me to thoroughly prove myself with this curveball. Fate could take its best shot.

This was my chance at redemption.

Unlucky? No. This sounded more like an opportunity at something pretty damn incredible.

Now I just had to figure out what I'd done to piss Bailey off so badly.

Since she clearly didn't want to see me right now, I chose to give her a cooling-down period and put my time to good use doing research. I spent the next several hours on the internet.

Huge mistake.

By the time I was done reading, I was convinced our baby—which I now knew was called an embryo—would be born with eleven fingers, three ears, and would resemble an alien. There were so many things that could go wrong, and Bailey and I had absolutely no control over most of them. The notion was terrifying.

I finally forced myself to close my laptop and proceeded to pace the living room trying to work out how in the world we'd be able to afford specialized care for our little alien. I'd just resolved to sell a kidney when my mom walked in from work.

She set down her purse, covered her mouth, and gave me "mom" eyes. Then she dropped her hand and jumped up and down like a damn teenager. "I'm gonna be a grandma!" she squealed before running over to tackle me in a huge hug. Despite myself, I had to laugh.

☘ ☘ ☘

Not wanting to throw a damper on my mom's excitement, I just told her Bailey went home for the night—I left out the part about our argument and how I'd basically been declared an idiot. I was still trying to comprehend that one the next morning as I helped lay new sod in a section of the Vaughn's yard. The design was looking great, and I couldn't have been happier with the project.

I knew I had the dreaded meeting with Tessa McGuire in the afternoon, so I took off early, after confirming with Ollie that he'd meet me there. I was in no mood for any interaction with an entitled rich girl—the only girl on my mind was probably sitting at work pushing pins into a Beckett-shaped voodoo doll. I parked on the street in front of the McGuire's home and looked around. No sign of Ollie or a Precision vehicle.

There was no way I was getting out until he showed, so I took the chance to send my second text of the day to Bailey. This time, she deigned to answer.

Jake: *You can try to ignore me but I won't go away. You may as well respond.*
Bailey: *I'm working.*
Jake: *Me too. Oh, look—we have something in common. I hear it's good for married people to have things in common.*
Bailey: *I thought you didn't want our child to grow up fatherless??*
Jake: *Uh, my point exactly.*
Bailey: *Then you should probably shut up before I run you over with my car.*
Jake: *Why are you so pissed off? Tell me and I'll apologize. That's a great offer!*
Bailey: *I have to go. I need to make a phone call.*
Jake: *Who could be more important to call than your baby daddy?*

I snickered to myself at that one.

Bailey: *The coroner.*

Oh. Well, it seemed she was still just as pissed and just as tight-lipped about the reason. I was about to respond when there was a tapping on my window. I looked up, and Tessa McGuire stood there with bright red lips spread in a wide smile and a tall glass of iced tea in her hand—complete with a decorative lemon slice. Shit.

I glanced around furtively hoping to spot Ollie, but the guy was a no-show. Dammit! Looked like I'd have to do this on my own. Forcing a smile, I rolled down the window.

"Good afternoon, Mrs. McGuire."

"Tessa, silly." She laid her arm across the window opening. Did she just refer to me as "silly"? "I thought you could use a drink. I'll bet you've been working hard today." She let her eyes slide down my body which was, indeed, covered in dirt and a fair amount of sweat.

"Yes, ma'am, but I'm all right. Just had some water. I'm waiting on a colleague and then we can both meet you in the backyard if that works for you."

Her smile froze. "A colleague?"

"That's right. I'm not sure if you've met him—Oliver—he'll be giving me some input. He's more cultured than I am, by far, so I think he'll be a great asset," I said, pulling that tidbit straight out of my ass. Ollie did the accounts and only helped out the crew when Jax was short. I had no idea, however, if he knew the difference between a croquet mallet and a crowbar.

She recovered her smile, although it was strained, thus telling me that my instincts had been spot-on. I was in deep shit. "Oh, well I'm sure he's wonderful, but that's entirely unnecessary. Come on into the backyard and I'll show you what I'm concerned about."

Come on, Ollie. Where the fuck are you?

"Sure thing," I responded. "I just need to send a quick text." I motioned for her to go on without me, but she stayed put. Crap.

I texted Ollie, threatening his very existence on this planet if he didn't show up in the next thirty seconds. No response.

I threw another glance at Tessa and she just tilted her head, the wide smile returning.

If I wanted to keep this job, I was going to have to get my ass out of the truck and suck it up. So I did.

Tessa tried to link her arm through mine on the walk to her backyard, but I pretended to trip on something and then told her I'd changed my mind about the tea. I grasped the glass and brought it to my lips, hoping to hell it hadn't been roofied.

She closed the gate to the backyard once we'd passed through, and I suddenly felt like a child who'd been lured into a molester van with promises of candy and puppies. Except in this scenario, the molester was a designer-clad young bride and I was the hapless gardener. I was guessing in her mind we were in one of those romance novels with the heiress and the stable-hand, except this stable-hand had a pregnant fiancée and a fucking career to keep afloat.

I looked around, hoping to see a big tree laying on its side across the yard, but no. I scratched the back of my neck. "What seems to be the problem?"

She walked into the yard, deliberately taking it slowly and shifting her hips in her tight skirt. Then she turned or, more accurately, whipped around in a dramatic move that sent her hair flying. It completely startled me and I took a step back.

Jesus.

Tessa started toward me again and only stopped when she was in complete violation of my personal space. Her finger touched my chest. "The problem, Jake," she began, and then—thank fuck—the gate latch banged and a flustered Ollie practically sprinted over to us. I sighed in relief. Tessa huffed in frustration and stepped back. I didn't know whether to kiss Ollie or punch him in the nuts for being late.

After Ollie made his grand entrance, Tessa had very little to say. She murmured about some changes she'd like to make to the plans, something that could have easily been handled over e-mail. Ollie and I just smiled and "yes ma'am"ed until we could politely get the hell out of dodge.

"Jesus, man, I'm so sorry!" Ollie said for the fourth time. We were sitting at the bar of one of my favorite hangouts, both of us in desperate need of a beer after that near-catastrophe.

I patted him on the back. "It's okay. I'm just glad you showed up when you did." I took a swallow of my beer and let the cool liquid slide down my throat, calming me.

Ollie readjusted his tie—why he wore one, I had zero clue—and took a pull on his own beer. "That woman is a viper. She looked like she was getting ready to poison you and drag you into her den."

I had to laugh at that.

Ollie looked sideways at me. "Why doesn't shit like that ever happen to me?"

That just made me laugh harder.

☘ ☘ ☘

Driving to the Vaughn's the next morning, I resolved that if I didn't get Bailey talking to me by the end of the day, I was going to enlist my mom for help. *I know*—it felt fairly emasculating, but I was getting desperate and she was the only other person who knew about the pregnancy.

There'd been another text exchange with Bailey the night before. She'd felt obligated to tell me about an upcoming doctor's appointment on Friday, but she was still unyielding regarding any other discussion of our situation.

I was so preoccupied by my dilemma that I didn't hear Mrs. Vaughn until she was standing right in front of me saying my name. "Mr. Beckett, are you all right?"

My head shot up from my work on the hedges. I noticed she was wearing another impeccable pair of trousers and a matching sweater set. Not a hair was out of place in her silver bob and her hands were clasped neatly in front of her. She was, at once, completely out of place in the filthy surroundings and completely at home wherever she decided to put herself.

"I apologize, Mrs. Vaughn." I stood up. "I'm a bit preoccupied." Sheepish seemed to be my permanent condition around her.

She smiled understandingly. "Did you find the answers you were looking for?"

I gave her a baffled look. Jesus, I was doing a bang-up job at impressing this client.

"The young woman," she prompted.

"Oh," I replied in understanding. I scratched my chin and tried to determine a good response, looking to the hedges for help. "You could say that, I guess." I gave a self-deprecating chortle.

"And that's a bad thing?" She inspected the box hedges with her long fingers.

I suddenly felt the need to unburden myself and, for some reason, I instinctively knew Mrs. Vaughn wouldn't mind. Before I could chicken out, I divulged the abridged version of events, including the secret of the gestating alien and Bailey's refusal to speak to me.

Mrs. Vaughn just looked at me, not unkindly, but speculatively. "Am I to understand you're happy about the baby?"

"Well, yeah, I guess. I mean, what's done is done. I can either be mad or happy, and since mad does nobody any good…I guess I'm happy." I shrugged.

"And are you happy about this Bailey being the mother?"

I didn't hesitate. "Absolutely. There's nobody else in the world I'd rather have this baby with."

She smiled. "Well then. There's your answer."

"Huh?" Damn, I was inspiring boatloads of confidence here. All I needed now was a piece of straw to chew on to complete the portrait of a jackass hick.

"Repeat that last sentence to your young woman and I think you'll get a more receptive response."

"Oh," was all I could think to say. Then comprehension dawned. "*Ooh.*" I nodded my head. Bingo.

She nodded as well. "Don't let her stew too long, Mr. Beckett. And might I suggest flowers? As you know, the hydrangeas are beautiful right now." She lifted a brow. "You may be unaware, however, of what they symbolize—both heartfelt sincerity and the gratefulness of the giver for the recipient's understanding." She nodded as she spoke, assuring I felt her full meaning.

"Are you by any chance a therapist, Mrs. Vaughn?" I asked with a grin.

She smiled and shook her head.

"A psychic then? No, a florist!"

She laughed outright. "No, Mr. Beckett. I am many things, I'll admit, but above all, I'm a woman." She lifted her chin and wished me luck.

Chapter Twenty-Three

THESE IRISH EYES AIN'T SMILING

BAILEY

I was completely at my wit's end. I'd run around and around in circles in my head for two days and I determined it was finally time to bring someone else into this clusterfuck. Or, more precisely, two someones. I swallowed hard and took a deep breath before opening the door to my childhood home.

"Dad?"

Please don't be home! I was hoping it would just be my mom, as I was guessing her reaction would be a bit easier to stomach.

"Bailey!" my father's deep voice boomed from the living room.

Damn.

I entered the room, crossing it to give him a hug. His tall frame and broad chest made me feel positively dainty, a rarity for me. His returning hug also made me feel cherished, and I hoped to God my news wouldn't change the way my father looked at me.

"What brings you here in the middle of the week? Not that I'm not happy to see you." He released me and looked me over. "You look tired," he declared.

I barked out a laugh. "Gee, thanks."

"Are you working too hard? Are you sleeping? What's going on?"

How did he do that?

"Nothing. For God's sake, can't a girl come over to see her parents?"

He pulled me in again. "You're my daughter. I worry—it's my job."

"I'm aware," I mumbled, my words swallowed by his shirt.

"Of course you are. 'A son is a son till he takes him a wife. A daughter is a daughter all of her life.'" He quoted another of his favorite Irish gems. Then he let me go and smiled. "And that one is especially appropriate given the recent nuptials!" He seemed rather pleased with himself as he sat down in his leather recliner and rocked a few times.

"So, is Mom around?"

"She's upstairs," he responded and followed that up with a holler. "ERIN! YOUR DAUGHTER'S HERE!"

I covered my ears and briefly wondered if the baby had formed eardrums yet, as they'd surely been rendered useless after that. My mother's footsteps sounded down the stairs.

"For goodness sake, Riordan! Would you please pipe down! I'm not deaf—yet." She crossed to me and gave me a tight hug. "Hello, sweetheart. What a nice surprise. Are you hungry?"

My mother was always trying to feed people. Unfortunately, she lacked any degree of culinary skill, and it was a wonder no one had ever been poisoned. I shook my head. "No thanks, Mom. I'm fine."

"Come into the kitchen anyway. I'll get you a drink." She

waved for me to follow her. "I'm glad you stopped by—it gives me an excuse to take a break from closet cleaning. You wouldn't believe the things I'm finding in there. I'd forgotten I used to be so trim. And to think I never stopped to appreciate it." She looked me up and down and sighed. I was tempted to tell her not to feel bad—that I'd be Shamu in a few months' time. That didn't seem like the most tactful way to announce my big news, though, so I refrained and took the glass of tea she held out.

My father's voice sounded from the next room. "She looks tired, Erin. Do something."

I wrinkled my nose. My mother inspected my face, no doubt noting the bags under my eyes. "He does have a point. Haven't you been sleeping?" She gestured for me to sit with her at the kitchen table.

"Um," I began, not quite sure where to start. The sudden urge to flee bloomed in my chest and I imagined leaving clouds of Road Runner–style dust in my wake as I darted to freedom. But, as I was far too aware, there was no outrunning this particular problem. Best to just face the music. I turned my head to the living room. "Hey, Dad, can you come in here?" I faced my mother again and saw worry etched on her brow. Shit, this was going to be hard.

My dad entered the kitchen seconds later, wearing a similar expression of concern. I motioned for him to sit.

There we were. This was the last moment I'd be the Bailey they knew—the Bailey who hadn't carelessly fucked things up and changed her future irrevocably. I inhaled deeply, steeling myself.

Like a Band-Aid, I thought.

I placed my hands flat on the table. "Well, it looks like you're going to be grandparents."

Crickets. Fucking crickets.

Just as I was about to jump into the silence, my mother whispered, "Sweet baby Jesus." She brought her hand to her chest. "She's pregnant already? Oh my word, this is so exciting!" Her voice rang through the kitchen and she grabbed onto my father's hand. Then she looked quizzically at me. "Wait, why are *you* telling us? Won't Laney be upset you spoiled the surprise? And why did they tell *you* before *us*? Everybody knows the grandparents find out first! I'll be having words with Nate, you'd better believe that!"

"Erin!" my father shouted. "For the love of God and all that's holy, be quiet!"

She smacked his arm. "Don't you speak to me that way, Riordan Murphy—"

He cut her off again. "I'm guessing the grandparents *are* finding out first, you daft woman." I could feel him look at me but I couldn't meet his eyes.

"I don't understand," she continued.

"Mom," I said, daring to meet hers. "He's right. Laney's not pregnant. I am."

The sound of my mother gasping and my father's fist hitting the table just about undid me. But what had I expected? We were Irish Catholics—well, at least they were. I wasn't quite sure what I was, but that was beside the point. Their reaction was very predictable and that was fine. It had to be. Just as I knew they were disappointed, I also knew they'd come around and love this child unconditionally. We just had to get through this first rough patch.

"Give me a name." My dad's voice was low and controlled.

I barely refrained from rolling my eyes. "Dad, I'm almost thirty years old, not sixteen. You're not beating anyone up."

"You're damn right I'm not. I'm gonna kill him. Name," he demanded again.

The sounds of my mother quietly weeping then registered and I had to decide which source of crazy to address first.

"It doesn't matter! I'm a grown woman and I can make my own decisions."

"It does matter! It matters a whole hell of a lot, young lady!"

Young lady? What was this, the morning after prom?

The weeping from the other side of the table was growing louder.

"Dad, I appreciate your concern and I will certainly appreciate you being an awesome grandparent to my baby. But that's it. There will be no shotguns and no fists. For God's sake, you had a heart attack a year ago and you think you're going to stalk around town beating up my boyfriends?!"

"Boyfriends? As in, more than one? What is the matter with you young people?"

I took a breath, begging for calm. "No. There is one guy—one father. But what he and I decide to do from here on out is our business. I just wanted to tell you because I thought it was the right thing to do. Maybe I was wrong."

I moved to stand when my mom's strained voice came across the table. "Bailey."

I finally looked at her and saw the tears washing down her face. And she was smiling. *Smiling.*

"Bailey." She gripped my hand tightly. "You're having a baby." Her voice broke on the last word.

I looked at our hands and then back to her face, unable to keep the smile from mine. "Yeah. I am." I shrugged.

She laughed, then I laughed, and then we both started crying because that's what pregnant women do all the fucking time, apparently. And then we were hugging.

Somewhere in there, my dad quietly left the room.

☘☘☘

An hour later, I drove home, still smiling over my mother's unexpected reaction to the defilement and sinful impregnation of her youngest child. I simultaneously ignored all thoughts of my father. He'd come around—I had to believe that.

It felt good having some solidarity. My mind was a little more at ease and I could think more clearly. I knew I'd have to talk to Jake soon, but I was dreading it.

What did you say to a guy you adored who announced he was marrying you because that's what a good guy should do? I was sick of never being good enough as just me—as just who I am. Anton had wanted me to be someone else, and Jake only wanted me because he'd knocked me up. Sure, he was attracted to my body, but I'd be selling myself short if I settled for that, right?

I'd had my rules for a reason and I'd foolishly let them fall to the wayside. Now I was going to have a baby and Jake would always be around to remind me of what I would never have. I was coming to understand that this baby truly did change everything. Not just every plan I might have had for my future, but any plan I may have had for protecting my heart. This baby came equipped with its own little sledgehammer to use on the Great Wall as well as the ability to assist my heart in tossing the damn rope ladder over to the other side.

My smile from the thoughts of my mother was long gone when I pulled into my driveway and stopped short. There, on my front porch, was not a container of delicious kimchi, but a very tall, very handsome, and very unwelcome Jake Beckett. I feared the rope ladder was being prepared for tossing at that very moment.

I groaned and opened the garage door. Clearly, my threats to his life and man parts had not been as effective as I'd hoped. I pulled in and put the car in park. No sooner had I stepped from my car when Jake pinned me against the door and planted a searing kiss on my startled lips.

There went any chance of clear thoughts for our upcoming conversation.

He pulled back after a few moments and presented me with a bouquet of flowers. I looked from the flowers to his eyes and then to his lips—because, let's face it, my mind was still on that kiss—before going back to his eyes. They were filled with emotion. I saw the heat from our kiss, but I also saw a different kind of longing, and perhaps apprehension. I didn't know what to make of it, so I looked down to the flowers again, accepting them.

"These are beautiful, Jake," I said quietly. "Nobody has ever given me flowers before."

You see! All clear thought—vanished! Why in the hell did I tell him that? It was so embarrassing.

"You can't be serious," he responded.

I ignored his comment. "So, I guess you still want to talk, huh." I turned to enter the house, assuming he'd follow. There was nothing I could do at this point. And even if I tried, he'd just kiss me stupid again and I'd probably agree to not only marry him but adopt twelve Burundian babies while we were at it.

I took the flowers to my kitchen counter, unsure what one did with flowers. I was sure I didn't have a vase. Jake, somehow understanding my predicament, opened one cabinet after another until he unearthed a water pitcher and proceeded to fill it at the sink. This gave me a moment to breathe again—and to ogle him from behind. He really was quite remarkable and I couldn't help but pat myself on the back a little for getting knocked up by a guy who would undoubtedly make a gorgeous baby.

He turned around and retrieved the flowers, placing them in the pitcher and setting the whole arrangement on my island. We both gazed at it. The flowers were pink and fragrant, and their puffy collections of little blooms filled the area above the makeshift vase.

"I need to tell you something," Jake said.

I steeled myself and forced my eyes to meet his. I nodded.

"I made a mistake."

My stomach dropped to the floor and my chest began to constrict before he cut me off with both hands out.

"Wait! That came out completely wrong. Shit. I'm terrible at this."

Well, that made two of us.

"What I mean is, I went about this all the wrong way. I was thinking about the baby and what he needs and I wasn't thinking about what you need."

I resumed a state of semi-normal breathing. That was a decent start, so I remained silent, anxious to hear what would come next.

"I want you to know that, yes, I want to be here for the baby and for you, but it's not out of obligation."

My heart started racing. Sure, this was no declaration of love, but it was a far sight better than the Neanderthal proclamations he'd delivered at his mom's house.

"It's more than that. Surely, you know that. I mean, why else does a guy call and text until he's in danger of losing his man card?" he teased.

I had to grin a little at that. I heard the faint sounds of a tiny sledgehammer.

"And if you want to take things slowly, I'm okay with that."

I smiled, but he quickly amended his statement.

"For now."

For now. I guess I could agree to that. What other choice did I have?

Chapter Twenty-Four

ALLOW ME TO HAND YOU YOUR ASS

JAKE

This was progress. I'd gotten her to agree to tolerate me for the time being, and I still had possession of my testicles so there was that. And that kiss. If I'd had any doubt about her body's feelings for me, they were completely put to rest. Even with all this craziness to figure out, she still wanted me. Now I had to get her brain—and her heart—caught up with her body.

We talked a bit longer and made arrangements for the doctor's appointment in a couple days. I was nervous as hell and knew Bailey felt the same. I refrained from telling her about my alien suspicions since things were otherwise going well. I even snuck in another kiss on my way out, and my body cursed me for not asking to stay. But she looked tired and we both had work in the morning.

It wasn't until my drive home that I remembered her comment about never having received flowers before. How was that possible? What was wrong with her previous boyfriends? I would have thought she'd have guys lining up to bring her things. I made a mental note to get her more gifts in the future. I was becoming downright domestic and the little alien hadn't even arrived yet!

☘☘☘

Late afternoon the following day, the shit decided it was time to hit the fuck out of the fan. It started with a text from Mark and went tits up from there.

Mark: *Heads up - you and your balls may want to move back to Florida - or maybe Canada.*
Jake: *Huh?*
Mark: *Riordan's here. Nice job knocking Bailey up, by the way. Asshole!*

Shit. Oh shit.
This was not good.

Jake: *Where are you?*
Mark: *Apartments on New Garden*
Jake: *On my way. Keep him there and DON'T tell Bailey.*
Mark: *Whatever you say...Dad. Asshole!*
Jake: *And if you can try to keep him from announcing Bailey's business to everyone, that would be great.*
Jake: *And, yeah, I am an asshole.*

This was most definitely not good. Bailey was going to flip the fuck out. I signaled to Tom that I had an emergency and needed to run. I'm sure I broke every speed limit and a few other laws in my attempt to get over there before Bailey's dad could do more harm. I had to find out what was going on, but my guess was he was looking for me.

When I got to the building site, I slammed the truck into park and jumped out. I could already see the tall frame of Riordan Murphy standing in front of several of the crew, gesticulating wildly, his voice carrying across the lot to where I stood. I may have spoken too soon regarding my sustained ownership of my testicles. Not only was the Murphy patriarch present, but the protective brother was as well. It was time to bid my balls farewell. If Riordan didn't hack them off, Nate surely would.

I cautiously approached, working out my game plan as I went. I could tell the moment Mark spotted me because he covered his eyes and shook his head. This caused Riordan and Nate to whip around and catch me in their twin death glares. I had no idea the old man could move so fast. Before I knew it, he'd lunged toward me and clutched the front of my shirt in one hand while his other formed a fist.

I found myself pondering the proper etiquette for this type of situation. It wasn't like I could really defend myself. I might injure Riordan in the process, and I'm sure I deserved whatever was in store anyway. I had, in fact, impregnated his daughter. Which meant I had, in fact, had sex with her. You'd think those would be considered one sin but I was pretty sure they counted as two. Riordan Murphy is an Irish Catholic father and Bailey is his only daughter. I was guessing my actions were grounds for justifiable homicide. Add in his ignorance of my feelings for his daughter—or even the fact that we were sort of dating—and I figured my chances here were not good.

"You dirty son of a bitch!" he yelled as he shook me. "I should have known it was you. Only been here two months and already turning things upside down!"

Nate was scowling beside us and doing nothing to help me or his dad, for that matter.

I could see the crew pretending not to listen and doing a piss poor job of it. Mark gestured to them to get back to work as he crossed over to join us. I looked at him in silent question.

How the fuck did this happen?

He shook his head and mouthed "*Later,*" before addressing his boss.

"Riordan, I know you're upset. No offense, sir, but this isn't really the time or place. Maybe you and Jake and Bailey can all meet up after work and have a talk."

"You'd better believe I'll be on that guest list too," Nate growled. I think he was deciding which of my organs to auction off first.

My shirt still in his fist, Riordan cut in. "Mark. I suggest you get back to work."

I decided to jump into the fray. "Mr. Murphy, I know this is a shock. It's a shock to all of us."

Nate scoffed, hands on his hips, his eyes skewering me.

Riordan cut me off. "Oh, it's a shock, is it? You put your filthy hands and your filthy," he paused, raising his eyes to the heavens and growling an indecipherable word before continuing, "on my daughter and you're shocked that she's with child? Are you stupid as well as a lothario?" Nate snarled in agreement.

"Nate. Riordan. This is crazy. You can't talk about Bailey like this without including her in the conversation," Mark began.

I wasn't sure I agreed completely. I didn't want her having to hear all of this. I was sure she'd be mortified.

"Shut your trap, Mark. This is between me and your brother." Riordan drew his fist back deliberately and there was nothing I could do. I would have to take the punch. Just as I closed my eyes and braced, I heard the spewing of gravel under tires and a slamming door.

"What in the holy hell do you think you're doing, Dad?! Let him go!"

Shit. I opened my eyes again to see the tall blonde storming over, hair flying everywhere and arms out wide in incredulity. The beast was unleashed. And it was both pissed the fuck off and hormonal. I almost felt bad for Riordan and Nate.

Almost.

"Bailey, stay out of it!" Riordan yelled but didn't take his eyes off me. "This boy knows what's coming to him." Before he could throw the punch, Bailey slid in between us. All of us tried to push her aside in some comical version of musical chairs where we all just wanted anyone but her in the middle. She shoved back and slapped at our hands, and it was finally Mark who physically lifted her and held her to the side while Nate, Riordan, and I continued to face off.

"You're being ridiculous!" she yelled. "And, Nate, I can't believe you're a part of this!"

"You're my sister. It was one thing when you were dating, but he got you pregnant, Bay!"

"Jesus. Why don't you guys just yell it a little louder? I don't think all the church-goers across the street heard you!" At that point, we all looked across New Garden to the church parking lot. There was, indeed, a small group of parishioners giving us the stink-eye. She had a point.

Nate managed to look a bit sheepish, but then shrugged. Riordan didn't budge, and his hold on my shirt tightened. I stood awkwardly with my hands hanging limply at my sides, having no clue what to do.

"Look, sir, with all due respect, this is really between your daughter and me, and we're handling it. I'm sorry if this is upsetting, but what's done is done."

He looked at me incredulously but didn't bring his fist back up. "Respect? Where was this due respect when you dishonored me and my daughter?"

"Oh, for God's sake, Dad. This isn't 1950 and it isn't Ireland. I'm a grown woman. God, this is so embarrassing—can't you see that?" She was still struggling to get loose from Mark. Thankfully my brother's hold was like a vice—I didn't want her getting inadvertently hurt if fists started flying.

"The only thing I find embarrassing is how this man should feel, not even asking for your hand! Not even coming with you when you told your parents! That is the embarrassing part." His eyes flashed in anger.

Bailey sighed. "Not that it's any of your business, but he didn't know I was telling you. And," she paused and sighed again, "he did 'ask for my hand.'" She made air quotes and pursed her lips in exasperation.

Riordan released my shirt, and he and Nate both took a step back at that.

"Is that true?" asked Riordan.

I straightened myself as well as I could. "It is. I would like nothing better than to marry your daughter."

As if some spell had been broken, Riordan clapped his hands together and declared, "Well then! It's settled!"

Nate seemed wary, having met his sister before and all.

"It's most definitely *not* settled," growled Bailey, making one last attempt to break Mark's hold. "Buffy, if you don't let me go I swear I'm going to borrow one of Fiona's stilettos and make you scream—and not in the good way." She finally wrested herself free and stood looking around at all of us. "I just want to say thank you for making this the most humiliating day of my life." She turned to Nate and Riordan. "Go home. You've done enough." Then to Mark, "I'm going to assume you're the one who told my dad about Jake and me?"

He tossed his hands out to the side. "He's my boss. And how was I supposed to know why he was asking? I didn't know my asshole brother had knocked you up!" He shot me a glare.

"God, would everyone just stop yelling that out?!"

"I would have fired him on the spot if he hadn't told me," said Riordan.

Bailey whirled around, "Why are you still here, Dad?"

"Don't talk to me that way, young lady."

"Bailey—" Nate tried to cut in.

"No! Everybody mind your own business. For the last time!" she practically screeched and I was done. I was getting her out of here. I started toward her when another voice cut into the melee.

"Which one of you is Mark Beckett?"

We all turned to see a young auburn-haired woman in a sleek business suit. She held an envelope in one hand and stood with her heels planted firmly on the gravel lot. Bailey hung her head in utter defeat and I continued over to put an arm around her.

The new arrival looked expectantly at the rest of us until Mark finally raised a hand. "That's me."

She marched over to him through the silent crowd, her sudden appearance having shut the rest of us up. She held the envelope out to Mark and he took it, giving her a quizzical look.

The woman looked him squarely in the eye. "Mark Beckett, this is to notify you you're being sued for assault and battery. If an acceptable settlement cannot be reached, we will be pressing criminal charges as well." Then she turned and strode to the edge of the lot where she dropped into the seat of her sedan and drove off.

Everyone stared dumbly at Mark. He just stared at the envelope. I was afraid I knew what this was about. And not only would it screw with Mark's life, but I was guessing it would secure us both firmly in Bailey's doghouse.

Fucking Anton.

The entire group was seated at a large high top at Jake's, our favorite bar. Given the name, it's obviously a cool place to hang out—but I can't take any credit for that.

From the look Mark had given me moments after receiving the damn envelope, I knew he and I were on the same page. We needed to get everybody else to go home and then we'd regroup to figure this out between the two of us. Our plan, however, went to shit—as usual.

First to stick his nose in was Nate, unsurprisingly. Then Bailey, then Riordan. He was followed up by a couple other crew members, including Trey. Nobody wanted to see Mark get into any trouble, and everybody but me insisted this must be some huge misunderstanding. There was lots of talking all at once, and questions were thrown like freaking confetti until Mark's voice rose above the din and told everybody to shut the hell up.

He assigned Trey the task of finishing up the day with the crew while the rest of us planned to reconvene at the bar. One tactical call to Erin, Bailey's mom, and Riordan was promptly uninvited. He left for home with promises that his dealings with me were far from over. Nate, of course, called Laney, who in turn called Fiona, and the female contingent descended on Jake's. It was a regular brouhaha.

The only upside, as I could see it, was that the lawsuit trumped the pregnancy news, so the guys agreed to keep their mouths shut for the time being. That didn't deter Nate from throwing me daggers every few minutes, however. I knew it only gave Bailey and me a few hours' reprieve, but I'd take it. The last thing we needed right now was for Fiona and Laney to incite baby-fueled pandemonium in the middle of Jake's.

I could see Bailey temporarily relax now that her focus was reassigned to finding a solution to a new problem. That would not last long once she discovered the reason for Mark's legal entanglement, though. Yup, we were up shit's creek and we'd been beaten to a bloody pulp by the paddle.

"Alright, now that everybody is here, can you tell us what the hell this is all about?" Nate asked.

"Wait, if you and Laney are both here, where is Rocco?" I was kind of proud of myself for immediately thinking about the kid's wellbeing. I figured this boded well for my impending state of fatherhood.

Laney waved me aside. "He's with Charlotte. Now, what's going on?"

I saw Fiona biting her lip as she sat next to Mark. I figured she must know something, given that she practically lived with Mark and had surely seen his abused hand after its meeting with Anton's face.

Mark opened the envelope, reading it over for what I guessed was the tenth time. He then handed it to me, seemingly unable to figure out what to say. I'd already read it once, but I still found myself wincing as I skimmed it again.

"So, Mark kind of punched this guy—who completely deserved it, by the way—and now the asshole is suing him for damages. If Mark doesn't settle, then the douchebag is filing criminal charges."

Questions came from all sides.

"What kind of damages?" asked Fiona.

"How much? Wait, when did this happen?" Nate chimed in.

"Who was this asshole and how did I not know about this?" Bailey asked.

Mark and I looked at each other and silently agreed to answer the easier questions first—a.k.a. the questions that wouldn't get us stabbed.

Mark sighed and I explained, "He's seeking compensatory damages for property loss, emotional distress, and loss of income."

"What the fuck? Who is this pussy?" came a voice from behind me. I turned to find Gavin standing there, beer in hand.

"Who invited you?" Mark asked.

Gavin pulled up a stool, ignoring the implied insult.

"Trey called. I wasn't about to miss this. Congrats, by the way." He gave a sly grin and threw a chin out to Bailey. Her face turned nineteen shades of purple as she attempted to maintain her cool and not embed her glass in his skull.

"Huh?" Laney said, looking from Gavin to Bailey.

I cut in, hoping like hell for distraction. "Unfortunately, the amount is $50,000."

"What the fuck?!" Nate and Gavin exclaimed in unison.

Mark's forehead hit the table and Fiona rubbed his back. "It'll be okay. This is all a mistake. I'll call my dad's lawyer and we'll get it sorted out."

His muffled voice came from under the table. "Thanks, Shortcake, but I don't think it's gonna be that easy." He brought his head up again and grabbed his beer glass with both hands. "I did it. I hit the guy, and there were witnesses."

"Shit," came the refrain from around the table.

"But these claims have got to be bullshit," insisted Gavin. "I mean who suffers 'emotional distress' from a punch? Not to mention the other stuff. This guy's just out to scam you."

"I'm afraid it's probably more than that," I muttered, drawing Bailey's attention.

"More than money, you mean?" she asked. "What else could it be?" Her gazed passed back and forth between Mark and me.

Mark closed one eye as if to shield himself from what was coming. "Um, pride?"

Bailey's face was the picture of suspicion as she sat up straight on her barstool. "I'm only going to ask this one more time and I want a straight answer. Who. Did. You. Punch?"

Mark and I looked at each other one last time before we both gave it up.

"Anton."

Chapter Twenty-Five

WILD HORSES

BAILEY

Mother fucking Anton. If the gasps and subsequent curses from Laney and Fiona were anything to go by, I'd say we were all in agreement that the guy definitely deserved a beat-down. But why did it have to be from my friend, and why did he have to get in such deep shit for it? *Mark, you big, dumb, wonderful dufus.* If I'd known what he was going to do—hell, I should have known—I would have warned him. Anton would never take humiliation lying down.

"Who the hell is Anton?" Gavin asked.

"Bailey's asshole ex-boyfriend and the reason condom factories exist. In fact, they owe the world an apology for not stepping in on that one in the first place," replied Fiona.

I put my head in my hands. Damn, I was the indirect cause of a shitload of drama these days!

"Mark, I can't believe you beat him up," I wailed.

"He didn't beat him up," Jake interjected. "He just punched

him one time in the face—once. And then we may have stepped on his glasses." His voice trailed off and his beer glass was apparently super fascinating all of a sudden. I should have known.

"You were there too?!"

"I plead the fifth on the grounds that I may incriminate myself."

"What the hell is wrong with you Beckett boys?!"

Truthfully, nothing was wrong with them. Absolutely nothing. I felt myself start to tear up and willed the damn hormones to give me five fucking minutes.

"If *somebody* had told me about this asshole, I would have taken care of him before now," Nate said pointedly. "How did I not know about this guy?" He looked almost hurt.

I just shook my head, unable to deal with any more emotion. "Laney can fill you in." I flicked my eyes to her. "I absolve you of the girl-code gag order or whatever it's called. Go forth and gossip," I told her.

Fiona nodded and Gavin just drank his beer, reading the lawyer's letter over Jake's shoulder.

"So, besides the glasses and maybe a black eye, what's with the rest of this? I mean, can't you just cut him a check for some new glasses and call it a day?"

I took a sip of my soda. "I have a feeling it won't be nearly that easy." Fucking Anton.

Fiona pulled her phone from her fancy purse. "I'm on it. We'll have that twatface begging for mercy when we're done with him."

"Thanks, Shortcake—my delicate flower, you," Mark said, kissing her cheek. She winked at him and tapped at her phone.

By the time Fiona and Mark got off the phone with her family's lawyer, I was exhausted. So I did something I'd probably regret later and let Jake take me home. My eyelids dropped as soon as his tires hit the highway and the next thing I knew, I was being carried into my house. Carried. As in, the man picked me up in his arms like an oversized child and carried me to my room.

"Jake," I tried to protest but I was shushed.

"Do you need anything before bed? Something to drink, maybe? Are you supposed to be taking vitamins?"

I smiled a little at his concern. "I take vitamins in the morning. I'm okay, but I need to get ready for bed."

"Okay." He took me into the bathroom and set me down. I looked up at him expectantly. He just held my gaze.

"Um, Jake. I need to go to the bathroom and brush my teeth."

"Got an extra toothbrush?"

I eyed him warily as he stayed put. "Probably in one of the drawers. Help yourself…when I'm done," I prompted, shifting my eyes meaningfully to the door.

"I don't mind. The door to the toilet closes." He moved to the counter and started opening drawers.

"*I* mind."

"Why?" He looked back at me as if I'd just told him I eat my own hair.

"I don't want you to hear me pee."

He laughed, finally unearthing a pink toothbrush. There was a reason it was still in its packaging. He tore it open. "Hey, Bailey, guess what."

"What?"

"Everybody pees."

"I think it's *Everybody Poops*," I said, citing the famous book.

"Yeah, that too. Guess what else."

"What?" I was terrified to ask.

"I've seen you naked, I've been inside you, and you're pregnant with my baby. I think I can brush my teeth while you pee behind a closed door."

Well, he did have a point there.

I huffed so he'd know I was put out, but I let him stay.

Once we were snuggled in bed together, I remembered how nice it was to have his warm body next to mine. I couldn't help it, I burrowed in like a hamster or one of those meerkats. Once I had sufficiently plastered myself to as much of Jake's body as I could access, I fell into a deep and peaceful sleep.

♣ ♣ ♣

"Rise and shine, Irish," a deep voice beckoned as I drifted into consciousness. My nose twitched as the scent of coffee invaded my senses. Ahhh. I finally opened my eyes and decided right then and there that I should keep a camera handy at all times around this man. There stood Jake, in only his boxer briefs, with two cups of coffee and a ridiculously sweet smile. His dark hair was mussed and his face was covered in a sexy scruff. I was dying to feel it against my skin.

I couldn't help but smile back. "Good morning." I stretched my arms above my head. I'd slept like the dead and had the best night's sleep in, well, possibly ever. Apparently, having a Jake to lounge on promotes healthy sleep habits. I mewled as I stretched again, "What time is it?"

"Nine-thirty."

I shot up in bed, immediately sending my stomach lurching, all thoughts of sexy-coffee-scruffy-nakedness vanishing instantly.

"Whoa, take it easy." Jake tried to push me back to the pillow, but it was too late. I jumped from the bed and ran to the bathroom, losing the contents of my stomach in the toilet. Pregnancy is just so glamorous.

I heard him set the mugs on the counter and then felt his hand on my back, rubbing circles over my spine. This was so embarrassing.

"Can I do anything?" he asked.

"If you could un-impregnate me, that would be awesome. Thanks."

He chuckled. "Can I do anything *else* for you?"

"Water, maybe? Oh, and can you take the coffee away? Sadly, I think the smell might make me puke again."

He kissed the top of my head and left me to die in peace, my face in the toilet.

I cleaned myself up and was brushing my teeth when Jake returned with a glass of water and some crackers. He held them up. "I thought these might help." He shrugged and I wanted to hug him.

I mumbled my thanks through the toothbrush and then spit and rinsed, feeling a bit better. "I have to get to work. And isn't that where you should be too? Either that or helping Mark?"

He tilted his head in question. "Uh, no."

I mirrored his look.

"Bailey, we have the doctor's appointment in thirty minutes."

"Oh, shit!" I scrambled about, not sure what to do first.

Jake stepped around me and opened the shower door. He turned the tap and then disappeared into the bedroom.

Right. Shower.

Should I lock the bathroom door? He still needed to get ready too. But then he'd come in and see me naked through the shower door. Why in God's name did I have a clear door and not one of those damn curtains?!

Shit. What was I doing? What were *we* doing? Gah!

There was nothing for it, so I stripped down and slid under the pulsing stream of hot water. Damn, that felt good. The water beat down on me and I closed my eyes, getting lost for a moment. The next thing I knew, a draft of cool air blew in as Jake opened the shower door and stepped in. Bare ass naked. I immediately tried to cover myself with my hands, and I squealed—actually squealed, you know, like a pig.

"What?" Jake asked, calm as can be, making zero attempt to cover his…anything.

"What are you doing?" I whispered, still trying to figure out how to cover two boobs and one hoo-ha with only two hands.

"Taking a shower. We have to leave in ten minutes." He began scrubbing his muscular chest with a bar of soap.

My knees threatened to give out on me. It occurred to me that if I did happen to collapse onto my face, the coverage problem would be solved. Of course, then I'd have a bump on my head and I'd have to use both hands to conceal my ass.

"Time's a wastin', Irish," Jake said as he set the soap on the ledge and brought his lathered hands to my belly, covering me in soap and circling his large hands around to my back. He drew me in closer as he caressed the skin of my lower back and moved right down to my ass, cupping both cheeks.

I sort of forgot why him being in the shower was in any way troublesome as my arms found their way around his waist and I pressed in. I could feel his hard cock against my belly and I might have moaned a bit.

"As much as I'd love to stay in this shower with you all day, we'll have to save playtime for later." He drew back and placed a gentle—and way too brief—kiss on my lips, before quickly wetting and washing his hair. Coming to my senses, I did the same, and soon we were drying off, sneaking looks at each other in the process.

I was in so much trouble.

"If you'll just place your feet in the stirrups, we'll get started."

The only thing more embarrassing than "spreading them" for a glove-wearing stranger is "spreading them" for an attractive, male glove-wearing stranger. Add your kind-of boyfriend/baby daddy to the audience and we go straight past embarrassment and right into utter mortification with a side of *just kill me now*.

Idiot me—when I'd booked the appointment with Dr. Jamie Sutton, I'd assumed the good doctor was female. I was mistaken. Not only was Dr. Sutton very male, he was also very hot. Not ideal, I can assure you.

I had practically seen Jake's blood pressure escalate when Dr. Sutton had walked in the room, and there was no indication it was headed down anytime soon. Every time the doctor asked me a question that was at all personal—and let's face it, all of them were when it came to pregnancy—Jake just grunted or scoffed. It was getting pretty ridiculous. I had to admit, though, the spark of jealousy did make me grin a little on the inside.

Thus far, we'd talked about vitamins and diet, and Dr. Sutton had asked all sorts of questions about my medical history. My height and weight had been recorded and my vitals were officially on record. The doctor had even calmed me after my near freak-out when I recalled my ill-advised night of drinking a couple weeks back—I left out the drunk texting part. He reassured me that as long as I didn't do it again, it wasn't likely to be a problem.

Then, it was the moment of truth. Or, in my case, the moment of humiliation. I scooted my butt down as far as I could on the damn table and put my socked feet in the cursed stirrups. My knees, however, remained locked together and completely covered by a sheet. Jake growled, and I noticed out of the corner of my eye that the doctor grinned, hiding it as well as he could by looking down. Hmm. Perhaps Jake wasn't the first psycho father-to-be this man had encountered.

"Now, *Bailey*, we'll get this exam over as quickly as possible and then we can move on to any questions you may have." I didn't miss the stress he put on my name, which was clearly not meant as reassurance to me, but to my frothing-at-the-mouth cohort.

I closed my eyes and spread 'em for the doctor to proceed, and he did so with great speed. Thank God. When he was done, he told me to scoot back up on the table while the sheets were rearranged so only my belly and the very top of my pubic area were exposed. Only then did I chance another look at Jake.

His hands were clenched and there was a thin sheen of sweat on his forehead. I fought hard against rolling my eyes. Did he think this was fun for me? Did he honestly think I was going to go home and call up Fiona and Laney about this? "Hey girls, there's this hot doctor giving out pelvic exams downtown—grab your speculum and let's go!" I huffed at the thought.

"Jake, you may want to come closer for this." Dr. Sutton interrupted my thoughts. He was holding a tube of something in his hand. "I'm going to spread this gel on your stomach and we'll see if we can find a heartbeat. It's still a bit early—you're only nine weeks—but we may get lucky." He proceeded to coat my belly with what felt like Aloe vera and then he picked up an instrument resembling some kind of electric shaver. "This is a fetal Doppler," he explained.

I felt Jake approach as Dr. Sutton ran the instrument over my lower stomach, using more pressure than I anticipated. All I heard was white noise from the attached machine. Then, when the doctor brought the device around to the lowest part of my left side, the machine erupted in a series of incredibly fast beats, almost like the pounding of wild horse hooves. The doctor nodded.

I looked to Jake.

His eyes found mine and we both smiled like idiots.

Chapter Twenty-Six

DOMESTIC LOOKS PRETTY GOOD ON ME

JAKE

Holy shit.

I suddenly forgot all about my brother's lawsuit and the damn pretty-boy who'd been putting his hands all over my girl. Instead, my ears were flooded with the sound of a tiny heart beating a mile a minute. My eyes were glued to Bailey, who looked just as awestruck as I felt.

We were having a baby.

And, by the sounds of it, he was as strong as an ox.

"Is it supposed to be so fast?" I asked Dr. Dawson's Creek.

He nodded and smiled. "Perfectly normal. Fetal heart rates are a lot faster than people assume."

"We still have a lot to learn," Bailey said, now gazing at her still-flat stomach. The doctor removed the instrument and turned off the machine. The room was suddenly too quiet. I wanted to have that heartbeat on repeat from this moment until that kid was born.

"I'll recommend some books and websites you might find helpful. But, be warned, don't read too much—you'll just freak yourselves out." He smiled.

Well, at least he had that part right. I thought about our eleven-toed alien and then forced the notion aside.

"Questions?" The doctor looked at us. Neither of us responded. "Okay, then. I'll get the paperwork and those recommendations sorted while you do your blood test. Sound good?"

We both nodded. I was sure we'd have a million questions down the line, but right now I was still consumed with that sound. My baby's heart. *Our* baby's heart. Damn, now wasn't that something.

We went to grab a bite to eat before both of us had to return to reality. There were stolen looks over our sandwiches, all followed by stupid grins. For two people who had no business having a baby, we sure were taking this pretty damn well. I was impressed as shit with both of us.

I drove Bailey to Mark's work site where we'd left her car amidst all the drama the day before. After a slow kiss, she took off and I went in search of my little brother.

"Not good. The specs call for three-quarter inch. You're gonna have to hold off till we get our hands on some," he was saying to one of the crew when I finally found him inside an apartment.

"Hey, man!" I called out.

"Hard hat!" he responded. "How many times do I have to tell you? I'm in enough trouble already, dickhead." He motioned for me to exit the building and followed me out. We headed to my truck where I leaned against the door and faced him. He had his hands on his hips and his lips were tight.

"So, any progress with the lawyer?"

He blew out a breath. "Yeah, we have a meeting set up on

Monday with Germaine and his lawyer to talk about the 'incident.' In the meantime, my lawyer's gathering more information so we can prepare for settlement negotiations."

"Shit. That doesn't sound good. Settlement sounds a lot like 'expensive.'"

"He's hoping they don't have a case." Mark shook his head. "But I don't know how that's possible. Fiona says to trust him, though, so I guess I will. What choice do I have?"

I put my hands in my pockets. "I feel really shitty about this, little brother. I mean, it could have been either of us to throw that punch. If memory serves, *I* was the one to threaten him."

"Don't worry about it." Mark's face lost its dour expression and split in a half grin. "It felt good to give that fucker some of what he deserved."

I chuckled and nodded. "Can I do anything to help?"

He shrugged. "Actually, Bailey may be the person who can help the most since she knows that pigfucker best. I'll let you guys know." I nodded again, determined to help in any way possible. I owed him that and a hell of a lot more.

A crazy-ass grin suddenly overtook Mark's face. "Speaking of the mother-to-be, what the fuck, man? Haven't you ever heard of a condom?"

"Haven't you ever heard of the dreaded two percent?" I pointed a thumb to myself.

"That's some shitty luck, big brother. Us Beckett boys are not swimming in good karma these days." He shook his head.

"I don't know if I would say that." I couldn't help my smile as I squinted in the midday sun.

"Ah, so it's like that, huh? I mean, I knew you were hot for Bailey, but being a daddy? I would never have guessed." He punched my arm a bit too hard. I pretended it didn't hurt.

"I'm as shocked as you are. I just came from a doctor's appointment—don't get me started on the doctor, though. We heard the baby's heartbeat. It was freaking nuts."

"Well, look at you, big brother. Getting all domestic and shit. How's Bailey taking all of this? I mean, no offense, but she's about as maternal as a cactus."

I scowled in her defense. "I don't really think it's hit her yet. We'll figure it out, though."

"So, it's true? You really did ask her to marry you?"

I rocked on the heels of my boots. "Yup. Can you believe it?"

"Not even a little." He grinned.

"Yeah, well, she said no, so I still have some work to do."

"Oh, this should be fun to watch." He threw his head back in a cackling laugh.

"Hey, you didn't tell Fiona, did you?"

Still snickering, he replied, "No, but Nate can't keep a secret from Laney to save his life, so the clock's ticking, man. Tell Bailey to gird her loins. The psycho female train is approaching the station and there's no stopping it."

"I figured as much." I winced at the thought of Fiona and Laney losing their ever-loving minds over the news. "I gotta run to work, but keep me updated on the lawyer stuff, okay?"

"Sure thing. Thanks," he said and turned to walk back to the building. Then he paused and turned around again. "Hey, bro!"

"What?" I opened my door and sat in the driver's seat, glancing back at him.

"Congrats!" He waggled his eyebrows like a douchebag and smiled as he continued back to the apartment.

After going home to change into fresh clothes, I went to the Vaughn's house where we spent the remainder of the day finishing up the central portion of the yard. It was looking fantastic, and it was going to make the perfect venue for the family wedding next summer. We tidied the entire site and loaded up the trucks since we'd be temporarily shifting our focus to the McGuire project the following week. I was praying the next week would fly by so I could return to safer waters and the company of a client who didn't want to eat me for breakfast.

I went back to my mom's house to clean up and make a few calls. I was working on securing another two clients and Jax was throwing numbers at me left and right. Apparently, Mrs. Vaughn had some friends.

My mom wasn't home, but she had left me a smart-ass note about my whereabouts the night before, along with some welcome news of Italian leftovers in the fridge. I finished my work between bites of cheesy lasagna and then called it a day.

Jake: *Have you had dinner? I can bring you lasagna...*
Bailey: *I'm good. Already ate.*

I waited for her to continue, not wanting to make assumptions about where I was sleeping tonight.

Nothing.

Jake: *So, do you want to do something tonight? It's Friday, after all. Date night?*
Bailey: *I think I'm just going to turn in early.*

Hmm. I didn't know if I should take this at face value or read something into it. I decided to call her.

"Hey there. You feeling okay?" I asked when she picked up.

"Yeah, just tired. You know."

No, I really didn't know.

"Okay. You want me to leave you in peace or should I come over?"

There was an awkward silence. I was guessing that was my answer. I didn't really understand this after last night and this morning—not to mention the heartbeat.

"I've just got a lot on my mind, Jake."

That was never a good thing to hear from a girl. It usually meant something along the lines of, "I've got something to tell you and you're going to like it about as much as hot sauce on your pecker."

I had to remind myself that I'd promised to take things slowly for the time being. I let out a breath, forcing myself to relax. "Okay. Can I call you tomorrow?"

I could hear the relief in her voice. "Of course."

"Get some sleep, Irish. I'll talk to you tomorrow."

"Goodnight, Jake." She hung up, but not before she could hide the affection in her tone.

♣♣♣

I woke up to the sound of a screech owl in the living room. I stumbled out of bed and promptly tripped over my boots in my attempt to reach the door. In my mind, I could see my mom battling the bird with a broom, feathers flying everywhere. I was picking myself up off the floor when the door swung open and a tornado of colorful silk and blond hair tackled me back to the ground.

"Oh my God! A BABY!!!" Fiona screamed in my ear as her arms tightened in a choke-hold that could rival one of Mark's.

I appeared to be the only one aware that I was dressed in just boxer briefs as my brother's girlfriend plastered herself to me and rained kisses down on my head.

"You have the sperm of an Olympic champion, my friend!"

I managed to catch a glimpse of my mother in the doorway, a smile spread wide across her face. "I tried to stop her, but, well…" There was no need to finish that sentence.

"Laney called me first thing this morning and we decided to split up to cover more territory. She and Nate and Rocco headed over to Bailey's and I headed right here to see you and Kelly. I can't believe this!" She kissed my cheek this time and beamed at me.

"Um, Fiona."

"Yes, *daddy*." Okay, that wasn't weird at all. *Ahem*.

I glanced meaningfully at the position of our bodies on my floor, and only then did she seem to comprehend my state of undress and her seat on top of me.

She blushed and scrambled off immediately, smoothing down her dress and stepping to the side.

"I mean, what would Mark think?" I couldn't help teasing her after the heart attack she'd nearly caused.

She sneered. "Don't even talk to me about Mark. He's dead to me." She turned briefly to my mom. "Sorry, Kelly." My mother just tsked and shook her head, maintaining her grin. "He's known since Thursday and didn't tell me—I had to find out from Laney! At least Nate knows how to treat his woman right." Then she eyed me. "You'd better not take any relationship advice from your brother or you'll find yourself thrown out on your ass!"

"Noted." I stood and shuffled over to my dresser to get some pants while she turned back to my mom.

"Do you want a boy or a girl?" Fiona asked my mom, not even letting her answer before continuing. "I'm dying for a girl. Just think—we'll buy her all kinds of cute clothes and take her for mani-pedis. Oh, and we'll teach her just where to kick boys when they get out of line. It's going to be so great!" She squealed again.

"I don't really care which it is, as long as it's healthy," said my mom.

"It's a boy," I told them.

Their eyes swung to me.

"Sweetie, I'm pretty sure it's too early to tell that," my mom responded. Fiona frowned.

"I'm just telling you. Oh, and he's definitely healthy."

My mom smiled indulgently.

"We went to the doctor yesterday and heard the heartbeat," I told them, pride filling my chest inexplicably.

"Aww," they both responded.

I proceeded to tell them about the visit with the overly handsome doctor, leaving out my resentment over him seeing or touching any part of Bailey. They listened with rapt attention and asked tons of questions, none of which I knew the answers to. Bailey and I had a lot of research ahead of us.

Fiona then decided to pay Bailey a visit before she and my mom reconvened later for a cocktail party they were catering. I showered and headed for the bookstore, the list of recommended reading in hand.

A huge part of me wanted to accompany Fiona since I knew all this attention had to be making Bailey uncomfortable, but I needed to keep the big picture in mind. Slow and steady wins the race. I was also guessing being a well-informed partner on all things baby-related wouldn't hurt either. So off to the bookstore I went.

Chapter Twenty-Seven

ADAM AND EVE HAVE A LOT OF EXPLAINING TO DO

BAILEY

I shut the door behind Nate and Laney and leaned against it. It was only noon and I was already exhausted. They'd paid me a surprise visit this morning—although it really wasn't much of a surprise. After my dad's stunt on Thursday, I knew it was only a matter of time before everyone in the Triad was informed of the bun in my oven.

Fiona had also stopped in briefly just to squeal in my ear and squeeze me half to death. Then she took off saying she had some investigative work to do. Normally, one would question a friend about something so bizarre, but this was Fiona, so we all let it go.

Laney had been similarly ecstatic about the baby, and Nate had offered more than once to kill Jake and hide the body. I told him to hold off, citing my need for Jake's earning potential to raise the kid. Nate seemed to find that answer acceptable. What I didn't tell him was that my need for Jake had very little to do with money and everything to do with Jake himself. And then there was the baby, of course. Which was terrifying to contemplate. All of this was the reason I kind of blew Jake off the night before.

I'd needed time to think. But every time Jake's face popped into my head I got all swoony and turned on. I was a little ashamed of myself, as I'm sure that's not appropriate mom-to-be behavior. But then I just said *fuck it* and had myself a little fantasy or two. *Are you allowed to use battery-operated assistance while pregnant?* You'd think the notion of impending motherhood would have killed the mood, but no. I wasn't really letting myself think about the end result of this pregnancy yet. I was afraid I'd have a full-blown anxiety attack if I did, and I was not ready for that. So my selfie stick and I had gone to bed together and focused solely on Jake's hot bod.

Once everyone left, I debated about calling Jake. I knew I had to pull my big girl panties up and make some decisions. Before I could even step from the door, though, I got a text from cheekbones himself.

Jake: *Mind if I stop by? I've got something for you.*

I sighed. How could I say no to a mind-reader bearing gifts?

Bailey: *Sure. You just missed the crazy train.*
Jake: *Oh, believe me, it made a stop at my mom's too.*

Of course it had.

Bailey: *I'm hopping in the shower, so let yourself in.*

I hit send and then realized too late how incredibly suggestive that had sounded. Shit. I dropped the phone on the entry table before he could respond, and I headed straight to the shower.

Ten minutes later, I emerged clean and dressed, to find Jake in all his handsomeness lounging on my couch. A large plastic bag rested on his lap and he was looking at me like he was trying to decide which part of me to snack on first. My knees buckled a bit and I grabbed onto the wall.

"Hi, Jake," I said, suddenly feeling shy.

"Well," he replied, "since I missed the shower, do I at least get a kiss or something?"

I felt like this was a test of some sort since I'd left things so vague the previous night. I suddenly had flashbacks to the wedding night when I wouldn't have hesitated to pin him down like a calf at a rodeo. Summoning all the courage I had, I walked slowly to the couch in what I hoped was a sexy manner. His pupils dilated and his jaw twitched, which I took as a good sign.

When I was about a foot away, he tossed the bag off his lap and pulled me forward until I sat straddling him. The next thing I knew, his lips were on mine and I melted into the kiss as he adjusted to the perfect angle. His tongue delved in and I didn't hesitate to meet it with mine as I threaded my fingers through his thick hair. He pulled me in firmly so I could feel the evidence of his arousal under me. I moaned and stroked my tongue against his again.

He tasted like mint and a hint of chocolate, and I wanted to pour him all over a giant bowl of ice cream and dig in. At that bizarre thought, my stomach rumbled loudly. We both pulled back, startled.

"That wasn't…the baby…?" he trailed off.

I scrunched my eyes shut in embarrassment.

"No. Not the baby. I guess I forgot to eat," I confessed, opening my eyes once again.

He reared back, a crease forming between his eyebrows. “You haven’t eaten anything today?”

I just shook my head. He motioned for me to get off his lap. Damn.

“That’s it. I’m taking you out to lunch and then we’re going grocery shopping,” he declared.

I did not like this turn of events. I wanted to get back to the kissing part.

“Come on,” Jake coaxed, “you heard what the doctor said—plenty of fruits and veggies and lean protein.”

That sounded unpleasant at best. “I thought one of the perks of being knocked up was that I got to eat whatever I wanted. You know, the whole pickles and ice cream thing?”

“Urban myth. I just read about it. Broccoli and Greek yogurt for you.”

I wrinkled my nose at that, but he just helped me up and held out a hand. Trying one more stall tactic, I asked, “What’s in the bag?”

“Ah!” He smiled, bending down to retrieve it. I peeked inside and it was full of books. Okay. “The books the doctor recommended,” Jake prompted.

I’d kind of been hoping for cheesecake, but I looked at his face and he seemed so pleased with himself. Not to mention it was all kinds of sweet that he’d gone and bought these books. I put one hand on my stomach and used the other to balance on Jake while I gave him a light kiss.

“Let’s take them with us to lunch.”

☘ ☘ ☘

“This doesn’t make any sense,” I said for the sixth time in thirty minutes. "The baby grows lungs and starts breathing, but doesn't drown in there. How is that possible?" I looked to Jake.

His dark hair was a rumpled mess. We were back from our outing, and he sat beside me reading his own book, a similar look of perplexity on his face. "You don't even want to know what I just read. Word to the wise, do *not* read the chapters on the actual birth." He scrubbed a hand through his hair again.

"Don't worry about that," I responded, lifting my water bottle to take another sip—I'd been ordered to hydrate. "I'm taking a box cutter to those chapters." I closed my book and sank back into the couch. This was worse than I thought. I could feel my blood pressure start to rise.

Jake closed his book as well and turned toward me. "Hey, we're in this together."

"Fine, then you carry this baby," I pouted.

"If I could find a way to do it, I totally would."

"You're just saying that because it's not a possibility. It's like me volunteering to give you my kidney, knowing we're not a match."

"That's completely untrue. If I could carry the baby for you, I would," he stated firmly. "Wait, if we were actually a match you'd give me a kidney, right?"

"Sure. Anytime," I said, pulling a face.

He grabbed my hand and kept his eyes on it. "Bailey, I don't think you know how important this is to me."

I wasn't sure if he was talking about me or the baby or even the damn kidney.

"I am going to be here every step of the way. I'm not going to let you or the baby down. I hope you know that."

I just nodded. I did know that.

"I'm not going to be that guy who makes a commitment and

then bails. I know what it feels like to be on the receiving end of that." His eyes moved up to mine. "My dad was a total asshole. I know you've heard all about it from Mark." I nodded and he continued, "But Mark probably didn't tell you *I* acted like an asshole too."

Huh? I looked at him in question.

"Remember me telling you I went into the Marines out of high school? That was me running away. I had to get away from my dad, and I left my mom and fourteen-year-old brother to deal with him on their own. And not just that—they had to handle *everything* on their own. The bills, the house, insurance…everything. And I just ditched them."

"Jake," I interjected, "you were a kid yourself. You didn't do it deliberately."

"Maybe not, but I should have grown up faster and come back. I'll never be able to undo what I did." He looked at me earnestly. "So, when I tell you I'm here for you and this kid, I'm *here*. I'm not going away. Not ever."

I didn't know what to say, so I just pulled him into a hug and held on tight. We stayed that way for a while.

After that, Jake seemed a little uncomfortable with his confession so I tried to lighten the mood. I got us both a snack—a healthy one (yuck)—and grabbed my sketchpad and pencils.

"Ever since I met you I've been dying to draw those cheekbones of yours." I smiled and plopped back down on the couch.

He grinned. "What cheekbones?"

"You've got to be kidding me. Have you looked in the mirror? You have beautiful bone structure."

His lip curled. "Don't ever call me beautiful again. That's just…wrong."

"Too bad. Now, sit still so I can get the basics down."

"Are you going to ask me to strip and wear a giant jewel around my neck?"

I snickered. "Not if you obey and be a good boy."

"I don't like being a good boy." He inched toward me and ran a hand up my bare leg.

I smacked it. "That's how we got into this situation in the first place, Captain Sperm Count. Now, sit."

He acquiesced, but only after letting his hand graze my inner thigh, causing goosebumps to rise on my skin. I sketched the main shapes of his face before I let him resume his reading. I tried to focus on the image as I glanced back and forth between Jake and the paper. But the tingling sensation from his touch proved to be quite the distraction.

"Wow," Jake declared a half hour later when I presented him with the finished sketch. "That's really good." His eyes flashed to my face. "You're pretty damn amazing, Irish."

I brushed his compliment aside. "Well, it's hard to mess up when my subject is so damn pretty." I jumped from the couch just as his hand shot out to grab me. I was too late and he smacked my ass.

"Ow! Abuse!" I yelled, unable to keep my laugh in.

He managed to get both arms around me and pull me back down so I landed on his lap. "If you liked that, I've got a thing or two I could show you," he teased.

My insides clenched. Hmm, that was new. Apparently, pregnancy came with a fetish or two.

My phone rang, interrupting the moment. I glanced at it where it sat on the coffee table and saw that it was my mom. I groaned.

"What?" Jake asked, and then looked at the screen. "Oh." We both stared at it for a moment while it rang. "Aren't you going to get it?"

I sighed and hit accept, raising it to my ear. "Hi, Mom."

"Hi, sweetheart. How are you feeling?"

As I was still seated on Jake's hard thighs, I was feeling pretty damn good, but I didn't suppose that's what she meant.

"I'm good. A bit nauseous here and there, and I'm sleeping a lot, but I'm good."

"Oh, my. I was so sick with both you and Nate. They say it's a sign the baby's healthy, though."

I scrunched up my face and looked back at Jake. He was focusing on my neck and preparing to lean in. I gave him a scolding look.

"Mom, I'm pretty sure that's one of those things people tell you to make your suffering more bearable. 'Hey, I see your severed limb is bleeding nicely. They say the more it bleeds the cleaner the cut. Good for you!'"

Jake pressed his face into my back and chuckled.

"Bailey Cathleen! I swear I don't know who raised you."

I laughed in response, always loving to get a rise out of my mom.

"Anyway, I was calling to invite you to Sunday dinner tomorrow." I heard a voice in the background and then the sound of my mom covering the phone. There was some muffled yelling and then she was back. "Sorry about that. Um, what I meant to say was could you please bring Jake to dinner tomorrow? I'm afraid it's the only way to avoid a repeat of your father's behavior at the job site."

I looked back at Jake again. Clearly, he'd heard my mother's voice because he suddenly looked serious.

"So, you heard about that?" Not surprising.

"Sweetheart, I think everyone heard about that. I have no

control over that man. At least this way we can keep it somewhat contained. What do you say?"

I gave Jake a pained smile as I spoke into the phone again. "Do we actually have a choice?"

"Um, no."

Jake shrugged. I sighed. "Then, sure. Jake and I would love to come over for dinner."

"Wonderful. Oh, and I'm making pork chops, so bring your appetite!"

I was more likely to bring my Pepto.

I would like to say that after I hung up with my mother, Jake and I screwed like rabbits and spent the entire night devouring each other repeatedly. But that would be a lie. We ended up having spaghetti and salad and watching a movie on TV. Correction: Jake watched a movie on TV. I promptly passed out and was, once again, carried to bed by Jake. This pregnancy thing was doing nothing for my sex life!

Chapter Twenty-Eight

THE IRISH GODFATHER

JAKE

I'd thought ahead this time and packed a bag, hoping I'd be spending the night. I got my wish, although Bailey fell asleep on me shortly after dark. But that was okay. I still got to sleep next to her sweet, warm body and wake up to her lazy, sleep-drunk smile. I was beginning to think I couldn't go another night without her.

I brought her tea—since coffee was apparently out—and some toast in bed so she, hopefully, wouldn't get sick again.

"This is really thoughtful, Jake. Thank you." She was uncharacteristically sweet and agreeable. I figured the sass would be back once she got her legs under her.

I felt a bit lighter today, having confessed my past behavior concerning my family and my feelings about it. I'd needed Bailey to understand where I was coming from so she'd feel more inclined to trust me and my intentions. So, things were looking up.

I was even considering broaching the moving-in topic again since the last day had gone so well.

The only difficulties weighing on my mind now were Mark's lawsuit and the upcoming dinner with Riordan Murphy. I should probably have taken out some life insurance, but it was a little late for that.

Bailey spent much of the morning painting while I ran a couple errands. On the way back I called Mark.

"All set for your meeting tomorrow?"

"Getting there. Hey, while I've got you, can you do me a favor?"

"Anything."

"I got a list of witnesses from my lawyer. I'm going to e-mail them to you and Bailey. Will you ask her to look them over and see if she recognizes any names? Best to have all the information we can get."

"Sure. That makes sense. I'm on my way back to her place now."

"Yeah, mom said you haven't been sleeping at home much. I take it things are going better?" Mark asked.

"I'm working on it. We've got dinner at her parents' tonight."

"Oh, shit."

"I know. I'm not looking forward to another run-in with her dad." I cringed internally at the thought.

"No. Well, yeah, that'll suck. But my 'oh, shit' was for a completely different reason. Do not eat the food, man," Mark said in a cryptic tone.

"What do you mean?" What the hell was he up to?

"Erin. Do not eat her cooking. It might kill you."

"Shut up, asshole. You're just setting me up." He was undoubtedly trying to get me to embarrass myself. As if I needed more awkwardness with the Murphy clan.

"Don't say I didn't warn you." He laughed and hung up.

What the hell?

♣ ♣ ♣

"Oh my God. This is unbelievable." Bailey scowled, smacking the arm of the love seat.

"Ashley, Hannah, Taylor, Michael—these are all Anton's groupies."

She was looking over the list of witnesses Mark had sent over.

"Of course they're going to side with him. They practically worship him." She tossed her phone down in a huff.

"Wait, are they his students or something?"

"Sort of. I mean, some of them have attended his guest lectures, but they literally follow him around like puppies waiting for scraps."

"That's great then, isn't it?" I asked, picking her phone up and reading the list for myself.

"What do you mean?"

"Well, that makes them biased witnesses. I don't think that's allowed."

Her face brightened. "We definitely have to call Mark."

"Great, but let's do it on the way to your parents'. I want to stop and buy flowers or something. There is no way I'm showing up empty-handed."

"Aww, are you scared of my big bad parents?" She smiled slyly.

"Yes, and I'm not afraid to admit it. Your father is going to either make me a eunuch or challenge me to a duel." I got up and grabbed my keys.

"God, he needs to just butt out," she grumbled. "I am so bad at standing up to him." She bent down to put her shoes on.

"I don't think that's true at all." I stopped and looked down at her.

She returned my gaze, confusion lining her brow.

"You should have seen yourself on Thursday. You were a beast," I teased.

She smacked me with a shoe.

"No, you got right in his face and told him to mind his own business. It was pretty hot." I shrugged.

She looked at the shoe as if it would aid her memory. "Huh. I kind of did, didn't I?" It seemed like some kind of revelation to her. She stood still for another few moments before donning her second shoe and following me out the door.

♣ ♣ ♣

"So, Jake, how do you plan on supporting my daughter and this child?"

Groans sounded around the entire table.

"Dad!" Bailey interjected, but I grabbed her hand under the table to silence her. Riordan had the right to this conversation. He was protective of his family, and I respected that—I respected it a lot.

"Well, sir, my business here in Greensboro is just starting up, but my practices are well-established and I'm partnering with a respected operation."

He grunted in response and Laney cut in. Yes, the whole family had been invited to witness my trial, even Rocco. He sat next to

Riordan, stuffing his face with rolls and singing to himself. "Erin, could you please pass the potatoes?"

The bowl exchanged hands until it reached Laney who winked at me. "Riordan, would you like some more?" Her tactic failed, although I appreciated the effort.

"Aren't you living with your mother?" Riordan scowled.

I almost choked on my water. I should have been prepared for this. Why hadn't I written note cards or something?

"It's a temporary situation. I need to establish a pattern of income before I can qualify for a mortgage. I have a plan, sir, I assure you."

"Dad, I have a condo of my own. Have you forgotten?"

"And what about insurance? Have you thought of that, Mr. Beckett?" Riordan challenged again.

"Bailey has the company's insurance, Dad, as you well know," said Nate, reaching for his own roll.

Everybody seemed to be loading up on potatoes and rolls. In fact, as I looked around the table, I realized I was the only one who'd taken an adult-sized portion of pork chops.

"And that will cover the baby too," finished Bailey.

I was about to speak up about my own insurance when Erin cut in. "Can we please talk about something else?"

"Yes, please," responded Bailey and Nate in unison.

"Is it too early to start planning a shower?" Laney asked.

"Ooh, so exciting! I don't see why we couldn't," replied Erin.

Bailey put an elbow on the table and covered her eyes. She spoke so only I could hear. "They're not going to let me out of that, are they?"

I smiled and squeezed the hand I still held under the table. "It's not looking good. We all have our crosses to bear," I teased. She squeezed my hand back—a bit violently, in my opinion.

"I don't understand why I'm the only person in this room who's concerned!" shouted Riordan, who was immediately shushed by Erin. He continued in a calmer tone, "What happens when the baby comes and Bailey decides to stay home with the little one? Are you going to be able to pay the bills?"

I admit I hadn't really thought about that. What if Bailey wanted to stay home with our kid? What if *I* wanted Bailey to stay home with our kid? Hell, what if Bailey wanted *me* to stay home?

"Dad, I'm not staying home, and Jake and I will work everything out. Can we just eat?"

He let out a harrumph, but Erin patted his hand and I took that as my cue to dig in. I forked a large bite of pork chop and brought it between my lips. It was only then that I realized I needed to listen better when my brother talked.

After several minutes of chewing, I managed to choke down the driest, toughest piece of meat I'd ever encountered. I then chugged my drink and set the glass back down, gasping. I believe there were even tears in my eyes.

"Here, have some more potatoes," Bailey said, holding out the bowl.

I looked around the table and noticed Nate, Laney, and Bailey all wearing shit-eating grins. Bastards!

"Hey, when can *we* get a baby?" Rocco asked. Erin clasped her hands to her chest in delight, and Nate and Laney immediately dropped their smiles.

Then it was my turn. I put on my brightest fucking grin. "Yeah, when *are* you guys having a baby?"

Bailey joined right in. "I think it would be swell if we had them close together, don't you guys?"

Subtle hand gestures were exchanged and we all went back to our food, the pressure thankfully off me for the time being.

☘☘☘

"I suppose it could have been worse," Bailey joked, joining me on the front porch where I'd gone for a much-needed breath of fresh air. Seeing her smiling face was all I actually needed, I realized. I turned to her and grabbed either side of her waist, pulling her closer. I ran my hands up and down her sides as we both smiled moronically at each other.

"You know, you may have Irish blood, but I'm the lucky one."

She just wrinkled her nose. "If you say so." She was cute when she was embarrassed. "Oh, and speaking of blood, my dad might still be out for yours. Just sayin'."

I pulled back a touch with false indignation. "How is this still my fault?"

"Uh, you kind of knocked me up," she teased back.

"Well, yeah," I pretended to blow that off, "but I proposed."

"No, you didn't." She glowered at me. The teasing tone was gone.

"I have a very specific memory of doing just that."

She tried to pull away. "You didn't propose, you ordered!"

"Same thing." I didn't release her.

"In fact, the exact opposite, Jake." She looked at me like I had the IQ of a doorknob.

"Fine, will you please marry me?" I forced myself not to roll my eyes. Yeah, in retrospect, my tone was not ideal.

"No!" She forcibly pulled away.

I grunted in frustration. "What do you want from me?"

She didn't bother to answer. She turned around and went back inside, slamming the door behind her.

"She wants you to love her," came a deep voice from my left.

I turned, startled, and saw Riordan's solid form leaning against the side of the porch. It seemed somebody else had needed fresh air as well.

How long had he been there? This was more than a little embarrassing.

“Excuse me?” I asked before letting his comment sink in. Then, “Oh.” Well, shit.

“Do you?” he asked, his eyes piercing me like daggers.

“Yes.” It was the truth. Such a simple word, but it said it all.

“Well then stop being an idiot and tell her.” He turned and walked into the yard.

Chapter Twenty-Nine

GRABBING JOHNNY'S ASS

BAILEY

I stalked upstairs to my old bedroom, angry with both myself and Jake. I kept letting my heart hope that he returned my feelings, but I should know better. I just couldn't be with him when he was doing it out of duty and some kind of quest for redemption. I threw myself on the bed like I'd done a thousand times in my misunderstood youth. I punched the pillow. I had some serious decisions to make.

"I've been falling in love with you since the moment your long-ass legs walked up that aisle in those damn stockings," Jake's voice came from the doorway.

I rolled over and sprang to a seated position.

What?

"It's true, and I should have told you before." He took a step toward me, his brilliant eyes pleading with me to listen. To believe.

I didn't know if I could afford to.

"That's ridiculous. That wasn't even me." There was no way I was admitting that I'd been similarly struck the moment I spied him at that damn wedding.

"What do you mean? Of course it was you." Confusion overtook his features and he stopped in his tracks.

"Technically, sure, but that was all Fiona's doing—the dress, the hair, the *stockings*. Everything." I tried to look away from him but I couldn't.

"Oh, I see. Was it Fiona moaning in my ear telling me she needed me?" His eyes freaking twinkled.

I fought a blush and lost. "Don't be ridiculous. Besides, that was sex. It was lust, not love." I threw out my chin.

"Maybe not then, but it is now." He took another step closer.

"I was playing a part. I was pretending to be someone I'm not." Shit.

His back got straight with tension and possibly anger. "What the hell is that supposed to mean?"

"Guys like you don't look at me, Jake." I shrugged. "That night, I was all done up and I was acting the part of a girl a guy like you would look at." He still looked angry—and baffled. I threw my arms out to the sides. "You are so far out of my league, I'm playing tee-ball and you're in the Majors. Don't you get it? I'm 'one of the guys' Bailey Murphy. I'm nothing special, and one of these days, you're going to realize that." My eyes flooded with tears. Goddamn hormones!

His head jerked back. "I don't even know how to respond to that."

I stood up, determined that this conversation had to end. "I don't really expect you to understand, but just trust me. I know we've made a mess of things by involving a baby in this, but we'll just have to work that out independently of our personal relationship."

He leaned forward so I had to look at him. "You mean the one where you refuse to be with me even though I love you and I'm pretty certain you love me?"

I whimpered and almost fell back on the bed. I was so fucking in love with him I didn't know how I was going to survive without him. And the thought of having to see him all the time because of the baby—Gah!

"That's what I thought." He grasped my face in his hands.

"Look at me and say you don't love me."

I couldn't do it. How could I possibly?

"Why won't you let me love you?" Jake pleaded. "I'm not going to walk away. I'm not going to hurt you. I'm not any of those other people who made you feel like you don't deserve to be loved for exactly who you are. I'm not. Please believe me."

How could he be so certain? How could I afford to believe him?

"I need to think," I whispered.

"Thinking is overrated." His hands moved down to gently hold my neck while his thumbs grazed my chin.

I blinked and fought the urge to lean in. "I can't think clearly when you're around."

He smirked. "I'll take that as a good thing."

"Jake," I pleaded.

"Twenty-four hours," he responded quietly. "That's your reprieve. And then I'm coming for you, Irish."

☘☘☘

I laid on my old bed for a while, weighing my options. Amazingly, both my parents left me alone apart from my mom poking her head in to ask if I needed anything. I was pretty sure I needed either a shrink or a shot of tequila, but neither was an option, sadly. I was confused and agitated, and nothing felt right. I was afraid I was going to have to do something drastic—something I'd never in a million years envisioned myself doing.

I was calling for a Girls' Night Out.

Since Jake had only given me a twenty-four-hour window, it was declared an emergency by Fiona. She wanted to have us over to her place, but I figured if we chose a public setting I was less likely to dissolve into tears. So, she swung by to pick me up and we met Laney at Gia for some tapas and a drink. Lord knows, neither Laney nor I had ingested much at dinner.

Once the girls had their wine and I had my boring old water, I filled them in on the latest developments. It wasn't long into my story when Fiona shot up in her seat. "Oh my God, you're Baby!"

Uh, I was well aware I was having a baby.

She noted my confused look and continued, "In *Dirty Dancing*. You're Baby and you think Jake is Johnny Castle!"

Laney gasped and nodded vigorously.

I just looked at them like a total idiot. I mean, of course I'd heard of that movie—who hadn't? But I'd never actually seen it.

Fiona scowled, clearly offended on a personal level. "Okay, so there's this girl named Baby," she began and I immediately frowned.

Laney cut in, "I know, horrible nickname, but you'd have to see the movie to understand."

Fiona continued, unbothered, "She's kind of a nerdy tomboy and she has this glamorous mother and sister—although, I gotta be honest, I thought the sister was kind of a dog." She pointed to her nose and grimaced. "Anyway, Baby falls for Johnny, this really hot dance guy who thinks she's just some meddlesome little-sister type."

I was in no way regretting my choice to skip this movie. "Really hot dance guy"? Ooookay.

"Only, Baby ends up saving his ass by volunteering to be his dance partner at this big shindig—long story. The point is, he starts to see who she is on the inside and totally falls for her—and they have a super-hot affair. In the end, he makes everybody else see her through his eyes."

Fiona and Laney both sighed. I felt more like retching.

"Anyway," Fiona continued, "my theory doesn't hold for the entire story. But, like I said, you think you're Baby, and Johnny Castle is never going to give you a second glance."

Laney interjected, "But you're totally wrong. Jake knows exactly who you are and he has from almost the very beginning. I think maybe this has more to do with you than him if you think you're somehow not worthy." She grabbed my hand.

Well, shit.

"And remember how he stalked you—I know we've talked about this before, but he didn't stop once he realized you prefer sneakers to stilettos," Fiona said.

"That was probably just a guy thing—all men want what they can't have. They see it as a challenge. And besides," I pointed to my gut. "Have you forgotten about the baby?"

"Whatever," Fiona continued. "You just need to be like Baby. Turn on some sexy music, grab Johnny's ass and tell him how you feel!"

What. The. Fuck.

Laney was nodding. "That was totally hot. I can't believe you've never seen that."

Fiona fanned herself. "Seriously, you just need to jump in there and get him, girl! He loves you, you love him. End of story. Go get your man!"

Laney laughed and nodded, "She's right. You deserve to be happy so go get yourself some happy." She smiled and squeezed my hand again.

I took a deep breath and looked at both of them again. "Okay, I'm doing it," I declared and they both erupted in whoops.

"Now, on to the next topic," I said. "Did Mark tell you about the witnesses in the whole 'incident'?"

Fiona set her glass down with a clank. "Yes! And I did some poking around myself. I am prepared as shit for this meeting tomorrow!"

"Would it help if I came since I know the witnesses?"

She grabbed my hand. "That would be awesome. I'll text you the address."

Laney declared, "You guys are going to kick that guy's ass. Again." We all snickered and dove into our food.

I was feeling confident—about both the meeting and my next move with Jake. I let out a breath and felt some calm come over me. Then I put a hand to my belly and did it again.

☘☘☘

I knew Jake would be calling later—I'd been given my warning, after all—but I didn't want to lose my nerve or my resolve, so I decided to track him down first thing in the morning. All it took was a call to Fiona since she had the schedule for everyone at Jax's business. After ordering me to "go get me some," she sent me to a posh neighborhood on the north side where Jake was supposed to be starting a project today. I knew it wasn't very professional, but I felt like I just had to see him. I promised myself I'd be discreet and would just have a quick talk with him. We could hash things out further when we both finished work for the day.

I saw his truck, along with two other Precision Landscaping and Lawncare vehicles parked along the street in front of a beautiful brick home with a lush green lawn. What could these people possibly need redone? This was suburban paradise—all that was missing was a racially insensitive lawn jockey.

I parked on the opposite side of the street and made my way down the driveway, hoping to spot Jake without alerting anyone else to my presence. No such luck.

Just as I was debating whether or not to let myself into the fenced-in backyard, a man came through the gate. A man I recognized.

"Hey, Ollie! What are you doing here?" Ollie did the books at Fiona's office and I'd gotten to know him and Jax a bit through her. He was dressed in his typical garb of khaki pants, a sweater vest, and tie. He often had a frazzled air about him, and today was no different.

"Bailey, hi! Just averting another crisis. A typical day in the life of an accountant," he joked, adjusting his glasses.

"Have you seen Jake around?" I went for casual but I doubt I pulled it off.

He gave me a knowing smile. Jesus H. Christ. Did everyone in this town know about the fruit of my freaking loins? I pursed my lips and gave him my best *don't fuck with me* face. "Around back," he answered quickly and rushed to his vehicle.

I proceeded to the gate and opened it, revealing what looked like a good acre of lush lawn and beautiful evergreens. Wow. I was so caught up in my surroundings that I didn't notice Jake at first. Or the dark-haired woman who was plastering herself to his sweaty t-shirt-clad chest. My jaw dropped as I saw her rise up and put her mouth on my fucking boyfriend/baby daddy/fiancé/who-the-hell-cares-cuz-he's-mine-you-bitch!

I stopped breathing. This wasn't happening again. No no no!

"Oh, shit" came a voice from behind me. A man wearing a Precision t-shirt rushed past me toward the slutty, cheating ho-bags. "Jake!" he called, and the woman quickly stepped back from Jake. The part of my brain that controlled speech had shut down completely. The part that controlled movement, however, shifted into high gear the moment Jake's eyes found me. My feet sprouted wings and ran faster than they ever had in my life. I made it to my car in seconds flat and peeled out of the neighborhood, surely leaving skid marks on the perfectly paved suburban-paradise street.

☘☘☘

I parked outside the address Fiona had given me. I was early for the meeting, but I didn't know where else to go. I didn't want anyone to see me falling to pieces.

How could he do this, after everything he'd said, everything he'd promised?

And then I replayed the scene in my head—as if I could ever erase it—and something hit me. That woman was touching *him*. That woman reached up to kiss *him*. Jake's hands were at his sides.

Shit.

I mean, still, he shouldn't have let her get near him, but it had been *her*—not him—instigating whatever the hell had been going on there. And that *her*, I was guessing, was the rich-ass client.

I don't know how I didn't see it from the beginning. I'm not stupid and neither is Jake. He wouldn't go there. It would be career suicide.

My momentary relief ground to a screeching halt. But, wait. What did it say about me—about us—that my first thought was that he would never do anything to fuck up his business? Why wasn't my first thought that he'd never do anything to fuck up our fledgling little family?

I knew what it said, and it wasn't good. Despite my new resolve that I would trust him and trust us, I didn't. Or wouldn't.

I put my forehead on the steering wheel and stayed there until I knew the meeting was starting and I was needed inside.

Chapter Thirty

AIN'T THAT A KICK IN THE BALLS

JAKE

Where the hell was she?!

I'd been driving around like a madman trying to find Bailey and was having zero luck. I was sure I'd broken a dozen different laws in my crazy zig-zagging trek across town, but I was getting nowhere. She wasn't at her office or condo, Nate hadn't seen or heard from her, and I'd even broken down and called her mom in my search. Nothing.

I thought about calling Mark or Fiona, but I knew they were in that meeting with the lawyers and that cocksucker Anton.

Wait! That was it! Bailey was probably there with them. She had the information on the witnesses so surely she'd be there to help. I called Laney in a last-ditch effort. She confirmed my guess and even told me where the lawyer's office was. I put the address in my GPS and took off.

How had I let this happen? I was a sorry excuse for loyal husband and father material.

The day had started out fine—apart from not waking with my girl in my bed. I knew working with Tessa McGuire would be a challenge, but we had all our ducks in a row. We were going to do a kick-ass job on her property, and I was never going to be alone with her. Obviously, that plan went to shit within the first two hours.

Tom and Luis were both on the site with me, and we were preparing to remove some sod when Ollie stopped by with some papers I needed to sign. Tom and Luis must have thought I was safe with Ollie there because they both went to their trucks for who the hell knows what. Ollie, thinking I was covered, took off and I swear Tessa McGuire had been waiting like a fucking snake to strike. As soon as that gate had clicked shut, she was all up in my personal space.

"Jake, I was hoping to get you alone for a minute," she said from behind me. I froze. She walked around in front of me and continued, "It seems I have a little problem and I was thinking you could help me with it."

I looked around, frantically searching for some way to get myself the hell out of this. "Mrs. McGuire," I began and she cut in.

"Tessa. I'm Tessa and you're Jake. Remember?" She ran a finger down my t-shirt.

Fuck.

"Mrs. McGuire," I insisted, "I am happy to help with anything related to your yard. That is all."

She put both hands on my chest and whispered, "I'm afraid that won't do…Jake." And then she leaned in and kissed me on the fucking lips.

"Jake!" I heard Tom's voice yelling from the fence line. Thank Christ. Tessa jumped back and I let out the breath I'd been holding.

I turned to talk to Tom, or maybe kiss him for stepping in—anything! And then I saw her.

Bailey stood behind Tom, her mouth agape. I could see the wet in her eyes from all the way over where I stood. If disappointment and heartbreak had a name, it was Irish. As soon as my eyes hit hers, though, she bolted.

I stammered my excuses as I ran after her, but I was too late. She was roaring down the street in her little coupe, away from the McGuire's and away from me.

I should have put Tessa McGuire in her place the very moment she laid her hand on my arm that first fucking day. Screw the job. Screw the money. What good was all that when it caused the love of my life to wear that look on her face?

Love of my life? You bet your ass.

♣♣♣

I pulled up outside the offices of Jefferson, Wheeler, and Schenk and parked my truck in the first spot I saw. Only then did I hesitate. What was I going to do, burst into this meeting and get down on my knees? That would just piss Bailey and everyone else off. I paced the sidewalk in front of my truck, trying to formulate a plan.

"Jake!" I heard a squeal.

Fiona.

"You're here! Oh my God, we totally kicked ass in there—you should have seen it!" she shouted in excitement. Then she saw my face and her smile dropped. "Shit! I knew there was something wrong with Bailey. What the hell happened?"

"Where is she?" I started past Fiona but she grabbed my arm.

"She's still inside with Mark. I just came out to get something from my car. Now, tell me, what the hell happened?"

I stopped trying to get past her and just leaned back on my truck. "I fucked up."

"How did you fuck up?"

"There's this damn client who's been hitting on me."

Her hand went to her hip. "Tessa McGuire. We're acquainted. I knew she was bad news." She smacked my arm. "What did you do?"

"Tessa somehow got me alone and she kissed me." I looked to the sky, still not believing this crap.

"That bitch! You didn't kiss her back, did you? And how the hell does Bailey know about this already?"

"No, I didn't kiss her back. I hardly realized what was happening. She kissed me and then I looked over and Bailey was standing *right there*. She saw the whole thing!"

"Oh, shit."

"Yeah. Oh, shit. But it's my fault."

She looked at me like I had a screw loose.

"I never should have let it get to that point. I knew that woman was going to pull something like this. I was so worried about losing the job that I think I lost Bailey in the process."

"Calm down, drama king. You haven't lost anything." She patted my arm this time instead of slapping it.

"Did she look bad?" I ventured.

"She didn't look good." Fiona's mouth twisted to the side. "I figured she had morning sickness or something. But she came through like a champ for Mark."

Dammit. Not only was I a shitty boyfriend, I was a shitty brother too. "So, you guys won the case?"

"Well, there was no case to win really. It was just a meeting. But we squashed that cocksucker like the bug he is, and he's dropping the suit."

I smiled for the first time in hours. "Yeah?"

"Yup. We'll tell you all about it later. Right now, you have some 'splainin' to do." She gestured to the door where Bailey and Mark were emerging. They were caught up in conversation and didn't notice me until they were about ten feet away. As soon as Bailey saw me, she turned around and headed back toward the building.

"Bailey, wait! I'm so sorry! It was not at all what it looked like!"

The smile Mark had been wearing dropped and he came closer to me. "What the fuck did you do now?"

Fiona grabbed his arm. "Don't worry, He-Man. It was just a misunderstanding. They'll work it out."

I brushed past both of them and went after Bailey. She had almost made it to the double doors of the building when Anton burst through the doors and came right at her. "You bitch! You just had to play that revenge card, didn't you? My reputation is going to be ruined and it's your fault!"

He grabbed her by both shoulders and shook her. "You weren't even worth the shitty lay!" This was not fucking happening. I sprinted in their direction.

"Get your fucking hands off her!"

I could hear Mark's footsteps pounding the sidewalk just behind mine.

"Stay out of this, lawn guy!" Anton said as he pushed Bailey and she stumbled back. I reached her just as she lost her footing and started to go down. My arms caught her in time and I righted her again. Mark got in Anton's face with Fiona not far behind.

"Don't you fucking touch her, cumstain!" That one came from Fiona.

"What are you going to do, hit me again?" Anton taunted Mark. The veins in Mark's neck popped out.

"No, but I will," came Bailey's voice right before she kicked Anton Motherfucking Germaine right in the balls.

He went down hard, and it didn't escape my notice that his new pair of glasses hit the sidewalk first.

♣ ♣ ♣

"Well that was fun," said Fiona an hour later. We'd all gathered at Bailey's condo where I'd insisted she come to rest. All the day's drama had to be putting stress on her and we weren't taking any chances with the baby.

"I have to say Bailey's battle strategy was better than mine. No cracked knuckles or visible injuries to the victim." Mark snickered.

"Speaking of," I said. "How the hell did you get away without having to pay that asshole off?"

Mark and Fiona looked at each other and smiled. "Well, big brother," Mark said, "it helps to have a kick-ass woman by your side."

Mark's eyes stayed on Fiona but mine went straight to the love seat where Bailey was passed out cold.

Fiona waved it off. "It was nothing."

They went on to explain that Fiona had done some digging and discovered Anton's little gallery show had not gone well. At all. In fact, he hadn't sold one single painting. The gallery was dropping him and he was broke. It turned out this little lawsuit was going to be his meal ticket. He whined to his lawyer about not being able to sleep because he was so afraid Mark was coming after him, and he wasn't able to create any more masterpieces because the stress was weighing on him too hard.

"He knew that in itself was a longshot, so he thought he had another ace in the hole."

"The glasses? They couldn't be worth much."

"No, he had it all worked out," Mark began and Fiona cut in, as usual.

"He got his 'witnesses' to say on record that he'd been carrying one of his 'priceless' paintings with him when Mark punched him. He even produced the damn thing right there on the conference table. There was a giant tear through the center."

"He didn't have a painting with him!" I raised my voice and then glanced over to make sure I hadn't woken Bailey.

"Calm down, Nick Cage, I know," Fiona threw back at me.

"So, how did you prove he was lying?" I quieted myself.

"I got us our own witness." Fiona rubbed her hands together, à la *mwahaha.* "Turns out, there was a class letting out at the same time of the alleged confrontation." She winked at Mark.

There was nothing alleged about it and we all knew it. He laughed.

"All I had to do was ask around. And, it just so happens that the professor of said class witnessed Anton conferring with his groupies right after the incident. He even heard them scheming."

"Damn. That's a pretty credible witness. Impressive, Fiona." I smiled at her and she preened. Damn, my brother had his hands full.

Mark continued, "So, with Bailey and the professor's statement discrediting Anton's witnesses—and, therefore, the 'priceless' painting he was claiming in damages—there was really nothing left."

Fiona interjected, "Well, he still could have tried pushing the battery charge since I'm sure his face looked like hell, but the idiot didn't even have any photographic evidence." She snickered. "You should have seen his lawyer. She was all kinds of pissed."

"When Bailey and I left, she was getting ready to remove Anton's balls with a rusty spoon," Mark added.

"I guess Bailey finished that job for her." I smiled.

♣♣♣

After Mark and Fiona left, I called Jax to see if I'd tanked our job with the McGuires.

"Well, if it isn't the Casanova of the Triad," he greeted. I did not smile at that. "Just giving you shit, man."

"I probably deserve it," I responded.

"No way. I assume you're calling for a status report?"

"You assume correctly. How badly did I fuck this up?" I pinched my eyes with my fingers as I waited for his answer.

"I'm not saying you didn't give it your best effort, but everything's copacetic."

"Huh?" I marveled in a most sophisticated manner.

"Look, I know women like Tessa McGuire. She doesn't want her husband finding out about her extracurricular activities any more that you do. I simply paid her a friendly visit and informed her that if she didn't want her husband knowing she was hitting on you, she'd better make herself scarce for the rest of the project and give you a wide berth. As in, restraining order size."

"Holy shit. And she agreed?"

"Hell yes, she agreed. She knows where her bread is buttered. Her husband's family is loaded, and she didn't always wear such fancy duds, if you know what I mean. In fact, she used to be more partial to pasties."

Holy fuck. Pristine, buttoned-up Tessa McGuire used to be a damn stripper.

"I don't know how you do it, but thanks for saving my ass again," I told Jax.

"Not a problem, brother. Just a day in the life, you know." He chuckled and I was sure he was leaning back in his chair with his feet up on his desk—shit-eating grin firmly in place.

Chapter Thirty-One

PUT THE SLEDGEHAMMER DOWN AND LET'S SETTLE THIS LIKE ADULTS

BAILEY

I awoke with my head resting on a very hard, very warm chest. Again. I groaned and stretched, causing my muscular pillow to shift and tighten. A glance up revealed Jake staring down at me.

"I'm so sorry," were the first words out of his mouth.

I gave him a half-smile but didn't respond to his statement. "What time is it?" I asked instead.

He looked at his phone. "Two-thirty."

I sat up, realizing that we were situated on the couch. He must have moved me while I'd been sleeping. "Crap. I have to get to work. I've missed too much lately."

"You needed your rest. We don't want to take any chances."

My lips tipped up again. "I know. But I really do have to go in. And I feel fine."

He sat up next to me, rearranging himself. "Can we talk first?"

"Jake, I know you weren't cheating on me. You didn't do anything wrong, really. Well, I take that back. I wouldn't have minded hearing you tell that bitch off, but I understand. You have to be careful with your business."

"No, that's just it. I should have put you and us before the business. And I'm so sorry I didn't."

"You were, in a way. I mean, we'd be kind of hurting if you had no income, don't you think?"

He laughed mirthlessly. "I guess, but you know what I mean. I'm really sorry. I told you to trust me, that I'd never let you down, and I failed at the first turn."

I reached for his hand, holding it in my own. "You didn't let me down. The whole thing just made me realize I need to find my own way to really trust us. To trust this." I looked to our joined hands and squeezed again.

"How can I help make that happen, because I really need that to happen. I love you, and I want us to be a family," he pleaded.

"I think I have to figure that out on my own, Jake."

"Irish…"

"I'm not kicking you out," I reassured him. "I promise I'm going to do my best to fix whatever is going on in my head."

He released my hand and took my face in both of his palms, locking his dazzling hazel eyes on mine. Then he leaned in and gave me the sweetest kiss. It brought tears to my eyes, and I kissed him back, wanting nothing more than to give all of myself to this man. But I had work to do first.

And I knew just where to start.

☘ ☘ ☘

"Hey, Dad," I said as I walked into his office. "Does Mom know you're working today?" I teased. It was well known that my mom did not approve of her husband spending much time in the office. She blamed his work habits for his heart attack last year. Personally, I blamed his former diet of fast food and Chinese take-out. But who could really blame him for his clandestine trips to the drive-thru when all he had waiting at home was my mom's cooking?

"Well, with you and Mark gallivanting about town, somebody had to work." He gave me a grin so I'd know he was teasing back. "I heard Mark is off the hook, thank Christ."

I sat down across from him. "Yeah. That's a huge relief."

"Well, sometimes a man deserves a good punch. If he can't take it, he's not much of a man."

"Another pearl of Irish wisdom?" I asked.

He gave me the eye. "Don't have to be Irish to know that one. It's just a fact."

I smiled back at him. I really did love the crap out of my dad.

"So, Dad, there's something I need to talk to you about," I began, bracing myself for the difficult conversation ahead.

"If it's about marrying that Jake, you already know my feelings. But it wouldn't hurt if he officially asked me for your hand. Not that he deserves you." His eyes went back to the papers on his desk.

I rolled my eyes when I knew he wasn't looking.

"It's not about Jake. Well, not directly."

He looked back up. "What is it, then?"

I paused and bit my lip. I could do this. After all, I'd stood up to him when he'd been having his hissy fit at the work site. It was time to grow up. Time to be decisive and take control of my own damn future.

"I don't want the company." Shit, I said it!

He shifted his head to the side as if positioning himself to hear better. "Come again?"

I straightened my spine, sitting up in the chair. "I don't want Built by Murphy. I want to be an artist—a real one. And I want to go back to school if I can. Either way, I can't keep working here, filling my days with building specs and space planning. It's just not me," I finished.

He was silent. He just stared at me.

I squirmed under his scrutiny. Then I began to lose my nerve. "I mean, I know with the baby coming and all, I'll need insurance and an income, but I'm talking long-term."

"I see," he said. "And exactly how long have you felt this way?"

I looked down at my hands and mumbled, "Um, forever."

I heard him sigh. Then there was more silence. I finally risked a glance up. My dad had his hands steepled in front of him and he was looking at me, not with disappointment, but with something else. I could be totally mistaken, but it almost looked like pride.

"Why didn't you say anything?"

"I was afraid to disappoint you—to hurt you."

"Oh, my Bailey." His hands dropped flat on the desk and he looked at me with nothing but love in his eyes. I felt the tears welling in mine. These hormones were going to be the death of me. How did women survive this without stabbing someone? "All I ever wanted was for you to be happy. You have to know that."

I nodded because I did know that.

"Sure, I want you and Nate to have your legacy, but not at the expense of your own dreams. If you need to find your own path, I'll be nothing but proud."

I smiled and he gestured for me to come around the desk for a hug. "You know what they say, 'You've got to do your own growing no matter how tall your father is.'"

He just had to get one in there. I hugged him tightly and kissed his cheek, a totally uncharacteristic move for old Bailey. But my body had been taken over by "Bailey the Girl," so I had little control.

I pulled back a bit. "I know I have a lot to work out, but I really appreciate your support, Dad."

"I have faith in you. And, though it kills me to say it, I'm sure Jake will help." He squeezed my arms.

I smiled a little at that. "If I don't totally screw things up with him."

My dad's brow wrinkled. "What do you mean? That boy is half crazy with love for you."

My eyes widened. "You really think so?"

"I know so. He even told me himself."

I swallowed hard. "But what if he breaks my heart?"

"Well, I suppose there are no guarantees in life, but sometimes you just have to jump in feet first. Otherwise, you're going to miss out on the good stuff." He squeezed my arms again. "I promise you that."

"So, I guess I just need to make a decision to trust him—trust us—and hope for the best."

"That would be my advice. Follow your heart, Bailey. 'Everything will be alright in the end. If it's not alright it's not the end.'"

I hugged him again and laughed. "You're a never-ending font of wisdom, Dad."

"And don't you forget it."

☘ ☘ ☘

After my big talk with my dad, I went to my office and tackled my inbox, all the while getting distracted by thoughts of Jake. He texted me around quitting time, asking if he should head back to his mom's or come over to my place. I told him to come to the condo.

It was time to nail this thing down once and for all. If I didn't take the risk and let him in, I'd always regret it—I knew that down to my bones.

But Jake wasn't the only one I had to trust; I had to believe in myself too. Baby or no baby, I deserved to be loved. And it wasn't up to my heart or the baby to let Jake over the wall. They could put their rope ladder and sledgehammer away. I was going to be the one to take my duct-taped heart and place it in Jake's hands myself. Because if he loved me, he'd not only be the first, but with any luck he'd be the last. And how could I throw that chance away?

By the time Jake knocked on my door, I was pulling a frozen pizza out of the oven. *Baby steps, people.* I dropped it on the cutting board and went to let him in. He stood in my doorway, dressed in a clean thermal and dark gray cargo pants. I wanted to eat him instead of the pizza.

I met his eyes and saw trepidation. I needed to wipe that shit out ASAP, so I got up on tiptoes and planted a hot kiss on his lips. It took him about a third of a second to put his arms around me and take control of the kiss. I felt him urge me back a few steps and then I heard the door shut. Next thing I knew, Jake was pressing me against the door, as he so loves to do. I grinned against his lips, and he took the opportunity to slip his tongue between my teeth. My tongue met his stroke for stroke and I felt everything south of the border burst into flame.

I grabbed at his hair, twisting it in my fingers as I began to pant into his mouth. Jesus, at least these hormones were good for one thing. Although, pregnancy hormones aside, Jake had affected me this strongly from the very beginning. My mind tripped back to our first night together and it hit me. Maybe I wasn't Bailey 2.0, but regular Bailey had been in that hotel too. And Jake had wanted her —wanted me. Just like he did now.

With a surge of self-assurance and good old fashioned horniness, I pushed him forward until the backs of his knees hit the arm of the couch and we both went tumbling onto it. I pulled at the hem of his shirt as he grabbed my ass with both hands. As soon as I revealed his bare skin, I brought my mouth down to have a taste. God, he was firm and hot and his skin was salty on my tongue.

He released my ass just long enough to remove his shirt entirely and then his hands were back, delving inside the back of my pants and granny panties—*I know, but don't ruin the moment for me.* I went back to my sensory exploration of his chest and stomach, flicking my tongue down his happy trail. Jake groaned and pulled me up by my asscheeks so I was straddling him. He quickly disposed of my shirt and bra and started on the button of my pants, only to get distracted by my breasts.

He took one firm peak in his mouth and bit down gently on my puckered nipple. I moaned and arched my back, silently begging for more. My breasts were so damn sensitive—another point going to team pregnancy. He licked over the spot he'd bitten before moving to my other breast.

By this point, he had my zipper down and I was reaching between us for his. I rose up on my knees to get better access and he used the opportunity to pull down my pants and underwear, shifting me so he could remove them entirely. I did the same with his and then he pulled me back on top of him, both of us naked.

His eyes devoured me and I fought a blush. I lost, of course, and a flush spread over my entire body. Jake's eyes were stormy with lust. His hands gently caressed me from the top of my breasts down to my knees, his eyes following his hands the entire time. I felt…worshipped. I'd never experienced this before.

His eyes finally met mine again. "You are so goddamn beautiful, Irish." Then he took my mouth again.

We were a frenetic tumble of limbs and mouths, each of us exploring every square inch of the other's body. At some point, Jake stood with me wrapped around him like a spider monkey, and strode to the bedroom where he deposited me on my bed. He proceeded to climb on top of me and hold my wrists over my head with one hand while his other went between us to find my clit. He circled it with his thumb while his mouth teased my breasts. I squirmed beneath him, but his hold was tight so I just went along for the ride.

He entered me with a finger and I could hear him groan into my breast. "You're so wet."

Of course I was! Did he not know what he was doing to me? Freaking Queen Elizabeth would be begging for him to take her at this point!

"Jake," I pleaded.

He used his fingers and thumb to whip me up into a frenzy and I climaxed with a sound I was sure would make my next encounter with Mrs. Kwon more than a bit awkward. I was panting as I came down from my orgasm, and Jake finally released my hands. I immediately wrapped my arms around him and held him to me.

"Bailey," he said on a sigh, and I could feel it. I could feel everything in his heart in that one word. He loved me.

I reveled in that moment for about five seconds before I grabbed his ass with both of my hands and rolled us over. He chuckled and let me straddle him, his rigid cock laying between my folds. I rubbed against him and his laugh turned into a moan. I rose up to take him inside me and felt his body stiffen. My eyes snapped to his. How could I possibly have misread this?

He opened his mouth to speak and then dropped his head back to the pillow, chuckling again. "I was about to tell you I didn't have a condom."

I snickered with relief. "The damage has been done, I'm afraid." I shook my head. "You'll just have to go without one." His eyes got lazy again and he grasped his cock, allowing me to sink down onto him. I swear I saw his eyes roll back into his head as he groaned at the sensation. Then he took complete control and I let him. He thrust up into me and I met him stroke for stroke, throwing my head back when he hit just the right spot.

We were both sweaty and breathless when he rolled us over and continued to thrust into me, settling himself on top of me and drawing my knees up. I wrapped my legs around him and melted completely.

His jaw was clenched and his thrusts were hard, and I was just on the verge of another climax when he bent his head and bit my neck. That was it. Stick a fork in me—I was done. I came on another high-pitched squeal. I didn't give one good goddamn how loud I was. Jake rode me while I rode my orgasm, and then I felt him release inside me, grunting into my neck as he let go.

When he finally stilled, I felt like laughing. Every emotion hit me at once, but the predominant one was joy. I'd just made love for the first time in my life. *We'd* just made love. And it was like nothing else I'd ever experienced.

I pulled Jake's head up from its resting place in the crook of my neck and looked him in the eye. I brushed my fingers over his ridiculous cheekbones and placed a gentle kiss on his mouth before dropping my head back again. “I love you, Jake Beckett,” I finally whispered.

He immediately dropped his forehead to my chest. “Thank Christ.”

Chapter Thirty-Two

CONFESSIONS OF A TOMBOY

JAKE

Her tongue poked out to capture the last drop of ice cream from her spoon. Yeah, we had pizza and ice cream for dinner. Dr. Pretty Boy would probably not approve, but I didn't give a fuck.

"So," Bailey said, setting down her bowl and picking up a throw pillow to tuck on her lap, "there are some things you should know before committing to me."

I smiled. There was nothing she could tell me to scare me off at this point. I moved closer to her on the couch, grabbing her feet and placing them on my lap. I had this overpowering need to always have my hands on some part of her.

"I'm being serious here," she scolded. I schooled my features appropriately. "Despite the impression I may have given a time or two, I'm not really a *girl*," she said.

As I had plenty of evidence to the contrary, I just raised my eyebrows and shot her a playful questioning look. Mark's comment from weeks ago floated to the surface while I waited for her to continue.

"What I mean is, the wedding and the pregnancy—those totally make me seem girly, but I am most decidedly *not*." She gestured down to the Captain America t-shirt and workout pants she was wearing. "I dress in messy clothes, I don't wear make-up, I drink beer." She started ticking items off on her fingers. "I prefer football to any kind of chick show, I don't like salad, and I don't giggle. Ever."

I just smiled stupidly at her again. "Well, that's good because I happen to like the easy access your work-out pants provide, I couldn't give a shit about make-up or giggling, and I also prefer beer and football. The one thing you don't get a pass on is the salad, though." I gesture pointedly at her belly.

"Oh, that's another thing. I'm terrible with children. It'll be up to you to keep this kid alive."

"Not a problem," I responded, "but I think you might surprise yourself." I let my hand wander up her leg toward my favorite spot on earth.

She swatted at me, but she did it smiling.

"And I never make my bed—ever." She scrunched her eyebrows and continued, "Actually, I don't know how relevant that one is. I don't know very many girls who make their beds—with the exception of Fiona. I assume filthy-mouthed little woodland creatures come in to tidy her room and straighten her sheets every morning."

I laughed out loud at that one.

"There's more," she confessed and then paused.

"Go on," I prompted, giving her legs a squeeze.

"I burp," she said. "And fart." She covered her eyes.

I tried like hell not to laugh. I pulled her hand off her eyes and leaned in, whispering, "Guess what? Me too." She screwed her lips up to the side. "Bailey, everybody does. As long as you don't actually do it *on* me, I think we're good."

She looked at me very seriously. "I don't know if I can promise you that. My body's been doing all sorts of weird things lately and it seems I have very little control over it. The baby is steering the ship and he or she is a very, *very* bad driver."

"It's a he," I informed her. "They are notoriously bad drivers at this age." I grinned at her.

She grinned back. Then I got her another bowl of ice cream.

☘☘☘

It had been one long-ass day and we both passed out in her bed shortly after dinner. We didn't have sex again, but that was okay. We had plenty more nights ahead of us. We did take a shower together in the morning, though, to make up for it, and I was going to insist we start every day that way from here on out.

There was no official talk about me moving in, but I was thinking it was a given after the previous night. I didn't want to sleep without her next to me, and Bailey seemed to feel the same.

We kissed each other goodbye at our vehicles like a perfectly domestic little couple and I couldn't keep the grin off my face on my drive to work. That was, until I pulled up outside the McGuire's. Tension poured into my gut, but I pushed it aside. I had a job to do and a family to support. I wasn't letting Tessa McGuire or anyone get in the way of that.

I opened the gate to the back yard and saw three of my crew

already setting up. A glance around the yard and deck revealed absolutely no sign of the little hustler. I felt myself relax. Jax had really come through, God bless him. I joined the crew and we got down to business.

When I returned to Bailey's that evening, packed bag in hand—I wasn't about to hide my intentions—I was surprised to see her at the kitchen table with Rocco. I walked over and she got up to give me a kiss, noting my surprise.

"Nate and Laney both had to work late, so I volunteered to hang out with Rocco," she explained.

I raised my eyebrows and she scowled at me. That just made me laugh.

"Don't make me give you the same treatment I give your stupid brother," she scolded.

"My mom said it's not nice to call people stupid," Rocco said.

I covered my laugh.

Bailey sat back down. "She's absolutely right. I shouldn't have said that about Mark." She gave me the finger behind Rocco's back.

Still smiling, I asked, "What are you guys working on?"

Rocco looked up at me. "Aunt Bailey's teaching me how to paint."

I leaned over and saw several paint-covered papers along with tubes of paints littering the space between Bailey and Rocco.

"Wow, you're pretty lucky. You know your aunt is an awesome artist?"

"I know," he responded. "She's gonna be famous one day, and then I can say she taught me how to make cool pictures." He nodded and then poked his tongue out the side of his mouth in concentration.

I looked at Bailey but her attention was focused solely on her nephew. "You're doing awesome," she said, pointing out a part he'd just painted. "You totally got what I was telling you before, dude."

I bent down and kissed Bailey on the head and then went to shower. When I came out twenty minutes later, it was to a very different scene. Rocco was standing in the middle of the kitchen, arms crossed.

"Because it's almost dinner time," Bailey was saying, her own arms crossed.

"But you let me have Pop-Tarts every day when you were staying at my house," he pouted. "You just said not to tell anyone. And I promise I won't tell anyone this time either."

Bailey shot me a glance that silently promised I'd be sleeping alone tonight if I dared to smile at that one.

"That may be so, but the answer is still no."

"You were a lot more fun last time," he said.

"Rocco," I interjected, but Bailey waved me off.

"I'm sorry you're not having any fun here, but I'm not letting you ruin your dinner and that's final." She turned to the counter where she had been preparing said dinner.

"I didn't say I wasn't having *any* fun," Rocco mumbled and went back to the table where his paintings lay.

Out of the corner of my eye I saw Bailey smile slyly. I approached her and wrapped my arms around her from behind. "Look at you being a hard-ass. It's totally hot," I teased.

"It's called being a parent…I think." She paused and then shrugged. "At any rate, I figured I could use the practice."

"Well, I, for one," I paused and kissed the back of her neck—she shivered as I continued, "am damn impressed."

She turned in my arms. “Maybe I should try bossing you around sometime.” She raised an eyebrow and grinned wickedly.

“Yes, ma’am.” I leaned in and gave her a proper kiss. Well, as proper as I could get with a six-year-old in the room. But I supposed we’d better get used to that.

I couldn’t wait.

Chapter Thirty-Three

REDEMPTION

JAKE

"You got a minute?"

"For you? I've got all the minutes." My mom smiled up at me and patted the chair beside her. Her dark hair was styled in long waves, and eyes the same color as mine flashed back at me.

I sat and leaned forward, elbows to my knees. I gave her a sidelong glance and let out a breath.

She chuckled and earned herself a playful glare.

"Jake," she prompted, a knowing grin on her face.

I drew in a deep breath. "I owe you an apology."

Her head tilted sharply.

"A big one."

This had not been what she'd expected me to say. I knew that, but I needed to tell her now. Before.

She shook her head, still confused. "What do you mean?"

"I never should have left. It was selfish and cowardly, and just plain wrong. And I'm so sorry, Mom."

She put her hand on my arm. "Jake, sweetie, I'm not sure I understand what you're talking about."

My eyes shot to hers again. "After high school. When I ditched you and Mark."

Understanding dawned and her confused expression turned sad. Fuck, I knew that look well and I hated seeing it on her. She'd worn it a lot when Mark and I had been growing up. When the asshole lived with us. And I knew I'd been the cause of a lot of her pain, even if it had been indirectly.

"Jake…" she began, but I cut her off.

"No, Mom. This apology is long overdue, and you deserve it. If I had stayed I could have gotten a job and helped you out. I could have helped Mark—let him go off to college somewhere. And, I don't know, maybe I could have made the old man leave before he did. I let you down, and I want you to know that I'm going to make it up to you."

"You know it's not the child's responsibility to care for the parent." She rubbed my arm in comfort I didn't deserve.

I nodded. "I do, but our situation was different." I didn't want to remind her of her years of depression, especially since life was so much brighter for her now. But that should have compelled me all the more to stay.

She just shook her head. "Jake, do you think I wanted you to stay?"

I looked at her sharply. I didn't understand her question.

She smiled. "I mean, of course I loved—and still love—having you at home, but I wanted you to find your own way in the world. If you had stayed, you would have become bitter and angry."

I huffed out a breath. She was not wrong.

"Your father," she began and then paused. "Your father was good at making you feel like you were never good enough. That you'd never *be* good enough. No mother wants that for her child. No parent should ever want that for their child. I should have fought for you then, but I didn't." She shrugged sadly.

I shook my head. She was trying to let me off the hook. But it wasn't her fault. She didn't have it in her back then to fight for herself, let alone anyone else. "Please don't. I never blamed you, not for a second. I could have stayed and made it work. Or, at the very least, I could have come back sooner."

"I was happy for you when you left. I wanted you to get a chance to be your own man." She gestured to me with both hands. "And look how well you turned out."

I let out a sharp laugh. "You're just biased. And I still want to make it up to you in any way I can."

"I'm not biased." She squeezed my arm. "Well, not much. You're a good man, Jake. You're here now and that's what counts. If you feel like you have something to atone for, just be the wonderful father and husband I know you will be. That's more than enough." She gestured to doors of the courthouse where the most beautiful girl in the world stood looking around.

For me.

I let that settle into my chest nice and deep.

I took Bailey in from head to toe. Simple ivory sweater-dress, tan heels. Nothing too fancy but absolutely perfect. Her hair was down and her blue eyes finally caught mine as I stood. She stepped forward and I moved to close the space between us.

"Hey, Irish." My eyes took in every feature, finally landing on her lips where I then placed my own. She smiled against my mouth.

"I can't believe we're doing this," she said once she'd pulled back.

"You'd better believe it."

"You look beautiful," my mom told her.

Bailey looked down self-consciously. "You think?" She smoothed a hand over her small baby bump. "I feel like I'm smuggling contraband in this dress."

My mom laughed at that and I put my hand over Bailey's. "You look perfect."

"I considered changing into maternity jeans and a sweater at the last minute, but, what the hell—you only get married once, right?"

Damn straight.

I wouldn't have cared if she'd shown up in flannel pajamas. It hadn't been easy getting her to this point. She'd insisted living together was good enough, but I wanted her to be mine. For good. So I'd worn her down and gotten her to agree to be my wife.

My wife. Crazy.

This had ingratiated me to her father to a degree that he no longer wanted to do awful things to me. I was considering it a huge win.

And since I'd gotten my way and Bailey had agreed to tolerate me as her ball and chain, I'd left the rest up to her. She chose a very simple ceremony at the courthouse with just our parents. She said she didn't need a room full of friends and family to be there when she promised herself to me. Just the people who'd brought us into this world and the little one we'd be welcoming into it as well.

Of course, this had not gone down well with anyone else. Fiona and Laney had pleaded and cajoled, Mark and Nate had both protested, and a long list of other people had given their two cents. But the bottom line was my stubborn girl was getting what she wanted and I couldn't be happier giving it to her. Look at me. I was getting really good at this.

"Sweetheart, you forgot your purse." Erin came up beside Bailey and handed her a small, sparkly handbag. Bailey growled.

"I told her I didn't want that damn thing." I didn't have to ask who *her* was.

"Fine, I'll hold it for you and you can have it back when we get to the party," Erin replied.

We may have been able to talk everyone into staying away from the courthouse, but there was no way they were letting us get married without at least some sort of accompanying celebration. So Fiona and Laney had channeled all their wedding-fueled bitterness into planning an "after-party" at Erin and Riordan's house. Casual, just like my girl, but everyone who wanted to would get the chance to celebrate with us, and Bailey could remain sane in the process. It was a win-win.

Riordan pulled Bailey aside and my mom took the opportunity to straighten my tie and give me a hug. When I pulled back I deliberately gave her a long look so she'd feel everything I wanted her to know. "Thanks, Mom."

"You're very welcome, sweetie." She smiled.

"Well, let's get this show on the road!" Riordan boomed, and it didn't escape my attention that he was wiping a tear from his eye. Bailey held his other hand and we all walked toward the chambers where Bailey Murphy, the girl I never saw coming, would promise to make me a husband, a father, and the luckiest son of a bitch there ever was.

EPILOGUE

BAILEY

Three Months Later

"You seriously expect me to eat this?"

Fiona just nodded, handing me a spoon.

"Just because I'm over the morning sickness doesn't mean I won't puke all over this damn place," I informed her.

She grimaced. "Gross. Do you have to talk like that?"

"I'm sorry, but how am I the gross one here? You just presented me with a buffet of diapers filled with melted candy bars that look like actual shit." I gestured to the incredibly fucked up baby shower "game" Fiona was trying to get me to participate in.

"You're the guest of honor—you have to play the games!" she insisted.

So far, I had tolerated having all the attendees guess how fat I was, I'd drunk apple juice out of a baby bottle, and I'd let every person in the damn restaurant rub my belly for luck. I was being pretty damn agreeable if you ask me.

But I was drawing the line at "Name that Poop." I'd heard rumblings about some game called "Bobbing for Nipples" that was coming up next. I assumed that would provide a bit of entertainment for the guys, at least.

Guys, you ask? Oh, yeah. This was a freaking co-ed baby shower. I couldn't believe Laney and Fiona had talked all the guys into coming to this shindig. Not that Jake and I didn't appreciate the sentiment and all the effort—we really did, but it was not necessary. At all. Still, I'd tried to keep a positive attitude. Until the poop. I had to draw the line somewhere.

"Fine," said Fiona, finally taking her tray of shit candy with her.

I felt a tiny bit bad. Fiona had really come through for me in more ways than one in the last few months. In addition to throwing this shower, she had completely overhauled my supply of "intimates"—I was told they're not called underwear when they cost more than ten dollars. I was looking forward to a time when I could look down past my belly and actually see the panties she'd purchased for me. But Jake assured me they were hot, so I was good. I had drawn the line at more thongs, however.

As if that weren't enough, she made a few calls on my behalf and I had an upcoming interview with the MFA board at the art school. Turned out Anton's arrogance and general douchebaggery had lost its charm with the board, and his opinion wasn't welcome anymore.

I think we all took more than a little pleasure in the knowledge that Anton was finally being given the true "starving artist" experience he'd championed for me. Laney said she'd give it about six months before we spotted him working at a Starbucks. I was thinking she was probably not wrong.

At any rate, Fiona had really gone above and beyond for me. I knew from past stories that she liked to play fairy godmother—her words, not mine—and I was now apparently one of the god-children or something like that. Whatever we were to each other, I was certainly grateful to have such a generous friend.

As for art school, I didn't know how I would swing it if I did get in, but having the chance was thrilling on its own. And as with everything, Jake and I would figure it out.

Laney approached, laughing. "Don't worry about Fiona. I told her nobody would want to eat that shit." I laughed at her comment and she put an arm around me. "I still can't believe you and Jake are having a baby. I mean, I know it should have sunk in by now, but I think I'm still in shock."

I rubbed my ever-growing belly where Dexter rested inside. Yes, we referred to the baby as Dexter. We still didn't know the gender for sure, but the kid's propensity to stab me sharply in every organ led to our nicknaming the little tyke after a serial killer. *What? Don't look at me like that.*

"That makes two of us," I told Laney, resting my head sideways on her shoulder. I was getting better at this mushy girl stuff every day.

Gavin walked up just then. "Did I hear something about nipple bobbing?" He rubbed his hands together, his brown hair a tangled mess and a naughty grin firmly in place.

Laney shook her head at him. "I don't think it means what you think it does, Gav." She patted him on the shoulder.

We both laughed at his crestfallen look. "Dammit. Anyway, I was sent to tell you it's time to open the gifts."

I gave Laney a panicked look. She knew I was not one to relish being the center of attention. She grabbed my hand and pulled me toward the table where Jake sat talking to Kelly.

"It'll be fine. Jake will make it okay," she said.

And I knew she was right. He made everything okay. He just *got* me. I relaxed as I made my way to my seat.

"Hey, Irish," Jake leaned in and kissed me as I sat. "You having fun?"

I glowered at him. "Ha ha."

"The good news is I hear we only get one baby shower no matter how many more kids we end up having."

Did I say he got me? I'd like to retract that statement.

He just chuckled at my look and kissed me again.

"First come the cards and then the wrapped gifts," Fiona announced cheerfully, all resentment from the shit game apparently forgotten. She handed Jake a small stack of cards that had been mailed to her address. These must have been the people who couldn't make it, although I couldn't imagine squeezing in one more person.

We were occupying a semi-private dining room at Gia. I couldn't believe the owners were allowing us to carry on with all the games and noise, but Fiona had a way of talking people into just about anything.

Jake proceeded to open the first envelope. He pulled out the card and a check fell from it, landing on the table. I went to grab it and discreetly tuck it away when I saw the amount written there. WTF?

Jake read the card to himself and then looked to me with a smile. I pushed the check over so he could see it. His eyes got wide. Thankfully, no one seemed to be paying much attention yet.

It was from Mr. and Mrs. Vaughn. They were the nice older couple who had propelled Jake's business to a level of success he'd never anticipated. They'd been his first clients in Greensboro and had proceeded to recommend him to pretty much everyone they knew. In fact, we were invited to their daughter's wedding this coming summer.

Jake handed me the card.

Dear Mr. and Mrs. Beckett,

I hope this note finds all three of you healthy and well. A baby is such a joy and a blessing, one I hope you'll cherish.

I don't think I ever told you, Mr. Beckett, but our darling Sophia is adopted. Mr. Vaughn and I never had the opportunity to have a child of our own, so we took it upon ourselves to go find our family instead.

While you two may not have been in search of yours, it pleases me to no end to see you embrace it when it found you.

We wish you nothing but the best in all things,

Michael and Emilia Vaughn

I looked up to Jake and then back to the check.

"Holy shit. You must be one hell of a landscape designer."

Jake looked back at me and we both burst out laughing.

He tucked the check in his wallet for safekeeping and we continued opening the gifts.

I made sure I oohed and awwed, and even I had to admit most of the stuff was pretty damn cute. Jake, in turn, raved over any of the baby items that included batteries. There was lots of chatter as we opened each gift.

Fiona made it clear she did not like being limited in her color selections since we'd decided to keep the gender a surprise—although Jake was absolutely positive it was a boy. Laney offered baby advice on the use of each practical item we received, as she was the voice of experience. And my dad announced to the room that the baby would be given an Irish name.

He was not wrong. We just weren't telling anybody what we'd chosen. And, in truth, the source of our chosen name was something precious to me that I didn't want to share with anyone but Jake. That was part of the reason we kept referring to the baby as Dexter.

As soon as I'd started showing, Jake had taken to talking to the baby, his head usually resting in my lap while he did so. He'd talk about me, making jokes about things I would and wouldn't tolerate ("You'll never have to make your bed, but you will need to close the door when you pee"), and he'd make promises to our baby—ones about love and loyalty and always keeping his word.

And then, one day, he'd stood in the doorway of our bedroom where I'd been resting. I didn't even notice him at first, but when I did, I had to do a double-take. No one, in my entire life, had ever looked at me the way Jake was looking at me. Not even close. When Jake had stared at me the first night we met, I'd been amazed to be on the receiving end of such a gaze. But it couldn't hold a candle to this one. Jake was looking at me like I was…everything.

And that's when I knew, without a doubt, that is wasn't about the baby at all. It was about me, Bailey Murphy of the skinned knees and stubbornness and snarky attitude—and tender heart. I was caught breathless for a moment and then Jake crossed to the bed, climbing on and placing his ear to my growing belly. But his eyes were on me when he started humming. It took me a minute to recognize the song, but once I did, I smiled.

And not that I can carry a tune to save my life, but I started to sing along to the old Loggins and Messina song about the love a man has for his wife and the son they're expecting. We smiled like idiots at each other when I got to the chorus and Jake took over the singing, reminding me why I loved that song so much. He had a surprisingly good voice. Yet another of the good genes I was crossing my fingers would be passed down to little Dexter.

But he wasn't going to be named Dexter after all. He'd be Danny. Just like the song. And if Jake was mistaken and the baby turned out to be a girl, I thought Dani worked just fine.

"Brita if it's a girl," my father announced. I didn't have the heart to tell him we were not naming our child after a water filter. "Cullen if it's a boy." Yeah, there was not enough time to explain vampire culture to a man in his sixties. I just mumbled to Jake that he could take the panicked look off his face and we continued with the gift opening.

Before we knew it, the last gift had been unwrapped and passed around, and I could sit back and enjoy my drink—out of a glass this time, not a baby bottle. I was somewhat surprised that none of the boxes had held a gecko or other such reptile. It seemed I'd been forgiven for introducing Pickles to the family—either that or Laney was just waiting until the baby was born to spring one on me.

I was just about to make my sixth trip to the bathroom when I felt someone approach from my side. I looked up and saw a red-headed woman who looked vaguely familiar.

She appeared a tad uncomfortable. "Hi," she greeted Jake and me. "I don't know if you remember me. Emerson Scott? We met—"

I cut her off, "Anton's lawyer. I remember."

She grimaced. "Yeah. I'm so sorry to interrupt." She gestured behind her to the main section of the restaurant. "I was having lunch with a friend and saw you here. I feel that I owe you an apology."

Jake extended his hand to her. "Jake Beckett."

She accepted it and continued, "It's nice to meet you, Mr.

Beckett. And it seems congratulations are in order." She gestured to the beach ball under my shirt.

"Thanks," I said, still a little leery.

"I won't take up any more of your time," Emerson said, smoothing the skirt of her suit. "But I wanted to give you my contact information in case Mr. Germaine ever tries to bother you again. I saw him push you, Ms. Murphy. Outside my building?"

Jake and I both nodded, his mouth pulling tight at the memory.

"I didn't know what a dishonest jerk he was when I took him as a client. I don't normally do personal injury cases. I guess I know why now." She shook her head to herself. "Anyway, I don't think he'll be stupid enough to come after any of you again, but if he does, please don't hesitate to call." She held out her business card.

"Thanks," I told her, accepting the card. The way I saw it, the breadth of Anton's stupidity was boundless so I was keeping that card in a safe place.

She smiled, finally seeming to relax, and it lit up her face. The sound of her phone ringing in her purse caused her smile to drop the next moment. "Would you excuse me?"

Jake and I nodded and she scurried to a corner of the room where she quickly brought her phone to her ear.

"Who in the name of holy spank banks was that?"

I turned to see Gavin standing across the table from us, drool practically dripping from his chin.

I laughed. "Don't even think about it, son. She is way out of your league."

Gavin's eyes remained glued to the red-head. I worried briefly that he'd stopped breathing.

"I'd guess she's a good five or six years older than you, Junior. Don't torture yourself," Jake added.

Gavin just mumbled something about feisty cougars and wandered off.

"Do we need to be worried about that?" I asked Jake.

"Nah," he shook his head. "Let Laney and Nate worry about him. We've got our own troublemaker to deal with." He ran his hand gently over my stomach. The kid kicked him in response.

"Ow," I said on a laugh. "You know, it's a good thing I love you so damn much or I'd have to kill you for doing this to me." I pointed at my protruding gut as the baby dug a foot into my ribs.

Jake bent down and stage whispered to my belly, "Your mom likes to say things like that but she doesn't mean them. She had to kiss a few frogs before she met her prince—they made her grumpy."

I huffed and smacked the back of his head. It only made him smile wider.

"Prince, my ass," I said, but I kissed the spot where I'd smacked him anyway. "I will admit, this falling in love stuff is not for wimps," I confessed.

"Well," Jake said, bringing his face up to my level and giving me a lingering kiss. "The good news is you'll never have to fall in love again. You're mine and I don't share well."

"I'm aware," I said and kissed him back.

But Jake was wrong on both counts. It wouldn't be the last time I'd give my heart, and he'd learn quickly how to share. Because three months later, when the doctor placed a screaming ball of naked fury on my chest, I fell in love yet again. Of course, this time, it was with a girl.

Just further proof that God has a fucking wicked sense of humor.

~THE END~

Continue the series now with ***The Game***, *Gavin & Emerson's story. Or stay tuned for an excerpt!*

Stay up to date on Sylvie's upcoming books and projects by subscribing to her newsletter! http://bit.ly/NewsSylvie

♣ ♣ ♣

Use these links to grab special **bonus** content!
http://bit.ly/BonusLuckyOne & http://bit.ly/LuckyOnePuzzle

ABOUT THE AUTHOR

USA Today bestselling author Sylvie Stewart is addicted to Romantic Comedy and Contemporary Romance, and she's not looking for a cure. She hails from the great state of North Carolina, so it's no surprise that most of her books are set in the Tar Heel state. She's a wife to a hilarious dude and mommy to ten-year-old twin boys who tend to take after their father in every way. Sylvie often wonders if they're actually hers, but then she remembers being a human incubator for a gazillion months. Ah, good times.

Sylvie began publishing when her kids started elementary school, and she loves sharing her stories with readers and hopefully making them laugh and swoon a bit along the way. If she's not in her comfy green writing chair, she's probably camping or kayaking with her family or having a glass of wine while binge-watching Hulu. Or she's been kidnapped—so what are you doing just sitting there?!!

**Winner of the 2017 National Indie Excellence Award for Romantic Comedy

**Winner of the 2017 Readers' Favorite Silver Medal for Romantic Comedy

Thank you so much for reading *The Lucky One* – I hope you enjoyed it. If you did, a **review** on your favorite book site is always appreciated!

✤✤✤

Want to stay updated on new releases, promotions and giveaways?
Subscribe to my newsletter! http://bit.ly/NewsSylvie

Want to hang out with me and my other readers?
Join my brand new reader group on Facebook: **Sylvie's Spot - for the Sexy, Sassy, and Smartassy!**
http://facebook.com/groups/SylviesSpot

Thanks! XOXO,
Sylvie

Keep up to date and keep in touch!
www.sylviestewartauthor.com
sylvie@sylviestewartauthor.com
Follow me on BookBub for sales and new releases!

facebook.com/SylvieStewartAuthor
twitter.com/sylvie_stewart_
instagram.com/sylvie.stewart.romance

THE LUCKY ONE PLAYLIST

You can listen to this playlist on Spotify!

- Danny's Song / Loggins & Messina
- Girl in a Country Song / Maddie & Tae
- Come on Get Higher / Matt Nathanson
- Different for Girls / Dierks Bentley and Elle King
- Sooner or Later / Mat Kearney
- Back to Where I Was / Eric Hutchinson
- Another Sunday in the South / Miranda Lambert
- The Girl You Think I Am / Carrie Underwood
- Something Beautiful / The Noms
- If There Was No You / Brandi Carlile
- Somebody Loved / The Weepies
- Tomboy / Miranda Lambert
- Never Seen Anything Quite Like You / The Script
- Inner Demons / Julia Brennan
- Danny's Song / Josh Gallagher

ACKNOWLEDGMENTS

Big shout out to my friend and editor, Heather Mann, and to my family and friends for being patient with me! Thanks, dudes!

Due to copyright expenses, I couldn't publish the lyrics to Loggins and Messina's *Danny's Song* but I encourage you to go listen to it. It makes me smile and tear up every time I hear it and it helped inspire this book. Look up my playlist for *The Lucky One* on Spotify—you'll find the song there, along with a country version of it. Cuz, you know, it's me we're talking about…

EXCERPT FROM THE GAME

Carolina Connections, Book 4

Chapter One: Patience Is a Virtue

GAVIN

I knew it was over before my shoulder even kissed the ground—before the crunch of metal and the burn of gravel registered in my brain and flesh. I heard nothing but the crack and pop of my bones, these sounds somehow isolated among what must have been an awful cacophony of scraping metal, squealing tires, and voices raised in alarm. It was over before it even began, and I had no one to blame but myself.

Hours later, when I awoke in the hospital, the well-meaning doctor informed me I was lucky to be alive. I begged to differ but kept my mouth shut, forcing both the physical pain and the self-loathing down as deeply as I could. My mother's tear-stained face, slack with relief, was no balm. Nor was the barrage of questions posed to the doctor by my father as he paced around the hospital room. Nobody had to tell me, but they did anyway.

In a steady, matter-of-fact tone, the doctor described the extensive surgery I'd undergo to repair the damage to my right arm and shoulder. Pins would be inserted and the healing process would begin. It would be long and arduous, not to mention painful, but I'd regain almost complete use of my arm with any luck.

They could cut the damn thing off for all I cared, because I had just thrown away the only thing I'd ever wanted or cared about—the thing I'd busted my ass the last ten years to achieve.

And all because I'd told myself nothing bad could ever happen on my birthday. There'd been a hot girl, cold beer, and a cool-as-shit motorcycle. One ride couldn't hurt. I was fucking Gavin Monroe, star pitcher, golden boy, and ripe to make my mark on the world, and hopefully that hot girl too. Instead, the only mark I left was on an isolated stretch of North Carolina country highway. That, and a deep scar on my future that could never be healed.

If I couldn't be a somebody, that meant I'd be a nobody. And I couldn't live with that. I was well and truly fucked. And not in the good way.

But life has a way of surprising us.

☘ ☘ ☘

- Four and a half years later -

"Hey, Junior! Where do you think you're going?" Mark yelled across the lot.

I let the douchey nickname roll off my back, something I'd gotten pretty good at over the last couple years. It wasn't my fault that I had boyish charm and youthful good looks. But, as is always the case with guys, you've got to pay your dues and put up with some hazing if you're ever going to earn the respect of those above you. Mark, while definitely holding a position of authority as my foreman, was also a friend, so I considered it my right and duty to put him in his place as well. Flipping him off seemed the most appropriate response in the moment.

"You wish!" was his reply, but I kept walking toward my Jeep, leaving the partially-constructed shell of the newest apartment building behind. I pulled off my hard hat and ran my other hand through my sweaty mass of hair, loosening the strands from the damp, tangled helmet they'd formed.

Mark knew good and well where I was going, he just couldn't resist giving me shit on the days I cut out before everyone else on the job site. But that was the whole point of working part-time. I admit, there may have been a time or two when I'd rubbed it in a few guys' faces that I'd be taking off after lunch while they slaved away under the hot Carolina sun. But, like I said, it's a guy thing.

I couldn't resist shouting back at him, "I'll tell Fiona you said hi!" That earned me a look that might make a lesser man shit his pants. Mark was built like a linebacker and was more than a little protective of his girlfriend. He made it too damn easy to rile him.

"You'll be doing it without teeth!" he growled. See, like I said —too easy.

I hopped in my Jeep and tore out of the lot, not bothering to secure my seatbelt until I was on the main road. The New Pornographers blared from my speakers, testing their limits, and possibly those of the passengers in the car to my left. I turned down the volume a smidge, probably prolonging the lifespan of my eardrums in the process. What can I say? I was in a good mood.

The workweek at my construction job was over and I'd be spending this afternoon and the remainder of the weekend on my second job—the one I was beginning to discover I was meant to do. I'd been working for the Baseball Academy for about a year and a half now, and despite my initial reservations, I was loving it. I got to spend my time playing ball and coaching elite players, some of whom had a real shot at what I once saw as my future.

Fate and poor judgement had gotten in the way of my dreams, but I could still be a part of it all by helping to coach these high-level players. I'm not saying it didn't still sting when I thought of what could have been, but it was getting easier as time went on. And I was learning a ton on the job. It's one thing to be a player and another to be a coach. I was starting to see a future I'd never allowed myself to envision before.

Before the Academy hired me, I'd been a bit of an embarrassment. Even I can admit it. I'd been crashing in my parents' basement since dropping out of college halfway through, and most nights were spent feeling sorry for myself and getting drunk with my best friend, Brett. How I managed to keep that shit up for over two years is beyond me. But I finally pulled my head out of my ass with the help of Brett and my sister, Laney.

She was way better at adulting than me. She'd had to be. Laney got knocked up her freshman year of college and still managed to finish her associate's degree, get a decent-paying job, and raise her son. I'm not ashamed to admit Rocco probably rivals Brett as my best friend, even though he's only six. We've got an awesome relationship—one Laney claims is so strong because of our similar levels of maturity. Whatever. He's a cool kid. I like to think I had something to do with that.

I was even teaching Rocco how to play ball, although at this point our goal was getting him to focus long enough to avoid getting hit in the head. One step at a time. Laney is…how can I put this? Hell, there's no good way—she's fucking hopeless when it comes to sports. Or anything requiring basic coordination. I can't even be in the car when she's driving. It was becoming clear that

Rocco's future as an athlete rested solely on my coaching abilities and anything his stepdad, Nate, could impart.

I pulled my Jeep into the staff lot of the Academy and spotted Gerry, one of the senior coaches, coming out the side door. As usual, his rotund belly preceded the rest of him through the doorway. I raised my hand in greeting as I parked and got out.

"Just the guy I wanted to see!" Gerry greeted me with his gravelly voice.

I grabbed my bag out of the back and threw him a chin lift. "Oh yeah?"

"Buzz and I need you to check out a pitcher this weekend. Sophomore at North—name's Miller. Two o'clock. Home game."

I wracked my brain trying to come up with a face, but the name didn't ring any bells. I prided myself on keeping track of the local high school talent. It was our bread and butter. I shot Gerry a questioning look and he nodded.

"Don't worry. You haven't been slacking. He's new in town." Gerry handed me a sticky note with just two words written on it. *Jay Miller*. Far be it from him to consider entering the digital age and shoot me a text or e-mail.

"And they let him on the team mid-season? Must be good." I raised an eyebrow.

"You tell me. I'm running out but I'll catch you later," he said, brushing past me. "And have a talk with Jameson—kid's getting too big for his britches!"

I groaned inwardly. Brad Jameson was an asshole, plain and simple. Spoiled kid with too much money and not enough talent. We'd tried several times over the last couple years to let him down gently and prepare him for a future that did not involve baseball—unless coaching little league counted. But the kid refused to listen, and his parents kept sending the payments to continue his training.

Things were going to come to a head at some point and I, for one, was not looking forward to it.

If anyone could smooth it over in the end, though, it was Gerry. He's exactly what you'd picture when you think of an old-school baseball coach—shaggy graying hair, ever-present cap, toothpick permanently clenched between his teeth, a gruff exterior, and not a man to waste words. He knew his shit inside and out, and I was lucky to have him as a mentor.

I waved him off and headed toward the staff locker room. I needed to shower the grime and sweat from the job site off before I changed into my uniform and started training. Just as I passed by the open door of the players' locker room, an object flew in front of my face, missing me by inches as it sailed by and landed unceremoniously on the floor to my right. A jock strap. You have got to be shitting me.

One glance into the room told me what I already knew. I stepped inside and crossed my arms over my chest.

"Maybe once they drop you'll be able to get some poor chick to suck you off." Brad Jameson stood with his back to me, guffawing at his own lame-ass joke and facing one of the younger guys whose jock strap Brad had obviously just tossed into the hallway. This was a quintessential Brad move. Who in God's name touches another guy's nut bucket? You just don't do that—it's an unwritten rule—unwritten because anyone with a dick knows that's the last place you want your hand. Except Brad, for some inexplicable reason. It's like the kid was trying to take douchebag to a whole new level. He was succeeding spectacularly.

Chris, the younger player, stood with a towel wrapped around his skinny waist, his face a deep crimson, further highlighting his unfortunate case of acne. He stiffened as he caught sight of me, but

I shook my head in a silent cue to leave my presence a secret for the moment.

"Doubtful," came another comment from someone hidden behind a row of lockers. Ah, Brad's lackey, Dell. The kid couldn't come up with an original thought to save his life. A couple players to my right occupied themselves by tying their cleats and pretending not to hear the exchange.

"True…he'd have to get it up first. Have you ever even had a boner, *Christian*?" Brad taunted and bent closer as the kid squirmed.

What an asshole.

"Well, ladies," I finally made my presence known. "Glad to see you've got extra time on your hands to gossip."

Brad stood straight and whirled around, clearly surprised at being caught. He quickly schooled his features, however, and assumed his usual "my shit don't stink" countenance, crossing his arms over his bare chest and shrugging.

I looked at my watch. "Fifteen minutes till batting practice. Should give you girls plenty of time to do shuttle runs. You've got sixty seconds to get dressed and get your asses out there." I knew if I didn't include Chris, it would just make things worse for him, so I made sure to address everyone in the room. I understood why kids didn't stand up for one another—it didn't mean I had to like it, but I understood it. The teenage hierarchy is a complex and fragile structure, and one you don't mess with lightly. I had to trust that the Chrises of the world would win out in the end, and it was my job to offer encouragement and a listening ear when the spotlight was off. It looked like I'd be having more than one conversation off the field tonight.

☘☘☘

"Yo!" I hollered as I walked in the front door to my townhouse. "Are we going to Jake's tonight or—" I stopped dead in my tracks and quickly spun back around to face the door. The briefest glance at the couch had revealed more than I'm sure the girl straddling Brett's lap would prefer.

"Shit!" Brett and I said simultaneously. I heard some rustling and whispering behind me.

"Hey, sorry guys. But you do know you have a room upstairs, right, asshole?" I said into the door.

Brett just grunted at me which made me grin. I had to say, the girl was pretty hot from what I'd seen.

"Oh, God, this is so embarrassing," I heard a female whisper just before the girl brushed past me and opened the door. Her shirt was still half off, but at least her bra was back on.

"I'll call you later, Ginger!" Brett yelled behind her. Something told me she may not be answering her phone for a few days.

I finally turned back to the room just as a *Men's Health* magazine whizzed by my face. What was it with people throwing things at me today?

"I wasn't expecting you home so soon," Brett said, giving his chin a good scratch. He was growing a beard—or attempting to—and had recently gotten gauges in his ears as well. It seemed the chicks were digging this new look. I had to say, before, he looked about eighteen instead of twenty-four, so it was time for a change.

"That's pretty obvious," I responded, smile firmly in place. "So, I guess you're free to go to Jake's then?" He threw a shoe at me this time, but I caught it, no problem.

"Why are you home so early? I thought you had training." Brett got up and walked to the kitchen. I trailed behind. We'd moved into this townhouse in High Point last year, and while it wasn't anything to write home about, we'd been pleased with the place so far. Living with your best friend always leads to some great times, and it was definitely a step toward overdue adulthood for me. I'd gone from my parents' house to my sister's before finally paying rent on my own place with Brett. Yeah, definitely overdue.

"I wrapped things up early so I could have a chat with that Jameson kid, but the little prick skipped out on me." I was still pissed off.

Brett handed me a beer from the fridge and we both popped ours open. I tossed my cap over my shoulder and straight into the open trash can. Brett's landed somewhere in a vicinity of the sink. I shook my head as if ashamed and, as usual, he completely ignored me.

"Somebody needs to hand that kid his ass," Brett said, shaking his head. He'd been my sounding board regarding the little shit on many occasions.

I laughed mirthlessly. "I wish to hell I could be the one to do it, but I kind of like being employed. I would suggest you do it, but, well…" I let that sit out there. Brett was damn scrawny and I loved giving him shit about it. But he was good at dealing back in kind.

"And you wouldn't want to mess up that pretty-boy face of yours anyway," he threw back at me. "Tell me, exactly how long did you spend getting ready this morning, princess?"

I punched him in the arm and he pretended it didn't hurt.

I told Brett about Brad's disturbing locker-room behavior, and he was appropriately appalled. I may not have caught up with Brad after training, but I had been able to pull Chris aside. I'd tried to share some tips on how to maybe fit in a little better without becoming an asshole himself. Truthfully, sometimes all it took was one new impression and a bully's attention could be diverted. I'd been half tempted to communicate the age-old prison strategy of beating someone to shit on your first day to keep people from messing with you, but even I knew that would be unwise.

"Hey, I'm going to check out some new talent tomorrow for Gerry and Buzz. You wanna come?" Brett and I had always shared a love of baseball—it was one of the main reasons we'd become friends in the first place. He revered the game almost as much as I did. He also had a damn good eye, even if he was kind of a shit player, so I often used his help.

"Got nothing better to do now that you've scared Ginger off." He set down his beer and pointed at my face. "You're gonna pay for that if she doesn't take my call, asswipe."

"Noted." My mouth tugged. It was good seeing Brett feeling more confident around girls these days. "But, just in case, let's head out in a bit and check out the talent at Jake's. Never hurts to have a back-up." I raised an eyebrow.

He sighed in resignation. "Whatever."

I headed upstairs, drink in hand, to take yet another shower before our night out. I had a good feeling.

♣♣♣

The good feeling from the night before had not panned out as I hoped. I'd had a decent time shooting the shit with Brett and a couple other guys, but I wasn't feeling any of the girls at the bar. I decided to attribute my positive premonitions to the player I'd be scouting today instead.

I found a parking spot up close by the field at North High School. It was a good day to play ball. The sky was clear and the temperature was ideal, sitting in the low seventies. I grabbed my notebook and headed for the fence to check out pregame warmup. Brett planned to meet me at the field later since I liked to show up early. I adjusted my cap and looked over the sea of uniforms for an unfamiliar number.

There he was. Number 52.

The kid was tall for his age, probably just under six feet, and he had a mess of dirty blond hair sticking out from under his blue cap. He was lanky as shit, but held himself confidently. His glove raised and lowered naturally as he and his teammate tossed the ball back and forth. It was impossible to see what kind of talent he may or may not have from just watching him play catch, but that was why I was prepared to stand against this fence for the rest of the afternoon.

I knew the starting pitcher for North, a senior named Wes Hartfield. He wasn't too shabby. North's record was 4-2 so far this season, and Wes had a lot to do with that. We'd worked with one of the coaches to try and set up some extra training sessions with Wes, but it was a no-go. His parents were set on him joining the family business out of high school and didn't want to shell out the money for a future they didn't see for their kid. It was a shame, but Wes didn't seem willing to fight them on it, so we'd let it lie.

His impending graduation opened up the spot for a starting pitcher on the team next season, and I could think of a couple guys who'd be gunning for it. I'd have to see for myself if this new kid could give them a run for their money.

The coach called the players in for a chat and I signaled one of the assistant coaches, a guy named Kirk. He jogged over, pulling his cap off and wiping his brow with his shirtsleeve.

We shook hands over the fence.

"Good to see you, Monroe," he greeted me.

I gave him a chin lift. "You too, man. Just wanted to give you a heads up that I'm here for Gerry and Buzz today. We're checking out the new kid."

His mouth lifted on one side in a knowing grin. "Damn, you move fast. The kid just got here last week."

"That means we're already a week behind," I threw back at him with my own grin.

That got a small chuckle out of Kirk. He settled his cap back on his head and looked to the side. "Well, patience will have to be your virtue today because he'll be riding the bench until probably the eighth. Wes has earned his time, and we got Anders and Bates fighting for relief pitcher already." He didn't look pleased.

"What's the story?" I asked.

Kirk didn't look at me or answer for several moments so I waited. Finally, he spoke. "You ask me, we could win the whole goddamn thing if we put Miller in starting today. But you know how this works—nothing's that simple."

I nodded. You can't escape politics, even in America's favorite pastime. "Well, Kirk, it's like you said—patience."

He nodded back and we both heard his name being called from across the field.

"Catch you later, Monroe. Make sure you stick around." He pointed at me as he turned and jogged toward the team.

Nothing was going to make me move from my spot today—not after that conversation.

☘☘☘

ALSO BY SYLVIE STEWART

The Carolina Connection Series:

The Fix *(Carolina Connections, Book 1)*

The Spark (*Carolina Connections* Book 2)

The Game *(Carolina Connections Book 4)*

The Way You Are *(Carolina Connections Book 5)*

♣ ♣ ♣

The Nerd Next Door *(Carolina Kisses, Book 1)*

Then Again

Happy New You

Game Changer *(July 2019)*

About That

Full-On Clinger

♣ ♣ ♣

Between a Rock and a Royal *(Kings of Carolina, Book 1*

Blue Bloods and Backroads (*Kings of Carolina*, Book 2)

THE FIX:

My life is a friggin' fairytale—just not the kind any single girl would ever want to star in.

LANEY:

Like any good heroine, I have challenges to face. Getting my son to wear pants is one; dealing with my snooze-fest of a job is another. Then there's the Beast, my freeloading brother who's worn a permanent dent in the couch at my new place. And no fairytale would be complete without a smoking hot prince, of course. Too bad he's a complete ass.

My instincts scream at me to steer clear of Nate Murphy. Because, if life has taught me anything, there is no such thing as happily ever after.

NATE:

I may not be a superhero, but I do my best to come to the rescue when I'm needed. And, hey, I just moved halfway across the country after a single phone call from my mom. But being back home and taking on the responsibilities involved makes me a bit cranky at times. Unfortunately, the one time I completely lose my cool is in front of the hottest girl I've ever met. I've got my work cut out for me if I'm going to fix this. But I *will* fix this.

I'll be anything Laney Monroe needs me to be … a superhero, a prince, or just a guy she might take a chance on.

☘ ☘ ☘

THE SPARK:

Mark Beckett is the most annoying, patronizing, arrogant jerk on the face of the earth. So, naturally, I can't get the damn man out of my head.

FIONA:

Like the old saying goes, I'm a jill of all trades but a master of none. What I lack in skill, however, I make up for in enthusiasm—something certain people (ahem) find irritating. But I have my reasons for living my life the way I do, for diving into one project after another and trying to make a difference. And if Mark Beckett doesn't like it, he knows where to find the door. I don't need his approval … or his panty-melting kisses.

MARK:

I enjoy the simple things in life: a job well done, a cold beer, a hot woman … you get the idea. But there's nothing simple about the mess I just found myself in. The last thing I need is a pint-sized princess sticking her nose in my business and pushing every damn one of my buttons like it's her job. But Fiona Pierce may be the only one with the tools to solve my problems—and the power to change everything.

Order your copy of ***The Spark*** today!

THE GAME:

They say opposites attract. Someone needs to tell that to Emerson Scott.

GAVIN:

All I ever wanted was to play ball. When an act of sheer stupidity took that dream away, I thought I'd never bounce back. But now I have the opportunity to coach an up-and-coming phenom, and I'm giving it all I've got. The fact that I've been lusting after his smoking-hot sister only sweetens the deal. Emerson may be buttoned up like a school librarian, but I play my best when I'm under pressure … and I *always* bring the heat.

EMERSON:

Never lose focus. Never lose control. Those are the first two rules in my carefully calculated plan for success. Finding myself thrown into the role of guardian for my little brother was *not* part of that plan. But I can adjust for Jay's sake; I'm not about to let one change make me lose sight of my goals. Too bad Jay's hot young baseball coach doesn't seem to give a fig about my plans. He has one of his own—and it includes me. Gavin Monroe may play like a pro, but that boy will never win this game.

♣ ♣ ♣

THEN AGAIN:

It's been two years since the divorce papers slapped Jenna in the face, and it's high time to dive back in.

Step one: find a romance-novel-worthy man for a hot summer fling.

How hard could it be?

But disastrously bad flirting, a failed honky-tonk hookup, and a mix-up with one of Sunview's finest have Jenna seriously doubting if this is all worth it. Maybe she's better off leaving the world of love and sex to others—or maybe she's just looking in the wrong place …

Order your copy of ***Then Again*** today!

www.ingramcontent.com/pod-product-compliance
Lightning Source LLC
Chambersburg PA
CBHW072204130726
47910CB00011B/1848

* 9 7 8 0 9 9 8 9 2 6 0 1 8 *